City Limits

Memories of a Small-Town Boy

Terry Teachout

Poseidon Press · New York

London · Toronto · Sydney

Tokyo · Singapore

SCRIBNER
Rockefeller Center
1230 Avenue of the Americas
New York, NY 10020

SCRIBNER and design are trademarks of Macmillan Library Research USA, Inc. under
license by Simon & Schuster, the publisher of this work.

Designed by Liney Li
Manufactured in the United States of America

10 9 8 7 6 5 4 3 2 1

Library of Congress Cataloging-In-Publication Data

Teachout, Terry.
    City limits : memories of a small-town boy / Terry Teachout.
        p.   cm.
    1. Teachout, Terry—Childhood and youth. 2. Missouri—Biography.
    3. City and town life—United States. I. Title.
    CT275.T377A3   1991
    977.8'04'092—DC20
        [B]   91-27550
                                                    CIP
ISBN 0-7432-4688-8

The text of this book is composed in Electra.

For information regarding the special discounts for bulk purchases, please contact Simon &
Schuster Special Sales at 1-800-456-6798 or business@simonandschuster.com

*To my parents, who knew about most of this,
and my wife, who knew about all of it*

*He knew for a certainty that
there was nothing great and
nothing little in this world;
and day and night he strove
to think out his way into the
heart of things, back to the
place whence his soul had come.*

—THE JUNGLE BOOKS

*New York, New York
Or a village in Iowa
The only difference is the name.*

—ON THE TOWN

Contents

1 | *Home and Away*

Ⅰt isn't easy to get from New York, where I live, to Sikeston, Missouri, my home town. Sikeston is a small town on the northern edge of the Bootheel, the part of Missouri that juts down from the southeastern corner of the state. If you want to go to Sikeston, you take a cab to the airport, fly to St. Louis, rent a car, and drive south on I-55 for about three hours. Direct flights from New York to the Bootheel are nonexistent; direct flights from St. Louis to the Bootheel are few and far between. They say it's a small world, but it starts to look a lot bigger if you're trying to get from New York to Sikeston in a hurry.

New York, of course, isn't exactly full of people trying to get to Sikeston in a hurry, and people from Sikeston aren't much more likely to go to New York, whether for a visit or for good. My father is a rare exception to this rule, for he went to a hardware convention in New York in 1964, returning with a reel of fuzzy home movies of the World's Fair, a plastic Statue of Liberty, and a commitment to never going back about which he has yet to change his mind. I listened to his tales of squalor and rudeness, but the home movies made a deeper impression on me, and I followed in his reluctant footsteps at the age of nineteen. My school, a Southern Baptist college just outside of Kansas City, sponsored a week-long expedition to New York every year, and I signed up as soon as I was eligible. It was a busy week. I haunted the museums. I went to the Metropolitan Opera. I saw my first *Nutcracker*. But my biggest adventure consisted of going by myself to the early show at the Café Carlyle, neatly dressed in a black suit that my mother and I had picked out at a factory outlet store in Bloomfield.

I went to the Café Carlyle because I was, believe it or not, a fan of Bobby Short, a cabaret singer who performs there regularly. I first read about Bobby Short in a piece Rex Reed wrote for *Stereo Review* back when I was in high school. Hungry for a taste of the glamorous life, I ordered *Bobby Short Is Mad About Noël Coward* and *Bobby Short Loves Cole Porter* from Collins Piano Company, the only place in Sikeston where you could place special orders for records. Going to see my idol in person seemed to me the perfect way to round out my trip to New York, so I booked a table for one and turned up half an hour before show time, blissfully ignorant of the fact that the Café Carlyle is an elegant watering hole intended for well-to-do New Yorkers, not teenage boys in ill-fitting black suits.

Not being much of a drinker, I decided to consume my minimum by having a late supper at my tiny table. I tore into my shrimp cocktail with gusto, unaware that anything was wrong until I put down my fork, looked around, and saw that no one else in the room was eating. I might well have died of embarrassment had it not been for the fact that Bobby Short, formerly of Danville, Illinois, spotted me for an out-of-towner the moment he walked through the door and came straight to my table to say hello, an act of kindness for which I am still grateful. I talked about it for weeks, though I knew only three or four people who knew who Bobby Short was, which took most of the starch out of the story after the first few tellings.

New York, as the song says, left me starry-eyed and vaguely discontented, but it never seriously occurred to me that I would someday live there, not even after I shook hands with Bobby Short. My big city was St. Louis, the middle-sized metropolis beneath which Sikeston is distantly suspended like a tiny pendulum. My family visited St. Louis every summer, and it was just possible for me to imagine living there when I grew up. New York was different. It was a place located far beyond the outermost limits of my youthful dreams. The idea that I might deliberately shape my life in such a way as to lead me there was alien; the idea that my life had already begun to take such a shape was, quite literally, unthinkable.

I've lived in New York for several years now, and I'm starting to get used to it. I don't carry a subway map around anymore. I take *The Nutcracker* and the Metropolitan Opera for granted now. I haven't been back to the Café Carlyle, but I do know somebody who knows Bobby Short, which is progress of a sort. Even now, though, I sometimes feel like an awe-struck visitor from a poorer planet, looking at the shiny world around me and scratching my head in hopeless confusion. I am forever conscious of being a Missourian in New York, a stranger fallen among fast-lane types who neither know nor care about the finer points of life back where I come from. Whenever I talk to native-born New Yorkers about the Midwest, I'm reminded of something that Philip Larkin, the English poet, told a reporter: "I suppose everyone has his own dream of America. A writer once said to me: 'If you ever go to America, go either to the East Coast or the West Coast. The rest is a desert full of bigots.' That's what I think I'd like: where if you help a girl trim the Christmas tree you're regarded as engaged, and her brothers start oiling their shotguns if you don't call on the minister."

I once wrote a book review for *The Wall Street Journal* in which, since the book in question had a small-town angle, I decided that it would be appropriate to say in my byline that Terry Teachout, formerly of Sikeston, Missouri, is an editorial writer for the New York *Daily News*, since that was what I was doing for a living at the time. But my editor, a native New Yorker, got his abbreviations mixed up, and the byline came out "Sikeston, Miss." instead of "Sikeston, Mo." I called him up the day the piece appeared and told him that he was more than welcome to answer any letters of complaint sent by irritated Sikestonians. He didn't get any, which isn't all that surprising; a *Journal* coin box stands proudly outside the Sikeston post office, but I've never seen anybody buy a copy. As for me, I got one letter. It was from a high school friend, a trumpet player with whom I had long ago lost touch. His note, written on the letterhead of an Oklahoma savings and loan, read as follows: "Dear Terry: *Mississippi?*"

I can't really blame my editor for being confused. Why should he have cared whether I came from Missouri or Mississippi? Either way, New York is my return address, and it's likely to stay that way for some time to come. It would be useless for me to pretend that I will ever return to my home town for good, or even for very long. I cannot pursue my hopes and dreams there. Sooner or later, people like me usually end up in places like New York, banging away at a battered typewriter or an out-of-tune piano, counting our pennies and waiting for the big break to come along. But it would be just as useless for me to pretend that I have become a true New Yorker, that my experiences have changed me in some fundamental way. I know better. Though it has been many years since I left Sikeston, I remain a small-town boy, uprooted and repotted, and nothing much has changed about me except the place where I happen to live. I still wear plaid shirts and think in Central Standard Time; I still eat tuna casserole with potato chips on top and worry about whether the farmers back home will get enough rain this year.

As dilemmas go, this one isn't particularly tragic, but it is still a dilemma, and it is constantly with me. I am glad to have two homes, glad to be able to catch a cab outside Grand Central Station and, six hours later, step out of a rented car and stroll up the driveway to the back door of my parents' house and sleep in the bedroom where I slept as a child. Once I thought I would spend the rest of my life in a place like that. I did not know when

I went off to college that I would someday stand at both ends of the long road that stretched invisibly before me, beckoning vainly across the continent to myself. I am like a million other Americans who grew up and moved away from the small towns of their childhood. We cannot go back; we are not at home where we are. We are exiles from the lost heart of the land we love.

I first began to understand the terms of this exile on a Saturday night several Decembers ago, not very long after I moved to New York. I had just fled the chaos of the closing of an issue of the magazine where I was working that year. I picked up the suitcase I had stashed behind my desk that morning, walked out the door and flagged a cab. Three hours later, I pulled out of the Hertz garage underneath Lambert International Airport in St. Louis, smiling to myself as I looked up at the deep blue Missouri sky, thinking happily about the long drive ahead. The night was clear, the air chilly and crisp, and every mile I put behind me brought me a mile closer to home.

As I drove by the I-70 interchange, I thought about the first time I went to Kansas City by myself. I remembered the careful directions my father gave me in his deep, grainy voice as we sat together at the kitchen table. ("Get in the left-hand lane at Wentz-ville, son. You don't usually do that to make an exit, but you'll have to there.") I remembered the fat yellow line he drew on the road map with a felt-tipped pen. I remembered what it felt like to drive through St. Louis during rush hour in a station wagon filled to the roof with books, records, socks, and clean underwear. I was sure that an eighteen-wheeler would run me down, scattering the accumulated debris of my sophomore year all over the eight concrete lanes of the highway.

I drove past the small green sign on the edge of St. Louis that says *I-55 South, Sikeston*. I made my way down the eastern edge of Missouri, almost within spitting distance of the Mississippi River. Twisting the dials of an unfamiliar radio with one hand, I picked up KSIM, a station that used to broadcast rock and roll and Sikeston Little League ball games and that now fills the air with the high, hard-bitten whine of steel guitars and the rueful lyrics of cheating songs. I drove past Ste. Genevieve and thought about the Saturday morning that I took a car full of noisy high school kids to the state student council convention, driving at speeds of up to eighty-five miles an hour. (We got to Ste. Genevieve fifteen minutes earlier than we should have, and the faculty adviser evened things up by yelling at me for just about that long.) I drove past Perryville, the town where I spent the first six months of my life and to which I have never returned, even though I pass by it every time I come home.

I drove past Cape Girardeau, the river town where, thirty-five years ago, I was born. "Cape Girardeau," Mark Twain said in *Life on the Mississippi*, "is situated on a hillside, and makes a handsome appearance. There is a great Jesuit school for boys at the foot of the town by the river. . . . There was another college higher up on an airy summit—a bright new edifice, picturesquely and peculiarly towered and pinnacled—a sort of gigantic casters, with the cruets all complete." Steamboats carrying jazzmen like Louis Armstrong used to stop at this tidy little port on their slow way up the Mississippi from New Orleans to St. Louis. The steamboats stopped coming half a century ago and the Jesuit school is only a memory, but Cape Girardeau is still the home of Southeast Missouri State University, where my mother used to bring me once a week to study violin. That was back when I thought I might grow up to be a concert violinist, an ambition that went the way of the steamboats. Now Cape Girardeau is just another stop on the long trip home.

I turned off at Benton and got on Highway 61, a hilly two-lane road long ago made obsolete by the interstate. (We call it "the old highway.") I drove past the run-down tavern where I used to watch my two best friends from high school shoot pool, feeling increasingly out of place with every ball they sank and every beer they downed. I drove past the First United Methodist Church, a structure known to irreverent Sikestonians as The Ark, and remembered the Sunday morning when Sour Mash, the country band in which I played bass, did Hank Williams' "I Saw the Light" for the offertory, a rip-roaring performance greeted by the longest silence I ever encountered in my entire career as a professional musician.

It was just after midnight when my headlights picked out the Sikeston city-limit sign. I drove slowly through town, memories trailing behind me like the broken pieces of a spider's web, feeling a sudden surge of love for my mother and father and brother and sister-in-law who were waiting for me, for the flat brown contours of southeast Missouri and the ugly plainness of the small town that will be my home until the day I die. I was startled by the strength of the emotions that seized me that night; like most people, I didn't know how much I loved my part of the country until I left it. As I pulled into the driveway of the house where I grew up, I asked myself: *What made me want to leave this place? How could I possibly have gotten from here to New York and back again?* That journey is what this book is about.

2 | *Down Highway 61*

One winter night when my plane got into St. Louis two hours late and I-55 was slick with fresh snow and dirty slush, I stopped at a pay phone and told my parents not to wait up for me. Then I drove to the edge of town and found a Super 8 motel with an empty room. Bone tired from the long flight, I dropped my bags in the corner and stretched out on the bed. I opened up the nightstand drawer, pulled out the Super 8 directory, and flipped idly through the pages, looking for Sikeston. I always look up Sikeston in motel directories. I do it to remind myself that my home town is not merely a fond memory but a real place, a spot on the map where weary strangers can pull off the road and spend the night.

I found Sikeston on page 111, but the entry didn't come to much: *63 units/Rodeo and Miner Fruit Market nearby/World-famous Lambert's.* What traveler would bother to pull off I-55 and spend the night after reading that drab list of bald facts? How could he know that all the important parts have been left out?

Rodeo, for instance, is not just any rodeo but the Sikeston Jaycee Bootheel Rodeo, started in 1953 by the Sikeston Junior Chamber of Commerce and known to everyone in the world who knows anything about rodeos. The Jaycee Bootheel Rodeo is not only an annual celebration of the manly art of cowpunching but southeast Missouri's very own country music festival. Had you gone to the rodeo the same year I spent the night at the St. Louis Super 8, you would have been serenaded, depending on your choice of evening, by Willie Nelson, Tanya Tucker, Earl Thomas Conley, or Charlie Daniels; had you stopped by the souvenir booth, you could have bought an official Jaycee Bootheel Rodeo belt buckle designed by my brother David, the novelties chairman, who set an all-time sales record that year.

Miner Fruit Market is nothing more than a big outdoor fruit stand, a good place to buy ripe peaches and watermelons and cantaloupes straight off the farm, but *World-famous Lambert's*, if not quite world-famous, is definitely a place worth telling your friends about: a rambling, souvenir-cluttered restaurant equipped with a lady who plays hot ragtime piano and a grinning proprietor who wanders through the main dining room tossing yeast-rising rolls at the customers, most of whom spend half an hour or more waiting for a table. Long before he invented "throwed rolls" and turned himself into a local celebrity, the owner of Lambert's Café was my high school gym teacher, a short, tough-talking man with an inexplicable fear of small white mice and a soft spot for clumsy kids with thick glasses.

You won't find any of this in the Super 8 directory, of course. Motel directories generally stick to the obvious, as do small-town boosters. The Sikeston Chamber of Commerce, eager to persuade you (or, better yet, your factory) to relocate, will gladly send you a fact-filled booklet called "Sikeston: A Community that Works!" Sikeston, it says, was founded in 1860 by one John Sikes and located on El Camino Real, an overland route connecting the cities of St. Louis and New Orleans that was laid out in 1789 by order of the King of Spain and is now known as U.S. Highway 61. Sikeston, it says, has 12 lighted baseball fields, 11 public parks, an airport with a 5,500-foot lighted runway and a population of 19,000, including 51 doctors, 11 dentists, and 46 "full-time public safety personnel."

I could go on, but why bother? In the end, you wouldn't know all that much more about Sikeston than 63 *units/Rodeo and Miner Fruit Market nearby/World-famous Lambert's.* The bald facts of a big city, its tall buildings and storied landmarks, give it a surface glamour that needs no explaining. (Imagine the listing for a Super 8 in the middle of Manhattan: *500 units/ Broadway and Grand Central Station nearby/World-famous "21" Club.*) A small town needs lots of explaining. It has no tall buildings, and the landmarks are all in your mind. When you look up, you see the sky; when you show somebody the sights, you see yourself. When I visit Sikeston Senior High School, I look at the aging brick buildings, but I see the place where I got in trouble midway through my senior year, when Charlie Waters and I hired Goode's Nursery to pull up all the bushes in the quadrangle and plant new ones. We wanted the sidewalks to look nice for the state student council convention, which was being held in Sikeston that year. We didn't clear it with Bob Buchanan, the principal. He paid for those scrubby little bushes, but he gave us hell, and the sidewalks, to no one's surprise but mine, wound up looking awful. They still looked awful long after I got my diploma and went off to college.

Memory is the key to a small town. A stranger driving through Sikeston would see nothing but schools, stores, and houses. Some are handsome, others nondescript, but all have one thing in common: the important parts are invisible, at least to eyes unaided by memory. This is why people like me never like to hear about how their home towns have changed since they moved away. Every change in the place where you grew up is an insult, a run in the homespun fabric of recollection. A couple of years ago, Sikeston was hit by a tornado that tore up dozens of houses and knocked out all the phones in town. I turned on the television that morning and heard an announcer say "Sikeston, Missouri." It scared me half to death. I knew that the only way my home town could possibly make *The CBS Morning News* would be if it were struck by a tornado or an earthquake, and I knew that both things are possible in the Bootheel, home of the New Madrid fault. As soon as the phones were fixed and I got in touch with my family, I made sure that no one I knew had been hurt. Then I asked: What buildings were damaged? Which ones were demolished? *What memories have I lost?*

Since there is no hiding from change, even in a small town, I am forever looking for stray details with which to jog my memory and restore the faded landscape of my childhood. Being a writer, I'm used to digging up such details in books, but nothing noteworthy seems ever to have happened in Sikeston, and the only book in which my home town can be found, so far as I know, is the atlas. Instead, I rely on the memories of my family and friends and on the various documents my parents have squirreled away over the years. Thanks to my father, who has been a camera bug for most of his adult life, the Teachout family archive contains hundreds of Polaroid snapshots, thousands of Kodachrome slides, and, best of all, dozens of home movies.

"If you're going to do something, son," my father always says, "you ought to do it right." Unlike me, he always does it right. My father is a man at home in the world of inanimate objects. When he packs a suitcase, he packs it to the brim and beyond, whisking suits and shoes into its maw with the debonair ease of a big-time magician. (He liked to pack my bag whenever I took a trip, and I never could figure out how to cram everything back into the same bag when it was time to come home. Sometimes I brought along an empty bag to catch the runoff.) When he became interested in home movies back in 1956, the year I was born, he bought a splicing block and a title kit and went to work in earnest. For ten years, he carted his gray Bell & Howell camera to family gatherings of every description. At regular intervals, he arranged his three-minute reels of film in chronological order, fitted them out with carefully typed title cards ("Introducing . . . TERENCE ALAN TEACHOUT"), and spliced them end to end into half-hour programs.

My father's movies are stored in a stack of round metal film cans kept in a hall closet known as "the camera closet," the graveyard of his ceaseless search for the perfect camera. We drag them out and watch them every year or so, laughing and pointing and passing a bowl of my mother's greasy, salty popcorn from hand to hand. Not all of them are funny. The earliest reels, taken before my father had quite figured out how to work his new camera, are full of oddly haunting glimpses of long-forgotten things: an open field, a country church, a birdhouse, a garden. Even the familiar scenes are lightly touched with mystery, for my father stopped making movies when I was ten years old, and I cannot remember any of the actual occasions on which he shot them. I know that I am the child on the flickering screen because I remember the Christmas toys that surround me: the two-story service station, the red International Harvester tractor, the wheezing toy organ that sits on a table in the basement, still playable, still out of tune. I was there, but I cannot recall a single one of these three-minute snippets of lost time preserved so faithfully by Eastman Kodak that my mother and father and I can watch them in our living room thirty years after the fact.

Though I love my father's movies, I find them more than a little frustrating, for he shot them from his perspective, not mine. He brought his camera to a half-dozen of my birthday parties, and I'm glad he did, but it never occurred to him to shoot an ordinary breakfast or dinner. That would have been a waste of film. ("Don't waste film, son," he used to tell me whenever I got hold of the camera and started taking pictures of sunsets, anthills, and the backs of people's heads.) I look at the screen and see my pregnant mother standing outside our house; a splice rattles through the projector and she is home from the hospital, holding my baby brother in her arms. The scene ends here, but I want more. I want to see the front yard. How high was the grass growing? What kind of car were we driving that year? My father's movies, lean and purposeful and full of unwasted film, cannot satisfy my longing for a movie made up of nothing but wasted film, a prosy, commonplace, uneventful movie whose only purpose is to show how Sikeston looked on an average day in 1950 or 1960 or 1990. . . .

A thin ribbon of grass grows out of a crack in the orange stripe that runs down the center of the concrete slab that fills the flickering screen. This is Highway 61, the old highway. You are now entering Sikeston, Missouri, gateway to the Bootheel. Turn right at the First United Methodist Church and you are on North Kingshighway, known to the Department of Transportation as Business Route 61, a wide, peaceful street lined with tall trees and two-story houses.

Look down the side streets and you will see rows of neatly painted wooden signs that advertise the services of doctors, lawyers, dentists, insurance salesmen. (Some of the signs have been repainted since I left town. They now bear the names of boys with whom I went to school, boys who went off to college and came back to Sikeston to work for their fathers.) A red granite marker tells you that you are driving down El Camino Real. *Erected*, it says, *by Missouri Daughters of the American Revolution AD 1915.* On your right is the site of the old First Methodist Church, where I went to kindergarten. The church was built in 1879 and burned down in 1968, leaving only six slender Ionic columns that stand there to this day, somber, solemn, and inscrutable, a stately monument to nothing in particular.

Turn right and there is Malone Park, shady and quiet, its sole ornament a chocolate-and-white bandstand built in 1912. Across the street is a granite bench into whose straight back an inscription has been carved: *Sikeston—A White Settlement. 1803. Platted by John Sikes. 1860. To know the story of this Missouri, look about you—here from swamp and wilderness, stumps and clay, our forefathers cut a home land.* The simple, sonorous words are impressive. They are also misleading. The words "A White Settlement" mean *No Indians*, not *No Blacks*, but nobody bothered to carve a footnote into the bench on the corner of North Scott and West North streets, and so the stern inscription stands uncorrected, waiting to be misunderstood by the next passerby with time on his hands who stops to read it.

Two blocks south of Malone Park is the Sikeston train depot, a vacant red brick building with white trim. Though it's been thirty years since a passenger train last stopped here, the windows of the depot are unbroken, the walls free of graffiti. You can lease it if you like, in which case a sign on the wall instructs you to get in touch with the Union Pacific Real Estate Department, Omaha, Nebraska. When the wind is right, you can smell the local bakery from here. It has changed hands since I left town, but the warm, yeasty smell remains the same and so does the product, a loaf of sliced white bread suitable for picnics and breakfast toast and sandwiches slapped together after you get home from choir practice or a football game or a hot date.

Look down at the worn cobblestones beneath your feet. Most of the streets of downtown Sikeston are covered with black asphalt, but the cobblestones of Front Street remain exposed, a reminder of what my home town looked like half a century ago. Look up at the granite markers embedded in the upper stories of the brick storefronts, silent witnesses to a town older than anyone now living can remember: MCCOY AND TANNER 1906. IOOF 1908. R. G. APPLEGATE. DERRIS. BLANTON. SHEPHERD. Look higher and you can see the microwave relay tower atop the phone company and, beyond it, the white water tower that says SIKESTON in simple black letters. I used to dream of climbing to the top of the water tower, but I never tried it. My brother got halfway up before his nerve ran out.

Once the farmers of the Bootheel came to Sikeston to buy the things they could not grow or make themselves. Then a shopping mall was built on the edge of town, and the downtown stores, one by one, started to sell off their stock and close their doors. Most of the stores of my childhood are gone now, sold or burned out or abandoned, though Kirby's, Sikeston's oldest greasy spoon, remains in business, filling the air with the sharp smell of fried onions, and Falkoff's and Buckner-Ragsdale are still the two biggest clothing stores in town. I bought my Cub Scout and Boy Scout uniforms at Buckner-Ragsdale; I bought a charcoal-gray pinstriped suit at Falkoff's the last time I was in town.

Just across the street from the depot is Legion Square, site of the Cotton Carnival, Sikeston's yearly salute to the Bootheel's principal cash crop. As small-town carnivals go, it's a pretty good one, complete with marching bands, dunking stands, a Ferris wheel, a Cotton Carnival queen and the American Legion hamburger stand, which sells the best fish sandwiches in the world, hot and moist and savory and wrapped in plain wax paper, the kind nobody uses anymore. In the center of the square, right by the flagpole, is a chunk of rock to which a tarnished copper plaque is bolted. *Legion Square*, it says. *In memory of those men of this community who made the supreme sacrifice in the world war.* Unlike the granite bench on the corner of North Scott and West North, this monument bears a footnote: a second, smaller plaque bolted beneath the first one and dedicated to the memory of those who served in World War II, Korea, and Vietnam. The Persian Gulf will doubtless be added before long. There is plenty of room on the rock.

Across the tracks and down the road are the old First Baptist Church and the American Legion post and the Masonic Lodge and Blackburn's, once a soda fountain, now an insurance office. The cluster of low-set buildings in the distance is Kingsway Plaza Mall, which sucked the life out of downtown Sikeston and is falling victim in its turn to a bigger mall outside Cape Girardeau, a mere thirty miles north. Just past Kingsway Plaza Mall are Wal-Mart and Memorial Park Cemetery (Choice Lots Available). Business Route 61 ends here, rejoining Highway 61 proper, which runs straight through the center of Sikeston, slicing the town in half. When I was a child, anyone who drove down Highway 61 had to drive through Sikeston. Then Dwight Eisenhower ordered the building of the interstate highway system, making it possible for a traveler to drive a thousand miles on well-kept four-lane roads without stopping at a single stoplight or seeing a single chocolate-and-white bandstand. An interstate highway, like a straight line, is the shortest distance between two points, and the dullest, too.

Off to the right is the Hampton Inn, formerly the Holiday Inn. I've never spent a night there, but Sour Mash used to play dinner music in the restaurant on Wednesday nights. We each got five dollars a night, plus tips and one free trip through the buffet line. (Seconds were extra for the help.) Forty years to the day after my mother and father were married, they showed up at the Holiday Inn for dinner, pulled open an unmarked door and found, to their amazement, a room full of family and friends gathered around a table loaded with punch and homemade hors d'oeuvres. The light fixtures were covered with blue crepe paper and a phonograph in the corner played Artie Shaw's 1938 recording of "Begin the Beguine." Standing in the doorway were my brother and his wife, who had spent three months planning the party, and my wife and I, who had flown to St. Louis and slipped into Sikeston the night before. I snapped a picture of my father as he opened the door and saw us standing there. It was the second time in my life that I caught him completely off guard. The first time was the day I told him I was moving to New York.

Off to the left is Kentucky Fried Chicken, formerly the Cyrus Restaurant. The Cyrus was segregated, and one of my earliest memories is of a little door out back over which a sputtering neon sign said COLORED. (*Sikeston—A White Settlement.*) Later on, the Cyrus became the Elks Club, scene of innumerable rowdy weekend parties. One night, the members of Sour Mash filed through what once had been the COLORED door, set up our instruments, and played for a room full of drunken revelers. Not long after that, the building was torn down and a new Kentucky Fried Chicken store, open to all, put up in its place.

A few blocks north is my old neighborhood, the Collins Subdivision, erected in 1961. Most of the streets in this part of town are named after trees: Mimosa, Maple, Elm, Pine. On your left is Matthews Elementary School, built in 1955. On your right is

Hickory Drive, a curving, tree-lined lane in whose bend you will find the house where I lived for twelve years, leaving in the fall of 1974 to go off to college, never again to return for longer than a summer. This street is full of summertime memories, most of them as plain as a picket fence and the sweeter for it. I can hear the tinkling bell that announced the cooling arrival of the Sno-Cone truck in the sticky heat of summer; I can smell the oily, mosquito-killing fog with which city trucks filled the streets of Sikeston; I can see the cold white lights that lit the streets where the children of Hickory Drive played tag between sundown and bedtime on hot summer nights.

Past and present come together in a small-town neighborhood like the rings of an old oak tree. You can sit on the front porch of our house and see the windows of my second-grade classroom, where Mrs. Jackie Grant, her voice trembling, interrupted an arithmetic lesson one November afternoon in 1963 to tell her students that the President of the United States had been shot and killed. If you stand on tiptoe, you can see Sikeston Senior High School, which looks just like Matthews Elementary School, only bigger: the same flat, ranch-style institutional architecture, the same concrete ramps and brick veneer and sickly blue-green trim. You can see, too, the round dome of the high school field house, where I ran laps every weekday morning under the tolerant eye of Coach Lambert, inventor of throwed rolls.

I graduated from high school in the field house, valedictorian of the class of 1974 and far too proud of myself for my own good. I gave a badly overwritten speech that night, sharing the stage with three of my classmates. One was Melodie Powell, a bassoonist who spoke French and wanted to be a translator at the United Nations; one was Mark Deane, the son of a farmer, who now works the land his father used to till; one was Charlie Waters, the class clown, a clever, sharp-tongued boy who went off to college to become a pharmacist. Charlie came back to Sikeston at the age of thirty-two to live with his parents, dying two years later. Melodie took up a collection to plant a tree in his memory in the quadrangle of the high school. I cannot see Charlie's tree from our front porch, but it fills my mind's eye as the screen fades to black and my movie comes to an end.

Though my home movie is imaginary, you could see just about everything in it if you took the trouble to fly to St. Louis and drive south on I-55 for three hours. Sikeston hasn't changed all that much since I moved away. In fact, it hasn't changed all that much since I was a boy. The street lights still sputter to cold white life at dusk. The crickets still quicken the air on hot summer nights. The cobblestones still sleep silently beneath their asphalt blanket.

A few things are different. The telephones have push buttons now, and you buy your milk at the grocery store instead of having it delivered to your doorstep every morning. The A&W Drive-In, which served Papa Burgers and Mama Burgers and cold, foamy mugs of root beer, is long gone. So is the old drive-in theater on the edge of town. So are the cotton patches. Quite a lot of Sikeston was planted with cotton and beans when I was a child. At 308 Powers, where I lived until I was five years old, there was a cotton patch out behind the house. I used to fill empty Kleenex boxes full of raw cotton and give them to my mother. Now that cotton patch is a ranch house. Most of the old cotton patches and bean fields within the city limits have been sold to real estate developers. Sikeston has become a community that works, a bustling little town with 46 full-time public safety personnel and a newly remodeled 189-bed hospital with a helipad from which my sister-in-law Kathy was swept away one summer afternoon and flown to St. Louis, there to give birth to my niece Lauren.

I haven't lost much sleep over any of this. It's the way people live that matters, not the way things look. Sikeston had a population of 13,765 in 1960, the year of its centennial. Another 5,000 souls live there now, but they live much the same way now that they would have lived then. Most people leave their car doors unlocked, and some people leave their back doors unlocked, too. Most people go to church on Sunday morning, and some people go to church on Wednesday night, too. Most people end up married for good, though it takes some of them two or three tries to get it right. A certain amount of hell gets raised after dark, but most people look the other way when they hear funny noises in the night, for they know that teenagers who smoke marijuana and listen to Metallica in high school usually end up drinking beer and listening to George Jones within a few years of getting their diplomas and going to work. Small-town life has a way of soothing the restless soul.

That is why I think about Sikeston whenever I find myself in a strange motel room late at night, flipping through a Super 8 directory in order to remind myself that some things in this world don't change very much. "Partialities," Mark Twain said after hearing the second officer of the S.S. *Gold Dust* describe Cape Girardeau as "the Athens of Missouri," "often make people see more than really exists." Partial as I am to Sikeston, I think I see it as it really is. Acts of God and small-time businessmen notwithstanding, Sikeston, Missouri, is still a place where people salute the flag and don't ask for receipts, where everybody knows who your parents were and what they did for a living. It is narrow and kind and decent and good, and I am blessed to have been raised in its shabby, forgiving bosom. It is my home town; it is your home town, too.

3 | *My Mother's People*

Oने night at a cocktail party on the Upper East Side of Manhattan, the hostess, a friend of mine known far and wide for her forthrightness, looked me in the eye and asked: "What kind of name is Teachout, anyway?" Startled by her unexpected interest, I automatically gave my standard answer: "I don't know. I've never looked into it. I guess I've never cared enough to bother." That wasn't good enough for my hostess, who started hauling down fat volumes from her well-stocked shelves in an attempt to shed some light on the origins of my last name. Though several guests offered to help, we got nowhere, partly because it was pretty late in the evening and partly because I was so taken aback by my hostess's curiosity that I forgot to steer her toward the one book in her apartment that might have been of some use: the Manhattan phone book. Unlikely as it may sound, you'll find at least one Teachout in the phone books of most big cities, and New York is no exception.

I have to confess that I've never called up any of these Teachouts, but I do get letters once or twice a year from people named
Teachout who see my name in a magazine and figure that I must
be a far-flung family member who might like to hear from another
branch of the clan. They're half right. Having spelled my last
name out loud a couple of thousand times for the benefit of
confused secretaries and telephone operators, it pleases me to
know about other people who are stuck with it. But I can't tell
you whether I'm related to any of the various Teachouts from
whom I have heard over the years, much less any of the Teachouts
who turn up in the phone books of America. I suppose everybody
in the world named Teachout must be related, but you couldn't
prove it by me. The only natural-born Teachouts I know personally are my father, my brother, and my niece.

The only other Teachouts to whom I am definitely related
live in Iowa. I got a letter from one of them the other day. He
told me that there were plenty of Teachouts in Iowa and that
they hold an annual family reunion which draws Teachouts from
all over the country. I don't know if I'm related to the Nancy
Teachout in the Manhattan phone book; I don't know if I'm
related to the fellow who gave his name to Teachout Creek, a
body of water in Colorado that my parents drove past and photographed many years ago. But I have good reason to believe that
I must be related to at least some of the Teachouts who go to
that reunion, for my paternal grandmother, a handsome, haughty
woman named Verona, who hailed from Omaha, Nebraska, was
married three times, and her first husband was an insurance man
from Des Moines, Iowa, named Harold Teachout.

Harold, who turns up in one of my father's earliest home
movies, died when I was a small boy, after which my father lost
touch with nearly all his other relatives. He has a half-brother
in Iowa with whom my mother exchanges Christmas cards. He
knows about the Teachout family reunion, but he has never
attended it. ("Are they blood relatives?" I asked him once. "Beats
me," he said, shrugging.) His complete lack of interest in other
people named Teachout, far stronger than a mere quirk, is easy

enough to explain. As a child, he was passed around quite a bit; at one point, he actually dropped the name Teachout for a few years and took the name of his second stepfather. As far as my father is concerned, his real family comes in three parts. The first and most important part is the one he has made for himself: his wife and children. Next comes Jim Moore, his other half-brother, with whom he has breakfast and goes to Sunday school every week. Then there is my mother's family, of which my father, unlike most in-laws, considers himself a full-fledged member in good standing.

The Crosnos, my mother's people, scratched their way through the Great Depression and World War II in Diehlstadt, a Bootheel town so small that most mapmakers have yet to hear about it. Albert, my grandfather, sold the family farm and went to work at the shoe factory in Charleston, while Grace, my grandmother, stayed home and raised their two sons and four daughters. Hard times drew the Crosnos close together, and when the children grew old enough to leave the nest, only one of them flew very far. Jet, who had a wandering eye, got himself a job in the construction business that took him to such exotic places as Puerto Rico and Fort Lauderdale, but Suzy, Dot, Peggy, and young Albert stayed closer to home. All of them have lived in Diehlstadt at one time or another, and three of them live there now. Suzy, in fact, lives in the old Crosno house, which got too big for my grandmother when her hardworking, banjo-playing husband had a heart attack and died back in 1962.

Evelyn, the most daring of the Crosno girls, graduated from high school in 1946 and moved down the road to Sikeston. She got herself a bachelorette apartment, a job as a secretary, and, in due course, a husband. She was young and beautiful, with the slightly plump good looks that were popular back in the forties, the decade of the pinup girl; he was young and handsome and just back from the Philippines, where he served in the Army Air Force during the last year of World War II. No sooner had they tied the knot than Bert Teachout discovered that his pretty young wife came equipped with something he had never had before: a half-dozen brothers and sisters who liked nothing better than to share a meal and chew the fat.

I imagine it must have taken my father a while to get used to the Crosnos. One of my earliest memories is of the sound of his deep voice raised in unmistakable irritation as we drove back from a Sunday afternoon visit to Diehlstadt. I can't remember what imagined slight set him off, though I'm sure that it was trivial and surer still that he forgot about it well before the next Sunday rolled around. In any case, his irritation grew milder with every passing year, and the day eventually came when his grumbles were not those of a mere in-law but of an honorary blood relative, intimately familiar with and fully accepting of the various eccentricities of six loving brothers and sisters and their husbands and wives. The truth was that the Crosnos were exactly what my father had been looking for all his life: an old-fashioned family. His own mother and father were long since dead; his relatives were scattered throughout the Midwest. Sikeston was his home and the Crosnos were his family and that was that.

When I was a child, Crosno family gatherings were as commonplace as church on Sunday. We went to Diehlstadt on Thanksgiving and Christmas Eve and the Fourth of July; we went because it was a sunny spring day or because Aunt Peggy had a new baby or because everybody simply got the simultaneous urge to sit down together and talk. Such urges were easy to gratify, for it took only twenty minutes to drive to Diehlstadt, a trip nicely suited to the finite patience of a restless child. With my father at the wheel, we turned right at the Sikeston Cotton Oil Mill and drove past Jon-Don Acres, the local mobile home park, out into the country. We read the battered Burma-Shave signs by the side of the road out loud ("He lit/A match/To check/His tank/And now/They call him/Skinless Frank/BURMA-SHAVE") and paid a visit to the fruit stand on the edge of Bertrand. Two turns later, we were bumping down the unmarked dirt road that led to my grandmother's house.

If it was the Fourth of July, we would pull into my grandmother's driveway early in the afternoon. My parents would go inside to sit with the old people and take part in the slow, steady talk that holds a large family together. (I thought of my aunts and uncles as "the old people," though they were no older than I am now.) I went inside to say hello, too, but I slipped away as quickly as I could, for there were better things to do on a summer day in Diehlstadt than sitting around listening to the old people talk. Sometimes I played softball with Mike, Bob, and Gary, my older cousins, in the empty lot next to Uncle Marshall's garage. Sometimes I shinnied up the low-slung mimosa tree next to my grandmother's house. Sometimes I walked down the road to Uncle Albert's house or across the street to Dot and Marshall's to gaze jealously at a new toy. Sometimes I hid out in Dot and Marshall's living room and spent the day reading about Huckleberry Finn or Captain Ahab.

Later in the day, the older cousins would start dipping into their private stashes of small-bore fireworks suitable for daytime use. Gary favored tiny cylinders that swelled into long, wormy spirals of ash that left huge gray-and-black smears on the front porch; Bob preferred little pellets that exploded with an ear-shattering *crack* when thrown at the nearest rock. Mike usually had a bag full of smoke bombs, and I liked those best. You put a little cardboard sphere in the middle of the dirt road, lit the fuse, and watched it belch forth clouds of foul green smoke. I had no fireworks of my own, for my parents were certain that it would be crazy to turn me loose with them, and they were probably right. So I watched and waited and tried from time to time to talk Mike into letting me touch the glowing end of a piece of punk to the stubby fuse of one of his smoke bombs.

After the last firecracker was lit and tossed, I crawled into the wooden swing on the crumbling front porch of my grandmother's house and rocked in the breeze. Once in a while I brought a book with me, for there are few things as pleasant as reading a good book while sitting in a porch swing on a breezy summer day. More often, though, I left my book in the car, especially after my spindly legs grew long enough to reach the concrete floor of the porch. Then I would sit at the very edge of the broad wooden seat, kick as hard as I could and push the swing higher and higher into the air, high enough that the soles of my sneakers scraped the ceiling and the heavy chains of the swing gave off a scary thump every time I fell back to earth. The higher I swung, the surer I was that the rusty bolts would gradually work their way out of the rotten wood of the ceiling, sending me flying through the air to a bloody but glorious death. Before long, one of the old people always came stomping out of the house and told me to cut it out before I cracked my fool head open.

In the middle of the long afternoon, the whole family gathered on the front porch to make ice cream. The older cousins took turns cranking the old wooden freezer. After half an hour of steady cranking, Uncle Albert unscrewed the lid of the freezer and scooped out rich, grainy, colder-than-cold bowls of pale yellow custard. I ate mine in silence, nursing an ice-cream headache. Then the aunts retired to the kitchen and the uncles set up charcoal grills in the front yard and built roaring fires. Dinner was served as the sun began to set. The old people ate at the dining-room table, the older cousins at a long folding table set up in the living room; the younger cousins sat by themselves in the kitchen. We wolfed down hot dogs, hamburgers, barbecued pork steaks, potato salad, creamed corn, hot rolls, and my mother's spicy baked beans. Then we cleared away the dishes and ate more ice cream and sat and talked until the last light had died away and it was time to cross the dirt road to the empty lot and shoot fireworks.

The old people gave each child a silver sparkler and a skinny brown stick of punk that filled the air with an incenselike smell when lit. As we waved our sparklers, Uncle Albert placed a squat, five-barreled cardboard cylinder on the ground. Mike approached it slowly and ceremonially, punk in hand, the other cousins looking on from a safe distance. We held our breath as he cautiously touched the fuse at the base of the cylinder with the smoldering stick of punk. Nothing happened. He touched it again. Was this one a dud? Then the fuse caught fire with a loud, rasping fizz and Mike darted away as a dozen red and green and blue fireballs shot into the air and exploded into a million golden dots of short-lived flame.

My father liked Roman candles, and I remember the first Fourth of July that he let me hold one on my own. First came the warning: "This isn't a toy, son. You could put somebody's eye out with it. Point it up and away and whatever you do, don't aim it at anybody. Do you understand?" I nodded, my heart racing with excitement. Then he lit the top end and handed me the slim cardboard tube. I pointed it up and away, but I knew that it was aimed at somebody, though I told no one that I was actually a mighty warrior locked in single combat with the evil forces of darkness. I shouted every time the sizzling tube went *crump* and lit up the sky with gaudy bursts of lightning, each one aimed squarely at the forehead of a giant monster from outer space. I dreamed of blue fireballs for weeks.

Like the Fourth of July, Thanksgiving in Diehlstadt was a festival of hot food and small talk. I spent the afternoon outside if it was warm enough; on cold days, the older cousins gathered around the kitchen table to play cards and call each other names. The important business of the day took place after dinner. After the dishes were cleared away, Aunt Suzy tore a sheet of paper into two dozen slips, wrote a name on each slip, folded it in half, and put it in an ashtray. One of the younger cousins proudly carried the ashtray around the room, and everybody pulled out a slip. The name on your slip was the aunt or uncle or cousin for whom you would buy a Christmas present that year. "If you draw your own name," Suzy always told us, "put it back."

The drawing of names was the first milepost on the road to Christmas. Next came the arrival of the Sears, Roebuck Christmas Supplement, an inch-thick volume filled with color pictures of toys of every imaginable kind. On the day that the Christmas catalogue came in the mail, I sat down with a sharp pencil and a pile of notebook paper and wrote down the name, price, and page number of each and every toy I could possibly want. Then I spent hours paring my list down to a reasonable length, a process that called for clear thinking and a cool head. If the list was too long, I might not get the toys I wanted most; if it was too short, I might get fewer toys than my brother David. (Neither catastrophe had ever happened before, but I figured I had to be ready for anything.) Once I finished drawing up the final draft of my Christmas list, I handed it over to my father, Santa Claus's agent and general manager of the Moore Company, a hardware-and-tire store owned by his second stepfather. My father could buy toys wholesale through the Moore Company, and he did so with childlike glee.

Not long after Thanksgiving, my mother would spend the better part of a Saturday afternoon making Christmas cookies and filling two round aluminum tins with dark brown squares of homemade chocolate fudge so rich that we were allowed to eat only one piece at a sitting. David and I cut the sticky cookie dough into stars and bells and silhouettes of Santa Claus and lovingly laid each piece on a greased cookie sheet. The Santa Claus cookies were special, for I took Santa Claus seriously. I left him a glass of milk and a plate of Christmas cookies before going to bed on Christmas Eve, and they were gone by sunup. When I was six years old, my family moved to 713 Hickory Drive, a house without a chimney. We had a long, tense family discussion that year about how Santa Claus would be able to get into our new house to bring us our presents. My father, a true man of the world, calmed me down by explaining that Santa Claus had a master key that unlocked the front door of every house on earth.

One terrible morning, my Sunday-school teacher announced in a matter-of-fact voice that there was no Santa Claus, a piece of news that left me choking back tears for the rest of the day. It took a little while for me to figure out that since the presents that magically appeared under the tree every year weren't coming from the North Pole, they must be stashed somewhere in the house.

That was when I gave up on Santa Claus and took matters into my own hands. I worked my way through all the upstairs closets. I opened every drawer and inspected every shelf that I was tall enough to reach. I spent whole afternoons quietly poking around the basement, a dark, cluttered cavern full of dusty shelves and moldy cardboard boxes, every one of which had to be opened and checked out.

Hunting for Christmas presents became an annual ritual, one that helped to ease me through a bad patch in my childhood: the year we added two rooms to 713 Hickory Drive. I don't think my parents ever quite understood how frightening it is for a child to see his home torn up and transformed right before his eyes. To make matters even worse, my very own bedroom was scheduled for demolition. After years of sharing a room with my brother, I had been allowed to move into the guest bedroom, which contained a phonograph and a long bookshelf and a double bed with flabby springs and a soft mattress. No sooner did the carpenters show up than this sumptuous retreat vanished in a cloud of sawdust. Before the week was out, my bedroom had become a hallway and four clothes closets. My father swore I'd have a bigger bedroom, but I didn't care. I was furious.

My fury softened after I moved into my parents' old bedroom, a bright and spacious corner room complete with half-bath, and it disappeared altogether as soon I learned that one of the new closets would be lined with cedar panels. I loved the tart, cinnamonlike fragrance of cedar, so much so that I occasionally sat in the closet and read books by flashlight. Within a few months, it was so full of clothes that I couldn't sit down anymore. By that time, though, I had a more compelling interest in the cedar closet, for I discovered one December afternoon that my parents were using it to hide Christmas presents. This discovery, about which I said nothing for several years, made it possible for me to keep track of the arrival of incoming presents. It also taught me how satisfying it is to keep a secret.

When the top shelf of the cedar closet was filled to the ceiling with toys, I knew it was time to bundle up, jump in the car, and drive down snowy country roads to spend Christmas Eve with the family. My grandmother started cooking when the sun came up, and by the time we got to Diehlstadt you could smell the turkey and dressing a block away. After the last roll was buttered and the last gooey dessert tasted, we loosened our belts and sat down in the living room, where a scrawny little Christmas tree shed pine needles on an enormous mound of gifts. My grandmother invariably bought pathetic-looking Christmas trees whose limp branches drooped toward the floor like the arms of a starving man. I can't imagine where she got them. Maybe she grew them in the root cellar out back.

As soon as the old people started talking, one of the older cousins would let out a fearful cry and chase me through the house. I headed straight for the two-way closet, an architectural marvel that linked the back bedrooms of my grandmother's house. Although there was a closet door in each bedroom, there was only one closet between them. I slid a door open, shoved aside blouses and skirts and mothballs and groped blindly for the other one. Whenever I found a stray cousin hiding in the closet, I hit him on the head with a wooden coat hanger and yelled for help.

Though I liked to play with my cousins, I also liked to be alone, and when I grew tired of running around the house, I would trudge across the snow-covered dirt road to Dot and Marshall's house and watch a little Christmas Eve television by myself. One year I watched Gian Carlo Menotti's *Amahl and the Night Visitors*, my first opera, and cried when the crippled shepherd boy offered his crutch to the Three Kings to give to the Holy Child; one year I watched the astronauts of Apollo 8, in orbit around the moon, open a Bible and read the Christmas story aloud to the whole world. I went out in the front yard afterward and stood in the ankle-high snow, looking for a long time at the silvery wedge that hung so far above me in the starry winter sky. Then I crossed the road again to eat warmed-over turkey and dressing with the rest of the family.

After dinner, the cousins gathered around the tree and the old people lined up to take pictures. We made funny faces and pinched each other as hard as we dared. The picture that showed the least amount of horseplay would be framed and given to my grandmother, who hung it in the gallery of grandchildren that covered one wall of her living room. Then the grownups took each other's pictures. First the in-laws photographed Grace and the six Crosno children, known since time immemorial as the "outlaws"; then the outlaws would take pictures of Grace and the in-laws. Soon every eye was swimming with blue flash spots.

Once the pictures were taken, the younger cousins started delivering Christmas presents. The old people opened their boxes carefully, folding the paper and putting it aside to wrap next year's birthday presents. The older cousins ripped their boxes open and threw basketball-sized wads of wrapping paper at each other. After I showed my gift to my parents, I waded through a sea of tissue paper and brightly colored ribbons, kicking empty cardboard boxes out of my way, and hugged whichever aunt or uncle had given me the heavy wool sweater or the handsome dress shirt. (I spent a half-dozen Christmases waiting in vain for *somebody* to give me a toy.) Then the aunts collected their covered dishes and the older cousins marched through the house, filling plastic garbage bags with red and green paper wads. I put on my coat and gloves, kissed everyone goodbye, and got in the car to go home. My brother and I huddled in the back seat, clutching our new sweaters and thinking about our Christmas lists.

Once we got home, David and I put out milk and cookies for Santa Claus and went to bed. Though we usually tried to stay up as late as we could, we never complained about going to bed early on Christmas Eve. We knew that the sooner we went to sleep, the sooner we would wake up and run down the hall to the living room in our pajamas and start tearing open presents, confident that this time there would be toys to go with the heavy sweaters and dignified dress shirts. My mother tucked me in and sang a chorus of "Winter Wonderland," my favorite lullaby. Then I closed my eyes tightly and listened for the faint rustle of boxes being pulled out of the cedar closet. Weary from the long, happy day, I soon fell fast asleep.

.   .   .

Small-town newspapers take a day off now and then, but most big-city papers are published every day, December 25 included. Not long after I went to work for the New York *Daily News*, I drew the short straw and had to stay in town during Christmas week in order to help get the paper out. Midway through December, my wife had to fly back to Missouri to see a sick relative. I spent an hour on the telephone that afternoon listening to five different ticket agents tell me that every scheduled flight from New York to St. Louis was booked solid for the evening of December 24. Even if I had been able to get a seat, I would have had to fly back to New York the next day. My heart sank as I hung up the phone for the fifth and last time, for it had become clear to me that I would be spending the holidays in a New York apartment with only my two cats for company, alone on Christmas for the first time in my life.

My boss opened champagne in his office at noon on Christmas Eve, and I sipped mine silently as my colleagues described the family gatherings to which they were headed after the last bottle was empty. I knew that I had a long evening and an even longer day ahead of me, but I was determined to make the best of it, though I wasn't quite sure how. When I got home that night, I found a box with a Sikeston postmark on my doorstep. The box bore telltale signs of my father's handiwork: it was wrapped in heavy twine and sealed with thick strips of reinforced tape. I had to use a butcher knife to get it open. Inside were four neatly wrapped Christmas presents and a familiar-looking round aluminum tin with a festive Christmas scene printed on the lid. It was one of the tins in which my mother had been storing Christmas cookies and fudge for as long as I could remember, and it was full of homemade molasses cookies.

I called home, catching my parents just as they were headed out the door for Diehlstadt. I called my wife. I popped a frozen pizza into the oven and went into the living room, which was bare of Christmas decorations. (It is as hard to put up a Christmas tree for yourself as it is to cook for yourself.) I put on a record of *The Nutcracker*. Then I curled up on the couch with my cats, my presents, and my tin of cookies and thought about the *Nutcracker* I had seen at Lincoln Center a few days before. Something told me that watching *The Nutcracker* in a theater full of children would cheer me up, so I chose a Saturday matinee. Kyra Nichols, my favorite ballerina, was dancing that afternoon, and I expected to enjoy myself. I did, too, but not in the way I had expected. George Balanchine's version of *The Nutcracker* begins with a Christmas Eve family party. The setting is a large, homey-looking living room filled with children who exchange presents, play leapfrog, and chase each other around. As the curtain went up and the children began to play, my eyes filled with tears. It was all so familiar. It had all been such a long time ago.

My wife comes from Trenton, a small town in the northern part of Missouri. We lived in Kansas City for the first few years of our marriage, and we fell into the easy habit of driving up to Trenton after work on Christmas Eve and going down to the Bootheel to visit my family a few days later. This habit persisted long after we left Missouri, and so it had been several years since I had spent Christmas Eve with my own family. It wasn't hard for me to settle into the cheerful customs of my in-laws, but doing so caused me to forget that there are only two Christmas rituals that can truly satisfy the soul: the one you learn from your parents and the one you teach your children.

My wife and I are childless, and my memories of Christmas Eve in Diehlstadt had grown pale and distant from disuse. But now, as I stroked my purring cats and ate molasses cookies and listened to *The Nutcracker*, those half-forgotten memories, stirred by my visit to Lincoln Center, sprang to life and filled the apartment with comfort and joy. Though the only ornament in sight was the cookie tin resting in my lap, a scrawny tree blazed merrily away in the corner of the room; though my loved ones were a thousand miles away, they sat by me on the couch, lifting my heart with their presence. I said a silent prayer of thanks and went to bed a happy man.

4 | *A Prig's Progress*

Every married couple finds its own ways to divvy up the endless labors of family life. One washes, the other dries; one spanks, the other offers bribes. My father took the pictures at our house, but my mother was in charge of the rest of the Teachout family archives. She scrawled an entry in the baby book whenever I did anything more interesting than sucking my thumb. She found a place of honor for the lumpy blue clay cup that I made in my seventh-grade art class. (It now sits on a shelf over the washing machine, filled with paper clips, postage stamps, and loose change.) In the course of the last thirty-five years, she has accumulated several pounds' worth of report cards, newspaper clippings, and programs from concerts, receptions, plays, assemblies, and graduations, all of it shoehorned into crumbling manila envelopes and stored in a cupboard in the living room.

I like to look at my mother's clippings, but I try to take them with a grain or two of salt. A family archive is a record of youthful success. The triumphs go into the scrapbook, the disasters into the wastebasket. If you went by the clippings, you'd probably come away thinking I was Sikeston's own Jack Armstrong, All-American Boy. Naturally, my childhood was more complicated than that, just as Sikeston itself is more complicated than *63 units/Rodeo and Miner Fruit Market nearby/World-famous Lambert's*. In order to understand the clippings, you have to read between the lines.

The last time I went through the living-room cupboard, I found a yellowed clipping from the *Daily Sikeston Standard*: "In Monday's paper under City League Baseball results it stated that KSIM had defeated Rotary 14–6 according to the score book. It stands corrected that Rotary did defeat KSIM in the Saturday night contest 14–6. Burrow picked up the win for Rotary and was aided at the plate with Teachout's three hits." You could have seen my head swell up from across the street as I read about that game. It had completely slipped my mind. I was the worst Little League baseball player of my time, possibly of all time. I spent night after night sitting in the dugout watching my teammates hit line drives. How could I have failed to recall my lone moment of glory? It seemed too good to be true. As I fingered the clipping, the worm of suspicion started gnawing away at my newfound pride. Maybe it *was* too good to be true. I turned the clipping over and looked at the date: July 15, 1970. I took a deep breath and let it out slowly. The date was wrong. The Teachout who had saved the day for Rotary twenty years ago was David, not Terry. I had forgotten that my brother played for Rotary, too.

If you want to know what my childhood was like, all you have to do is imagine the flush of pride I felt as I read about those three nonexistent hits I got off KSIM a quarter of a century ago. Yes, I got good grades; yes, I won my share of prizes. But I was also an awkward, nearsighted little boy whose idea of a really good time was a trip to the public library, and I would gladly have barbecued my library card at high noon in Legion Square in order to impress the other kids on my block. My brother, a feisty, red-haired troublemaker who fixed old cars and drove in winning runs with insolent ease, had no trouble impressing his friends. With me, it was different. I was the one who put my hand up in class every time the teacher asked a question. I told the other kids how good my grades were. I never tattled on anybody, but I committed a far greater offense: I refused to cheat. Cheating was a sin against order, and I was an orderly child. From kindergarten on, I did as I was told and made no bones about it.

To top it all off, I was totally lacking in what my father called "common sense," an elusive quality that most Sikestonians (and all of my relatives) seemed to have in frustrating abundance. *You haven't got a lick of common sense, son,* he said to me over and over again. How I hated that. I told myself that I was *full* of common sense and that anybody who thought otherwise was just plain wrong. But those who thought otherwise were right, and I proved it on the afternoon that I poured myself a glass of water from the kitchen tap and noticed with surprise that it was muddy brown. I don't know why I was so surprised. Sikeston's tap water turns brown every once in a while, usually because the fire department is flushing a hydrant somewhere in the neighborhood, a procedure that lets a little rust into the water mains. Any normal boy would have dumped the water down the drain and gone about his business. Not me. I decided that something was wrong with the water supply, and I decided to do something about it.

This is where common sense comes in. Had I been adequately endowed with it, I would have called up the Sikeston Water Department, asked them why the water was brown, and delivered an oral report on The Problem of Brown Water in class the next day. But that was the year I memorized "Paul Revere's Ride" for extra credit, and it was all too typical of my younger self that I drew my solution to Sikeston's water problem from Longfellow instead of life: I saddled up my bicycle and spent the rest of the afternoon telling every housewife in the neighborhood that the city water supply was polluted and that they shouldn't drink any more of it until further notice. More than a few of them believed me, and I'm not surprised, either. How could such a serious-looking child have made up so bizarre a story out of whole cloth?

It took the water department a couple of hours to catch up with my mother, who tracked me down about fifteen minutes later. I'll leave it at that.

My parents, both of whom were perfectly normal in every way, were puzzled by the creature they had spawned. I seemed ordinary enough in Diehlstadt, where I played tag, climbed trees, and even joined in the fruit fights that took place in my grand-mother's backyard every summer. Mike, Bob, Gary, and I would stand in the four corners of the yard and throw overripe plums at each other until one of the old people told us to lay off before we broke a window. (Guess who finally broke a window?) But what worked in Diehlstadt never quite passed muster in Sikeston. Bad as I was in Little League, I was even worse as a Boy Scout. I actually fainted from sunstroke during an overnight hike at Shiloh National Park. I earned only one merit badge in the course of my short, unhappy life as a member of Troop 43; it was for cooking, an activity about which I knew nothing whatsoever. After spending the morning poring over *The Boy Scout Handbook*, I dug a pit in the backyard, whittled a crooked spit, built a fire, and proceeded to roast the toughest shish kebab imaginable. Not only did I make my parents eat it, but I insisted that my father call up Roy Nall, the scoutmaster, in order to confirm that it would be all right for me to start the fire with a match instead of by rubbing two sticks together. Had he said no, I'd probably still be rubbing sticks together in the backyard of 713 Hickory Drive.

I was, in short, a born prig, and I could never leave well enough alone. There were always bigger and better apples to polish. It wasn't enough, for instance, that I was a good speller; I had to enter the local spelling bee, and I had to win it. One thing led to another, and before I knew it, I was in St. Louis, spelling my heart out on KPLR-TV before a viewing audience of about twelve. (The St. Louis Blues were playing a Stanley Cup match that afternoon, and nobody in town was interested in the state spelling bee. Even the monitors in the control room were tuned to another channel so that the technicians could watch the game.) My luck ran out that day, for a girl named Sally Shoemaker spelled me into the dirt and went on to the national finals, leaving me the second-best speller in Missouri, an honor that ranks right up there with being an unsuccessful vice-presidential candidate. Sally went to a Catholic school, and I like to think that wimpled nuns beat her with rubber hoses whenever she spelled a word wrong.

Looking back, it seems to me that the biggest problem of my childhood was that I was afraid of experience. I can't tell you how I got that way. Perhaps I charmed too many aunts at too many family gatherings; perhaps I was clobbered by Mike Griffith, the schoolyard bully, once too often. Whatever the reason, I was the very worst kind of Goody Two-Shoes. I went to church every Sunday and paid close attention to the sermons. Not that there's anything wrong with that, for a good sermon never hurt anybody, and the sermons at Murray Lane Baptist Church, preached in a ripe Tennessee accent by a good-hearted minister named Wade Paris, were top-notch. But an important ingredient was missing from my budding moral imagination: a sense of scale. Like a true Christian, I didn't kill anybody or covet my neighbor's wife. In addition, though, I never threw a roll of toilet paper over a neighbor's tree, stole a garbage can, or smoked a cigarette. Worse yet, I was terrified at the thought of putting myself in a situation where I might be unexpectedly called upon to perform one of these mortal sins.

Whenever I showed signs of being able to do something that might actually have impressed the kids on my block, I usually found a way to get it wrong. Take the fifth-grade music test. Every fifth-grader in Sikeston was given an aptitude test as a screening device for the music program. I aced the test, meaning that I could play any instrument I wanted. I could have picked trumpet or tenor saxophone, or, best of all, drums. No such luck. I chose the violin. While everybody else took band in the school cafeteria, I scraped away in a tiny cubicle of my own, wrenching bloodcurdling shrieks out of my Roth student-model violin. That December, the Matthews Elementary School Concert Band appeared at an all-school assembly, playing a simple arrangement of "The Little Drummer Boy" that sounded not unlike the performance of Beethoven's Minuet in G that Professor Harold Hill, the hero of *The Music Man*, coaxed from the children of River City, Iowa, a town not unlike Sikeston, Missouri, by using the Think Method. Richard Powell, my violin teacher, transposed a clarinet part for me, making it possible for me to sit in with the band. It was my first public appearance as a musician. It was also the last time I played with a band until I was a senior in high school, by which time it was far too late for me to get any social benefit out of the experience.

I don't mean to make light of my discovery of music. It was the most important event of my adolescence, if not my whole life. It's just that it served to isolate me even further from my peers, none of whom was even remotely interested in classical music. My interest, on the other hand, was passionate. No flesh-and-blood love affair could have been more thrilling. (That's what I told myself, anyway.) I remember the first time I listened to a whole symphony from beginning to end. It was a recording of the Tchaikovsky *Pathétique* by Eugene Ormandy and the Philadelphia Orchestra, and I bought it at Collins Piano Company for $5.98 in nickels, dimes, and quarters hoarded from my weekly allowance. I was twelve years old. As I played the first movement, I felt as if I had stepped through an unmarked door and fallen headlong into another universe. I never looked back.

By the time I was thirteen, I was eating and sleeping music. I practiced the violin constantly. I listened to plenty of rock and roll, but I also checked classical albums out of the Middle School library, carted them home in the library's green canvas bags, and played them in my bedroom. In one corner hung a portrait of Abraham Lincoln; in another, a garish poster purchased from a Cape Girardeau head shop. I changed it every few months in an attempt to add a touch of color to my life. The most imposing piece of furniture in the room was a cabinet radio-phonograph of uncertain vintage, a hand-me-down from my grandmother Verona known in the Teachout family as "the monster." The monster was the size of a food freezer and almost as heavy. I wore out five sapphire-tipped needles playing the *Pathétique* and *Appalachian Spring* and the slow movement of the Gershwin Concerto in F on that two-ton piece of junk.

As I sat in my bedroom listening to one record after another, I tried to figure out who I was and what I wanted to be. The answer to the second question seemed plain enough, though my father and I had different ideas about it. I wanted to be a musician; he wanted me to become a lawyer. The first question was trickier. On the outside, I was loud and pushy, lashing out at my classmates before they had a chance to reject me. On the inside, I was painfully shy, and nothing embarrassed me more than the fact that I was capable of falling flat on my face at a moment's notice. One day I was chatting with two girls on the third-floor landing of the junior high school, known in Sikeston as Middle School. I was trying to act blasé, that being my idea of how to flirt, when my foot slipped. I slid down a whole flight of stairs, landing squarely on and demolishing my olive-drab briefcase, which exploded in a white cloud of fluttering sheets of notebook paper. The girls doubled up with laughter and ran off. It was a month before I could look either one of them in the eye.

Much to the relief of everyone who knew me, I began to loosen up during my second year in Middle School. I fell in with a circle of kids from my neighborhood who walked home from school together and who stopped off every afternoon at Little Man Lambert's, a hole-in-the-wall diner run by Coach Lambert's father, to sip a Coke and eat a bag of potato chips. Even though I was the smartest kid in school and wore horn-rimmed glasses and a tight crew cut, Terry Presley, Mark Deane, Jim Bob Dixon, Drew Matthews, and David Crites were more than willing to put up with me. They were the first children of my own age who treated me in the same matter-of-fact way they treated each other, and their friendship helped me get up the nerve to put a fist through the hard candy shell of my priggishness for the first time in my life.

My new friends were startled by some of the qualities that

lay dormant beneath my shell. I was, like many nice boys, unexpectedly tough. Not that I could have held my own for five minutes in a fistfight, but once I made up my mind to do something, I would go through with it or die first. My niceness also concealed a deeply repressed streak of mischief. (Why else would I have told a hundred housewives that the Sikeston Water Department was dispensing cyanide cocktails right out of their kitchen taps?) Encouraged by my friends, it wasn't long before I found an opportunity to turn that hidden streak loose. Having toted hundreds of highbrow books and records back and forth from the library, I had become something of a minor-league aesthete. One of the principal objects of my disdain was the annual Middle School talent assembly, a gruesome succession of amateur acts. I decided that somebody ought to break it up, and I figured that it might as well be me. Being a prig, though, I had to figure out a way to do this without actually getting in trouble, or getting anyone else in trouble. So I did something characteristic: I spilled my guts to Bob Nelson, the teacher in charge of the talent assembly.

For once, luck was with me. Mr. Nelson, an unabashed child of the sixties, had longish hair and a scraggly beard. He used to bring his guitar to my eighth-grade social-studies class and sing Beatles songs. He loaned me records by Judy Collins and Joan Baez and listened soberly to my elaborate interpretations of the songs of Bob Dylan's middle period. He understood how much I wanted to break free of my inhibitions, and his relaxed, easygoing demeanor had an electric effect on me. Inspired by Mr. Nelson, I let my tight crew cut turn shaggy, fighting with my father over every extra inch. Assigned by Mr. Nelson to write a term paper on the most important event of the last half century, I produced a fifteen-page exercise in wishful thinking called "The Pill" to which he gave the highest possible marks. (I don't think I ran that one past my mother.)

I discovered, not entirely to my surprise, that Mr. Nelson shared my low opinion of the talent assembly. With his encouragement, I enlisted Terry Presley as my confederate and went to work. On the morning of the assembly, the entire Middle School student body trooped numbly into the gym and braced itself for the familiar parade of dance routines and baton-twirling girls. After the second act, Mr. Nelson took the stage and announced an unscheduled addition to the program. Without cracking a smile, he told the audience that Terry Teachout, whom everybody knew, had graciously agreed to deliver the speech with which he had recently won the local Optimist Club oratory contest. A copy of this speech can be found in the Teachout family archives, but you can take my word that it was long, pretentious, and badly delivered. Had I actually given it that morning, I would have been branded an apple-polisher for life. Fortunately for me, I had something else in mind.

The janitor pushed a podium to center stage and I strode up to it, snappily dressed in a jacket and tie and carrying an inch-thick pile of papers. I heard a chorus of groans from the back of the gym as I straightened my tie and cleared my throat. Then Terry Presley slipped through the curtains behind me, a cream pie balanced in one hand. As I opened my mouth to speak, Terry threw the pie at me, rubbed the plate in my face, and ran off. The silence that followed was as thick as the whipped cream that was dripping off my nose and chin. Then the gym exploded in laughter, loud, delicious laughter, all of it aimed at me. I clasped my hands above my head in a gesture of triumph and strode off the stage, leaving a sticky trail of whipped cream in my wake.

It wasn't long before I got up the nerve to strike another blow in the name of normality. The Army has a pithy word for official acts of priggishness: *chickenshit*. Polly Hanks, the Middle School librarian, committed an act of chickenshit when she announced that students who wanted to check out library books would henceforth have to sign two cards instead of one. It was a modest offense, but it irritated me, and it also irritated several of my friends. Over lunch that day, we discussed various ways and means of teaching Mrs. Hanks a lesson. Several suggestions were made, all of them too complicated to pull off on short notice. Then I spoke up. I suggested that we demonstrate our love for reading by checking out three books apiece that afternoon—and encouraging all our friends to do the same. A solemn hush settled over the table. Then we shook hands and marched off to war.

I strolled up the stairs two hours later, planning to saunter casually by the library and see how things were going. I didn't get that far. A line of noisy students stretched all the way from the stairwell to the circulation desk. By the time I pushed my way through the crowd to the door of the library, the mound of checkout cards on the desk was two feet high. Mrs. Hanks, who was no fool, figured out that something fishy was going on when she noticed a particularly knuckleheaded athlete lugging a biography of Edgar Allan Poe to the circulation desk. She immediately ordered everyone out of the library and bolted the door. Half an hour later, the school intercom rasped to life. Six students were told to report to the principal's office on the double. I wasn't one of them.

I understood at once what had happened: Harley Barnes, the vice-principal in charge of discipline, had simply rounded up the usual suspects. He was right on the money, too, for all six of them had been eating lunch with me that day. The only culprit he missed was the ringleader. It never occurred to Mr. Barnes that a well-behaved young man like me could have dreamed up so flagrant an act of youthful rebellion. I knew my friends would never rat on me, but it didn't matter, because I didn't give them a chance. At long last, I had done something really outrageous, and the six class clowns who got credit for everything were getting *my* press. This would never do. As soon as the bell rang, I stomped down the stairs and marched into the principal's office, briefcase in hand. Puffed up with a rich sense of self-righteousness, I threw open Mr. Barnes's door and demanded punishment. Never did any student in the history of Sikeston Middle School enjoy staying after school as much as I did. I think my parents were almost as pleased as I was, though they would never have admitted it.

The Great Middle School Library Book Checkout, as it came to be called, was not without its long-term repercussions. On my first day as a freshman at Sikeston Senior High School, I went to the library to pick up my textbooks for the coming year. As I stood in line, the head librarian, a portly gentleman named Frederick W. Huff, pulled open the door of his office, ambled over to me, shook a finger in my face and informed me in deep organ tones that he knew who I was and what I had done the year before and that there'd be the devil to pay if I tried anything like that in *his* library. Then he turned on his heel, strode back to his office, and shut the door. Only one response to this lordly gesture was possible: absolute loyalty. I spent the next three summers working like a dog for the high school library, passing the job on to my brother when I went off to college. It was worth it. Mr. Huff had gotten my high school career off to an ideal start by chiding me in public for gross misconduct. My classmates decided that there might be hope for me yet.

5 | *Anatevka, Mo.*

The most important building in a small town is the house where you grew up. The second most important building depends on who you are. It may be the church where you were baptized or the bank where you worked during the summer of your junior year or the school where you learned to read. Several buildings may vie for your loyalty; indeed, your heart may belong to a building that no longer exists, one that was struck by lightning in the middle of the night and burned to the ground years ago. But somewhere or other, be it on Front Street or in hallowed memory, there is a building that deserves the prize.

My building, the Sikeston Middle School Gymnasium, was built, so the cornerstone says, in 1925. By the time I got there, it was a dingy-looking pile of faded bricks and scuffed white tiles. My father played basketball and ran laps there when he was a teenager. Back then, it was the Sikeston High School Gymnasium. When the new high school was built three decades later, the old high school was turned over to Sikeston's seventh- and eighth-graders, in much the same way that a good winter coat is passed down from brother to brother. Though I labored there for two years, trying without success to unravel the mysteries of basketball and volleyball and gymnastics, it was the stage that made the gym the most important building in town for me. Like most small-town gymnasiums, the Middle School gym was equipped with a modest stage. It had no fly gallery and hardly any backstage space at all, but it did have four dressing rooms, a shiny velvet curtain, and a proscenium arch. On top of all this, it was the only stage in town situated in a building large enough to hold a good-sized audience, for the city fathers had failed to include an auditorium when they drew up the specifications for the new high school.

This oversight gave the Middle School gym a central place in the daily life of my home town. If you wanted to put on an indoor show in Sikeston, you did it in the gym or you didn't bother. The Sikeston Community Concert Association, for example, held its concerts in the gym, and I heard my first piano recital there. It was given by a dashing young man named David Bar-Illan. I still remember the program: Beethoven, Weber, Liszt, and Leonard Bernstein. Bar-Illan spoke to the audience between pieces, and his clipped accent fell strangely on my small-town ear. It was the accent of a well-educated man born in Israel and living in New York, but I didn't know it at the time, never having met anyone from either Israel or New York, well-educated or otherwise. A few years later, I reviewed a Bar-Illan recital for the Kansas City *Star*; he was playing in a synagogue and wearing a yarmulke, neither of which seemed at all strange to me by then. A few years after that, I read a magazine article by Bar-Illan and dropped him a note to say how much I liked it, mentioning in passing that his had been my first piano recital. He wrote back promptly, and I was surprised (and not a little pleased) to learn that he remembered the occasion quite well.

Sikeston Little Theater performed in the Middle School gym, putting on two straight plays and a musical comedy every year. I knew about Little Theater long before I first saw it in action, for my Uncle Jim played the King of Siam in *The King and I* one year and shaved off all his bushy red hair in order to look more like Yul Brynner. The show ran far past my bedtime, so I didn't get to see it, but the sight of Jim's bald head is firmly lodged in my memory. The Sikeston High School Drama Club, also known as the Harlequin Players, performed in the gym, too, and they gave a special weekday matinee performance of Noël Coward's *Blithe Spirit*, the first play I ever saw, when I was in eighth grade. It seemed to me the very height of urbanity, but it was also *funny*, as funny as Jack Benny or Red Skelton, and I found the paradox baffling and exciting. I was no less excited by *A Thurber Carnival*, which the theater department of Southeast Missouri State College brought to the gym later that year. Even though the boomy acoustics of the gym blotted out most of the punch lines, I loved every minute of *A Thurber Carnival*, and it made a big impression on me.

As soon as I entered high school, I threw myself head first into every outside activity for which I was eligible and at which I imagined myself to be even remotely competent. Staff slots on the *Bulldog Barker*, the school newspaper, were reserved for seniors, so I spent most of my spare time making music. I played in the orchestra and sang in the Concert Choir and Moderne Chorale. I prepared violin solos every year for the District Music Festival in Cape Girardeau. I taught myself how to play double bass and guitar. But my first extracurricular venture was at once the most predictable and the least likely of all: I tried out for a part in the fall play, William Archibald's *The Innocents*, a Broadway version of Henry James's "The Turn of the Screw." I had never read "The Turn of the Screw" and didn't know who Henry James was, but "Miles, age 14" was clearly an appropriate part for a skinny young freshman with a high-pitched voice, so I charged ahead.

It was, to put it mildly, a silly thing for me to have done. I knew that I lacked the physical presence that is as basic to the young actor as the ability to tell one note from another is to the young musician. I probably would have done just as well trying out for the football team. But I was drawn to the stage in spite of everything, and for a perfectly good reason: I wanted to try being somebody else for a change. That, after all, was more or less what I had done when I let Terry Presley plaster me with a cream pie in front of the entire Middle School student body, and it had worked. I made new friends through my audacity, and they belonged to *me*, not to the laughing fool covered with whipped cream. I had no illusions about being able to act. It didn't matter. I wanted a mask to hide behind—and, perhaps, to live up to.

As it turned out, I did better than I had any right to expect. The three lead roles in *The Innocents* were double-cast; Stephen Skalsky, my best friend from Middle School, played Miles on Thursday and Saturday nights, while I played him on Friday night and at the Saturday matinee. Barbara Brown, the faculty adviser, insisted that one cast was just as good as the other, but I knew better. Nobody was cruel enough to tell me how bad I was, though one of my friends did threaten to break up the Friday night performance by sitting in the back row of the Middle School gym and slowly rolling empty soda cans down the aisle.

Playing Miles was not the transformation for which I had hoped. It was still me on that little stage, and everybody knew it, myself included. But something far more important happened during the six weeks we spent in rehearsal: I got my first taste of the intimacy shared by the cast and crew of a play. We spent long nighttime hours working together in a cavernous building into which no stranger was allowed to set foot. We concentrated intensely on each other on stage and talked endlessly to each other off stage, exchanging the self-conscious confidences of adolescence in the shadowy corners of the gym. After every dress rehearsal and every performance, we drove to Sambo's, an all-night restaurant on the edge of Sikeston, and we went with faces unwashed and makeup intact, that being the badge of membership in the most exclusive fraternity in town.

I had never before made friends so easily, and the experience turned my head. No sooner did the curtain come down on the last night of *The Innocents* than I was ready to do it all over again. I got a small part in the spring play, *Harvey*, and the charged atmosphere of collective intimacy was no less heady the second time around. The only problem was that the crowd that had adopted me wasn't the crowd with which I wanted to hang out. Like most high school theater crowds, the Harlequin Players imagined themselves proud outcasts from the pettiness of small-town life. They saw Sikeston as hopelessly provincial and treated their classmates, especially the popular ones, with a lofty disdain that was rather convincing at times. I wasn't above this kind of role-playing, but I was still enough of a prig to be horrified by the fact that several of my colleagues were openly experimenting with sex and drugs. This put me in an impossible situation, or so I thought. Priggishness and tolerance don't mix, and it never occurred to me that I could simply do as I pleased and let my friends do the same. Instead, I decided to change my friends. Luckily for me, I didn't have to look very far to find new ones. I didn't even have to change buildings.

It takes a special kind of person to keep going back to a run-down gymnasium year after year, putting on greasepaint and pretending to be somebody else for the amusement of paying customers, some of whom are his friends and neighbors. Such people are in short supply in any small town, and the turnover tends to be brisk. For this reason, any teenager who takes a more than casual interest in the activities of a small-town theater group is likely to be greeted with a good deal of enthusiasm. That, at any rate, was what happened when I tried out for a part in *Oliver!*, Sikeston Little Theater's 1972 musical. The regular members of the company were clearly as glad to have me as I was to join them, and I put the Harlequin Players behind me without a second thought.

I knew that trying out for a musical comedy was a long shot at best. Though I had perfect pitch and could carry a tune easily, my voice was small and uninteresting, and my shyness kept me from singing out. Still, I had managed to get into the Concert Choir, and I was highly motivated, largely because the director of *Oliver!* was a cheerful, buxom woman named Carole Sue Clayton, wife of Buddy Clayton, my favorite high school teacher. I adored Buddy not only because, like Fred Huff, he took a genuine interest in me and did his best to help me over the hurdles of high school life, but because I had a crush on his older daughter, a leggy, outgoing girl named Lee. Lee liked me well enough, but I never dared to ask her out. Instead, I sought to impress her from a safe distance, and 1 suspect that this was the main reason why I decided to try out for the part of the Artful Dodger.

My chances were better than I knew, if only because everybody knew me. I was the champion of the local spelling bee and the Optimist Club speaking contest, a sound young man who could be counted on to work hard and show up on time. My voice had not yet broken and was high enough to manage the part. After two plays with the Harlequin Players, I knew how to get around a stage, and I was clever enough to do something that nobody else who wanted the part bothered to do: I memorized my big number, "Consider Yourself," before showing up for the audition. I don't know what kind of competition I had, but I got the part, so it must not have been very stiff. I quickly set about learning my lines and trying to figure out how not to embarrass myself too badly on stage. My anxieties disappeared when rehearsals began. The huge cast and crew offered plenty of opportunities for companionship, and the constant and reassuring presence of adults kept things from becoming frighteningly rowdy.

All of this changed when my mother went into the hospital a few weeks after *Oliver!* went into rehearsal. She had been suffering for months from headaches so severe that she sought the advice of specialists. At one point, she even consulted a Cape Girardeau psychiatrist, who spent half an hour chatting with her in the coffee shop of the hospital where I was born. The psychiatrist told my mother that whatever was wrong with her, it wasn't in her head. Figuratively, he was right; literally, he was dead wrong. One sunny March morning, not long after I had darted out the back door and headed for school, my mother collapsed in the bathroom. As I dissected a frog in biology class, an ambulance rushed her to the hospital, where the doctors concluded that her headaches had been caused by a cerebral aneurysm of long standing that had finally burst that morning, wreaking grave damage to her brain. Since no one in the Bootheel knew how to perform emergency brain surgery, they put her back in the ambulance and sent her to Baptist Memorial Hospital in Memphis, Tennessee.

I was given a sanitized version of the day's events after I came home from school that afternoon. (Aunt Suzy chose not to tell me that my mother had stopped breathing and had been revived in the nick of time by a paramedic.) I took the news in stride. My mother had been in and out of hospitals in the course of the last couple of years; I thought it entirely possible that the doctors in Memphis might cure her once and for all. So I fixed myself a peanut-butter sandwich and went off to the Middle School gym, where I was picked up an hour and a half later by two grim-faced neighbors who stuffed me into the back of an empty ambulance that was returning to Memphis that night. I was told months later that the purpose of the trip had been to give me a last look at my mother before she died. This came as no surprise to me, for I had guessed as much when I saw her. Her head had been shaved in preparation for surgery, and as I took her hand, she called me "Albert," the name of her oldest brother.

I was stunned. I was also unprepared. No one close to me had ever died before, and my mother was closer to me than anyone. I had always been intimidated by my father's cool competence in the world of tools and jobs and common sense. I went to my father whenever I wanted to learn how things worked; I went to my mother whenever I had a secret fear to confess. She did her best to teach me how to laugh at myself. She was the sturdy house that sheltered me from unknown terrors. The roof of that house fell in on me when I saw her lying in the intensive-care ward of Baptist Memorial Hospital, bald and helpless. I looked for the first time on the blank face of death, and I trembled at the sight.

Much to the surprise of her doctors, my mother didn't die that night, or later, either. In fact, she recovered completely, though her wits were temporarily scrambled and it was months before she relearned the many things that vanished from her mind when the aneurysm burst. She was still calling me Albert when *Oliver!* opened on May 4; she was too weak to go to the gym and would scarcely have known what she was seeing in any case. By staying home, my mother missed out on one of the most embarrassing moments of my life: my high-pitched voice, shakily balanced on the fulcrum of puberty, changed abruptly into a bass-baritone in front of a thousand people, right in the middle of the first verse of "Consider Yourself."

In spite of this catastrophe, I had a terrific time doing *Oliver!* For reasons unknown to me, I was widely praised for my performance as the Artful Dodger; I also discovered, much to my delight, that the miracle of communal friendship I first experienced with *The Innocents* was even more intense within the vast womb of a musical-comedy cast. I got to know people my own age, and I got to know adults in a way that was impossible outside the grubby white walls of the Middle School gym. I wanted more, and so I decided to take part in Little Theater's 1973 musical, *The Fantasticks*, the inaugural production of the new Sikeston Activity Center.

I suppose "new" is putting it too prettily, for the Sikeston Activity Center was really only the old First Baptist Church, located just across the railroad tracks from downtown Sikeston. The First Baptist Church was built in 1915, expanded in 1949 and 1956, attended by my family for a few years during the early sixties (it was there that I learned the truth about Santa Claus), and abandoned in the fullness of time for a brand-new church on the outskirts of town in 1971, at which point somebody had the bright idea that the sanctuary of the old church could be converted into a halfway decent theater. After lengthy consideration, the city bought the building and did exactly that. Black plastic letters reading SIKESTON ACTIVITY CENTER were bolted over the granite facade into which were carved the words FIRST BAPTIST CHURCH. The stained-glass windows were removed and the long wooden pews carted away. The floor was slightly raked, the back-stage space ample, the balcony reasonably well-suited to the installation of theatrical lighting. Since the budget wasn't big enough to pay for a real curtain, we tie-dyed a dozen bedsheets, stitched them together, and started rehearsing.

The Fantasticks, which opened off Broadway in 1960 and is still running, turned out to be perfect for our purposes. It had a hit song, "Try to Remember"; it had a small cast, which allowed us to concentrate on learning how to use our new stage efficiently; it required next to no scenery; and it was absolutely actor-proof. The only thing wrong with *The Fantasticks* was that it contained no role suitable for a clumsy teenage boy with a newly changed voice. Having just talked my parents into buying me a bass guitar, I chose instead to offer my services as bassist for the three-piece "pit orchestra." Gordon Beaver, director of the Sikeston High School Concert Choir and my beloved piano teacher, and Richard Powell, director of the high school orchestra and my equally beloved violin teacher, had always accompanied Little Theater musicals, but both men were too busy that year. No other bass players volunteered, so I got the job.

The pianist for *The Fantasticks* was Bonnie Harris, a junior in high school whom I had long admired from afar. Bonnie was widely considered to be the best student pianist in the Bootheel. As slender as a dancer, she had long, frizzy hair and arms so thin that it hardly seemed possible for her to play any louder than a whisper. She was soft-spoken, even a bit dreamy, and she had a vague reputation for being wild, at least by small-town standards. This merely served to enhance her allure, and since she was a perfectly serious musician, I was more than willing to put in long hours of rehearsal with her and Bryan Crites, a freshman and a very good drummer. (It was Bryan's brother David who had threatened to roll soda cans down the aisle at *The Innocents.*) By the time the show opened, the cast of *The Fantasticks* was riding on a musical carpet of nearly professional quality.

Adolescence had me firmly in its moony grip by this time, and I spent a lot of time imagining what it would be like to be in love with "the kind of girl designed to be kissed upon the eyes," that being the way in which Luisa, the fey heroine of *The Fantasticks*, describes herself. No such girl turned up, but *The Fantasticks* gave me something almost as good: a chance to make music with a small group of my peers. "Making music" seems the wrong way to put it, for a musician doesn't make anything, and when he stops playing, nothing is left behind. But he is a craftsman all the same, for the object he "makes," though it vanishes in the air, lingers in the memory, and he lavishes on it the same intensity and skill and respect for the tools of his trade that a carpenter lavishes on a mahogany cupboard. I had spent the better part of my life doing my best to make little clay mugs and hit line drives, and my best had never been good enough. Now I had found a craft of my own, and I quickly grew to love it with a fierce passion. I had discovered the incomparable joy of doing something really well.

After *The Fantasticks* closed, the Little Theater board decided that it was time for a splashy, full-scale Broadway musical, one with costumes and familiar tunes and, most important of all, a large cast whose members could fill the Sikeston Activity Center with at least three relatives per cast member. But Little Theater had already run through most of the better-known Broadway shows, and the musical comedies of the seventies were poorly suited to the special needs of a small-town company. (Try to imagine the outcry from the Sikeston Ministerial Council if we had chosen to do, say, *A Chorus Line*.) There was, however, one smash hit we had managed to overlook, perhaps the last great Broadway musical to be suitable for small-town production and consumption: *Fiddler on the Roof*. Somebody suggested it, and off we went.

I looked forward to playing bass again for Bonnie, but Hope Terrell, our resident musical-comedy director, needed me for something else. There were only two good violinists in Sikeston, and one of them, Elisabeth Dupont, was unwilling to sit on a roof and wear a false beard. That left me. Hope told me that I would be the fiddler on the roof when the script called for it, slipping into the pit to play bass when it didn't, which was most of the time. Elisabeth became one of Tevye's daughters, and Jean Dupont, her father, was cast as Tevye, with Carole Sue Clayton playing Golde, his wife. Dr. Dupont, a heart surgeon from Dallas who had moved to Sikeston with his large and musical family a few years back, had done a good job as Fagin in *Oliver!*, and everyone was sure that he would be an ideal Tevye.

Fiddler posed only one problem, but it was a big one: what possible business did we have putting on a show about Russian Jews and arranged marriages and pogroms in a deconsecrated Southern Baptist church located squarely in the middle of the Bible Belt? The only thing we had going for us was the absence of anything remotely resembling anti-Semitism in southeast Missouri, and this was a purely negative virtue; there was next to no anti-Semitism in southeast Missouri because there were next to no Jews in southeast Missouri. Our innocence, morally admirable though it may have been, left us floating in a dramatic void. Not knowing anything about anti-Semitism, how could we understand the Cossack pogrom that breaks up the wedding at the end of the first act? Not knowing what it meant to be exiled from the land of our birth, how could we convey the pathos of the second act, in which the residents of the little village of Anatevka are cruelly dispersed to the four corners of the earth? Not only did we know nothing about Jews, most of us didn't even know how to dance. It was surely no accident that the name of Jerome Robbins, the theatrical genius who conceived, directed, and choreographed *Fiddler on the Roof*, appeared nowhere in the printed program of our production.

Impossible though our task was, we did our best, and it wasn't bad. Though we weren't Jewish, most of us took our religion seriously enough to have some notion of what was going on in *Fiddler*, even if Jesus failed to figure in it. Jean Dupont had lived in enough big cities to get at least part way under Tevye's hide.

Hope Terrell rented authentic-looking costumes for the stars. And we had an ace in the hole: David Friedman, the owner of Falkoff's, Sikeston's upper-class haberdashery, the place where you went to buy extra-special Sunday clothes, rent a tux for the senior prom, or purchase the white dinner jacket worn by members of the Concert Choir. Mr. Friedman was a respected member of the local business community, and the fact that he happened to be Jewish was generally regarded as little more than a curiosity until Hope invited him to serve as "technical adviser" for our production, in which capacity he painstakingly explained to us how to wear our costumes, how to simulate plausible-sounding accents, and what the story of *Fiddler on the Roof* was all about.

The article about *Fiddler* that appeared in the *Daily Sikeston Standard* a few days before we opened bore the unmistakable stamp of our technical adviser, for it ended with the following tribute to cast and crew: "This is worth their time and great effort to perform, and definitely worth anyone's effort to watch and love. *Mazel tov!*" Thanks to that story and to the relentless salesmanship of the cast, we had the whole town on our side by opening night. To go to *Fiddler* would not only entertain you but make you a better, more cosmopolitan, more *tolerant* person. It was a sales pitch worthy of Madison Avenue, and it worked like a charm. We sold out on Friday and Saturday and had a nearly full house on Thursday.

As for me, I was in seventh heaven. Not only did I get to play bass again for the mysterious Bonnie Harris, but I also got to play the title role in a musical comedy without having to sing or speak a blessed word. All I had to do was sit on the roof of a makeshift shack, dressed in a peasant costume, playing mournful little tunes on my violin as the cast frolicked at my feet. There was only one catch: Hope told me that I would have to get rid of my glasses for the production, not only because they were out of place (I wore wire-rimmed photograys) but because the spotlights made them glitter distractingly. I did my best to talk her out of it. I would never have dreamed of venturing out of the house without my glasses, much less onto a stage, up a prop ladder, and onto the roof of a rickety wooden shack. But Hope insisted, and she was the director, so I swallowed my doubts and gave in.

I got through the dress rehearsal and the first two performances without mishap, but I was pushing my luck, and it ran out on closing night. The next-to-last scene of *Fiddler on the Roof* takes place outside Tevye's house, with the fiddler perched overhead on the roof, after which we dropped our tie-dyed curtain, allowing the entire cast to assemble for the singing of "Anatevka," which I accompanied. When I heard the stage manager hiss "Places!," I pressed my glasses into the hand of the nearest crew member and scuttled up the ladder to the roof. Jean Dupont played his scene. The curtain came down to rousing applause. I put my foot on what I thought was the top rung of the ladder. I was wrong. I plummeted straight down to the stage floor, frantically holding my violin over my head in order to keep from smashing it to bits. The resulting crash was no louder than any of the other strange noises that filtered through our tie-dyed curtain between scenes, and only two people out front suspected anything out of the ordinary. My mother, hearing an unexpected thump back-stage, was certain that her clumsy son must have had a hand in it. And Bonnie, banging away in the pit, heard me mutter, faintly but distinctly, a single word: "*Shit!*"

Waving away all offers of help, I scrambled to my feet and immediately fell back down again. I had turned my ankle badly, and it was beginning to swell. Instead of marching around in a circle with the villagers during the last scene, I stood in the center of the circle, putting all of my weight on my good leg and praying that Bonnie would have the sense to play a little faster.

As I limped off the stage of the Sikeston Activity Center, I decided to call a temporary halt to my life as an actor. I didn't do another play until my junior year in college, by which time I had stopped looking for masks to hide behind; I had begun to feel comfortable with the person I was in the process of becoming, and I acted purely for the sake of friendship, which I found in happy abundance in the theater department of William Jewell College. Some of the shows I did were better than others, but all of them were fun while they lasted, though I'm grateful that none of them was filmed for posterity, especially *The Man Who Came to Dinner*, in which I attempted to impersonate, of all people, Noël Coward. I brought my theatrical career to an end by composing and performing an original musical score for a student production of A *Thurber Carnival*, a stroke of autobiographical symmetry so neat that I never again felt the need to grace a stage with my fumbling presence.

Theatrical friendships, like shipboard romances, rarely survive the light of day, and it's been years since I heard from any of the friends I made in the Middle School gym and the old First Baptist Church. I never saw Bonnie Harris, Hope Terrell, or Carole Sue Clayton again, though my mother tells me that Hope and Carole Sue recently starred in a Little Theater production of *Steel Magnolias*. I did keep up with Buddy, Carole Sue's husband, who became her ex-husband shortly after I left town. I saw Buddy for the last time at a high school football game in Sikeston a few years ago. As usual, he was hanging out in the broadcast booth. We ignored the game and talked about old times; I gave him a big hug and told him, just in time, what he had meant to me. I sent a check to the scholarship fund that was set up in Buddy's name after he died of a heart attack that winter, and his daughter Lee wrote me a thank-you note. We are still in touch.

I don't know what Jean Dupont is doing now, but I hear that his daughter Elisabeth plays violin in an orchestra down south, and I know that his son Stephen, our Rabbi in *Fiddler*, is now a rising young basso at the Metropolitan Opera, for I saw his picture in *Opera News* the other day. As for David Friedman, he still runs Falkoff's. I saw him there not long ago, his black hair turned iron gray. I couldn't think of a graceful way to remind him of the small but important role he had played in my awkward age, so I bought a suit instead.

6 | *Truck Stop Days*

W hen I was a small boy, my parents and I went to dinner every Saturday night at the Charcoal House, a restaurant on the north side of town. I always ordered filet mignon. I liked saying "I'll have filet mignon, please" to the waitress, lingering over the unfamiliar-sounding words and trying to imagine what it would feel like to be able to speak French fluently; I liked pulling out the charred toothpicks that held the filet together and slowly unwinding the limp strip of grilled bacon in which it was wrapped. I also liked the sign in the parking lot of the service station next door to the Charcoal House: HALFWAY POINT BETWEEN ST. LOUIS AND MEMPHIS. It seemed incredibly romantic to me that I should be eating filet mignon in a restaurant located exactly halfway between two distant cities. It was like visiting the Berlin Wall or the North Pole.

What made the sign outside the Charcoal House so romantic was the fact that the claim it made was absolute and unequivocal: it was *exactly* halfway between St. Louis and Memphis. Eating filet mignon in a restaurant approximately halfway between St. Louis and Memphis would have been only slightly more exciting than staying home and eating my mother's pot roast. Even if the sign was off by a few miles, it must have been fairly close to the mark, since it takes three hours to drive from Sikeston to either St. Louis or Memphis. But I never questioned its accuracy. As far as I was concerned, the Charcoal House was located at the geographical center of the world as I knew it.

As I grew older, I became more conscious of the distance that separated my home town from the rest of that world. A three-hour drive is serious business, especially for a family with small children. People who live in Sikeston don't just pop up to St. Louis for dinner and a show on the spur of the moment. But even though Sikestonians tend to stay close to home, most of them try to keep in touch with life outside the Bootheel. I certainly did. I subscribed to *Time,* joined the Book-of-the-Month Club and was a regular patron of the "New Books" shelf of the Sikeston Public Library; I went to see every movie that came to town, even though new movies rarely made it to the Malone Theater until several weeks after I first read about them in *Time.* And I watched television, especially *The Ed Sullivan Show.*

Everybody I knew watched *The Ed Sullivan Show* during the sixties and early seventies, the years when I was growing up. No matter what kind of entertainment you liked best, Ed Sullivan gave it to you by the carload: jugglers and acrobats, magicians and ventriloquists, wisecracking comedians and slender ballerinas in silky tutus and stocky tenors direct from the stage of the Metropolitan Opera House. I learned a lot from *The Ed Sullivan Show.* One Sunday night, when I was doing my homework at the kitchen table, my mother called out to me, "Come in here, Terry. I want you to see something special. This man won't be around forever. Someday you'll be glad you saw him." I trotted dutifully into the living room and sat down in front of the television set, where an old man with an ear-to-ear smile was singing "Hello, Dolly." His white teeth and white handkerchief and golden trumpet lit up the room, and his raucous, gravelly voice made me feel good inside. As usual, my mother was right: I'm glad I saw Louis Armstrong, and I never forgot it.

Oddly enough, I don't remember seeing the Beatles make their American debut on *The Ed Sullivan Show*, but I remember the next day very clearly, because the girls in my second-grade class were all talking about how wonderful the Beatles were. They sat around at recess arguing about which one was cutest. (Paul won.) Not surprisingly, I turned my nose up at the Beatles, and I didn't start listening to rock in earnest until I was in seventh grade. It took me long enough, but when I finally got around to discovering rock and roll, I promptly became an avid fan. Songs like "Maggie May," "Fire and Rain," and "The Weight" have the same effect on me that "Moonlight Serenade" and "I'm Getting Sentimental Over You" have on my mother and father. Whenever I hear them, the years fall away and I am a teenager again, worrying about my pimples and anxiously hoping that Theresa Schuchart will let me take her home from Moderne Chorale practice.

Being a musician, it wasn't long before I became interested in playing rock myself. Throughout the late sixties, Sikeston was full of amateur rock groups, the kind known to members of my generation as "garage bands." My friend Drew Matthews played rhythm guitar in a garage band, and I soon decided that I wanted to join one myself. But my interest in playing rock and roll had nothing to do with its musical value. I noticed that there was something special about kids who played in garage bands: the moment they strapped on their Fender Telecasters and started bashing away at "Purple Haze" or "I Can See for Miles," their adolescent gaucheness disappeared and they became confident and self-assured. That never seemed to happen when I played a Brahms sonata. Maybe it was time to give Jimi Hendrix a try.

Only one thing stood in the way of my becoming a rock and roll star: I played the violin. What I needed was an instrument capable of being played at decibel levels approaching the threshold of pain, and so my father, after months of relentless begging, took me to Shivelbine's Music Store in Cape Girardeau and bought me a cherry-red Fender bass guitar and a big black Bass-man Ten amplifier. He meant well, but he was too late. All the garage bands in town had broken up by the time I mastered my new instrument. There was no one left with whom I could play rock and roll, and there was nothing else I wanted to play. I had recently discovered jazz, but I didn't know anybody who could play it, and I had no use for country music, the only possible alternative. None of my friends listened to country music. It was strictly for people who drove pickups, ate at truck stops, and watched *The Porter Wagoner Show* and *Hee Haw*. I didn't hang around with people like that, and I saw no reason why I should bother with their music, either.

If that sounds snobbish to you, it's probably because I was a snob. Big cities haven't got a thing on small towns when it comes to snobbery. In a small town, everyone knows where you live and how you live, and they talk about it all the time. But if it's true that there's no snob like a small-town snob, it's also true that you end up rubbing shoulders with just about everybody in a small town if you live there long enough, and you learn, if you have any sense at all, not to judge people by their addresses or their accents. I had not yet learned that lesson, though, and I'm sure I would have fallen down dead if somebody had told me I'd be playing country music and hanging out in truck stops before the year was out.

It all started one afternoon before orchestra practice. I was warming up with a Vivaldi concerto, playing the flashy parts over and over in a shameless attempt to impress my fellow string players. None of them paid me any attention. They were too busy listening to another violinist, an upperclassman named Greg Tanner, who stood at the other end of the rehearsal room, briskly sawing away at a piece I didn't recognize. I went over and asked him what he was playing. He said it was an old hoedown tune called "Boil Them Cabbage Down."

It wasn't the first time I had noticed Greg. He caught my eye shortly after I came to high school and started playing in the orchestra. I was struck by the fact that we were as different as two people could be. Greg was the first person I ever knew who acted as if he didn't give a damn what anybody thought of him. Two years older and a hundred pounds heavier than me, he spoke with a strong rural accent, the kind my friends called "hick." Though he liked to play the fool at rehearsals, it was clear to me that he was extremely bright, something he went to a great deal of trouble to hide from his friends, acquaintances, and teachers. Greg never seemed to take much of anything seriously. The only thing that interested him, as far as I could tell, was country music. His open contempt for all forms of established authority excited me; the fact that he chose to conceal his intelligence behind the mask of a buffoon fascinated me.

I had never heard anything quite like "Boil Them Cabbage Down," and I asked Greg to show me how it went. I expected him to tell me to buzz off. Instead, he spent the next couple of days painstakingly teaching me "Boil Them Cabbage Down" and a half-dozen other fiddle tunes of similar vintage. Richard Powell saw us practicing together one day and asked if we'd like to play a few hoedowns the next time the orchestra gave a concert. Once again, Greg surprised me: he said he'd love to. Greg and I performed a medley of hoedown tunes at the winter concert of the Sikeston High School Orchestra, accompanied by another violinist named Terry Hupp, a tall, cadaverous teenager who looked like a middle-aged farmer just back from the dust bowl. The crowd ate it up.

Not long after that, Greg introduced me to his best friend, a gangly fellow by the name of Ken Harbin. Ken wore a green baseball cap on his head and a slightly belligerent expression on his face, as if he were daring you to try to knock the cap off. I saw at once why Ken and Greg got along so well. Like Greg, Ken affected a who-gives-a-damn attitude toward life; like Greg, he was bright and chose to hide it. But Ken, unlike Greg, had a reason to play the fool: Sam Harbin, his distinguished-looking father, was superintendent of the Sikeston public school system. It was bad enough, God knows, to be a teacher's kid, but to be the *superintendent's* kid must surely have been the worst of crimes. Any youthful desire Ken may have had to please his elders would have been beaten out of him long before we met.

Ken viewed me with outright suspicion, since I had a well-deserved reputation as a teacher's pet, and I was pushing our slender acquaintance pretty hard when I asked him if he could possibly give me a lift to an all-day choral festival in Cape Girardeau in which we were both taking part. Ken's first impulse, he later confessed, was to tell me to go screw myself. Instead, he told me that I could come along with him as long as I kept my mouth shut and didn't act like a stupid little jerk. Otherwise, he said, I could walk home. Knowing a major concession when I saw one, I promised to do my best to keep out of sight. We wound up spending the whole day together, and by the time we got back to Sikeston that night, we were well on the way to becoming friends.

One lovely Saturday morning that spring, Greg called me up and told me to borrow a stand-up bass from the high school band shell, throw it in the back of my car, and drive out to Ken's house for "a little picking." I knew that Ken played guitar and that he and Greg played country music together for fun, but this was the first time I had ever been invited to join them. I said, somewhat stiffly, that I'd come as quickly as I could. "The hell with that soon-as-I-can shit," Greg replied. "You haul your little candy ass out here *right now*. Got it?" Before I could think of anything clever to say, he hung up. I grinned a Louis Armstrong–sized grin, told my mother I'd be late for dinner, and sprinted out the back door.

I spent the rest of the day picking with Greg and Ken. Greg knew hundreds of old songs, few of which I had ever heard before. Most of the ones I liked best, it turned out, were by a man named Hank Williams. They had spare, no-nonsense titles like "Hey, Good Lookin'," "Move It On Over," and "I Can't Help It (If I'm Still in Love with You)," and they kept running through my head long after I went home that night. I liked the way we sounded playing them, too. Greg was a passable country fiddler and a fine lead singer; Ken was a solid rhythm guitarist, and his light tenor voice blended nicely with Greg's mournful-sounding baritone. I stuck to playing bass, since I didn't know the words and wouldn't have been able to sing them convincingly in any case. It didn't matter. I was having the time of my life, and when Greg popped open a beer toward the end of the long afternoon and casually suggested that we seemed to have the makings of a pretty good group here, I found myself hastening to agree.

I spent many more afternoons and evenings that spring running through song after song with Greg and Ken. Though Greg favored the hard-edged honky-tonk sound that dominated country music in the late forties and early fifties, we ended up playing a little bit of everything. We did old classics by Hank Williams and new ones by Buck Owens; we did watered-down versions of bluegrass standards like "Uncle Pen" and "Orange Blossom Special"; we did high-stepping love songs and snappy truck-driving songs and hokey tears-in-my-beer songs. Ken kept a list of songs taped to the back of his guitar, and every time we learned a new one, he added it to the list. I can still close my eyes and see that list. The titles alone sound a lot like one of those ballads of lost love that Greg sang so well: "Key in the Mailbox," "Roll in My Sweet Baby's Arms," "I Didn't Know God Made Honky-Tonk Angels," "Your Cheating Heart," "She Thinks I Still Care," "Today I Started Loving You Again," "Heartaches by the Number," "I Saw the Light," "A Shoulder to Cry On," "Six Days on the Road," "Faded Love," "Carry Me Back."

As we practiced together, my longing to play in a garage band gradually faded away. Fond as I was of rock and roll, it had little to tell me that I didn't already know. Country music was different. It was about plain people who worked hard for a living and who knew from bitter experience the corrosive effects of sin, temptation, and regret on the human soul. "When a hillbilly sings a crazy song," Hank Williams once said, "he feels crazy. When he sings 'I Laid My Mother Away,' he sees her a-laying right there in the coffin. He sings more sincere than most entertainers because the hillbilly was raised rougher than most entertainers. You got to know a lot about hard work. You got to have smelt a lot of mule manure before you can sing like a hillbilly." That was what I heard in the songs Greg and Ken taught me: they reeked of the harsh, smoky odor of real life, something about which I knew very little. Ignorant of the world around me, I looked for truth in the lyrics of the songs we sang. I could have done a lot worse.

Greg decided after a few weeks of rehearsing that we needed a fuller sound, so he went out and recruited a guitar player named Chuck Hanna. Though Chuck preferred to play rock and roll, he had recently acquired a banjo, and working with us would give him an opportunity to practice on the job. Chuck never quite figured out how to pick his banjo in proper three-finger Scruggs style, but he was more than good enough for our purposes, and he sang well, too. With Chuck on board, we sounded like a bluegrass band that played honky-tonk songs, and sometimes, sitting in Ken's backyard on a warm spring day, it seemed to us that we played them very well indeed. All we needed was a name, and Greg came up with "Sour Mash" late one evening, after having consumed quite a lot of it. Ken's mother painted the words *Ken Harbin of . . . SOUR MASH* in fancy red-and-white script on the front of his guitar case, and that made it official: we were a real band.

We didn't have to wait very long for our first gig. The manager of the Holiday Inn invited Sour Mash to play in his restaurant for three hours every Wednesday night. We didn't know three hours' worth of music, so we faked it. Chuck brought along his electric guitar and played a medley of "Johnny B. Goode"–type rock tunes from the fifties; Ken sang a few solos by John Denver and James Taylor. Since Greg was our lead singer, that left me the only member of Sour Mash without a featured spot of my own. I was glad to stay in the background, but Greg felt that each of us needed a turn in the limelight, so he came up with an ingenious solution: I borrowed Greg's fiddle and played an old Jimmie Rodgers song called "TB Blues." Somewhat to our surprise, we wound up spending the better part of a year playing dinner music at the Holiday Inn. The crowds didn't flock to hear us, but they didn't stay away, either. Though the pay was lousy, the tips weren't bad, and we sounded better and better with every passing week.

By this time, Sour Mash was the only group of kids in Sikeston who were making music together on a regular basis, and since we were willing to play for anybody who asked us, we became something of a local institution. Despite the fact that we played country music, most people seemed to regard us as a reasonably amusing novelty. We performed at elementary school assemblies and at private parties; we played a weekly gig at Pasquale's, a student hangout, working for free pizza and the applause of our friends; we appeared at Moderne Chorale performances as a special added attraction. When the *Bulldog Barker* ran a picture of us playing together in the school cafeteria, an anonymous headline writer captioned it "THE ILLUSTRIOUS SOUR MASH." We had arrived.

After we had been playing together for a year, Greg's father lined up our most ambitious engagement to date: we toured southeast Missouri and northeast Arkansas as the opening act for a pair of genial con men who fronted for a tight little honky-tonk band. Earl and Roy had developed an unorthodox but effective way of augmenting their income. Before every concert, they went to the smallest radio station in town and cut a deal with the program director: if he would broadcast their concert live, they would donate their services free of charge. Then they visited every store they could find and talked the unsuspecting proprietors into buying advertisements to be read on the air during the broadcast. At the end of the show, Earl grabbed the microphone and spent thirty seconds or so rattling off a lengthy list of local businessmen who had "helped to make tonight's concert possible." This was the "advertisement" for which the businessmen in question had shelled out good money. Once the list was read and the show was over, Earl and Roy would pack their bags and hit the road, keeping an eye on the rearview mirror.

Sour Mash made half a dozen appearances as the opening act of the Earl and Roy Show, one of which was a concert held in the Bertrand high school gymnasium and broadcast live over KSIM, Sikeston's country-music station. We hurriedly parted company with our new colleagues when we figured out what they were up to, but it was fun while it lasted. We learned a lot about working a crowd from Earl and Roy; we learned even more from their band, a quintet of hardened professionals that made us sound like the likable amateurs we were. And we were paid in full and on time, suggesting that there really is honor among thieves. I lost track of Earl and Roy years ago, but I wouldn't be surprised to hear that they're still working the high school gymnasium circuit in Arkansas, selling ads and keeping their motor running.

Opening for Earl and Roy in Black Oak, Arkansas, was as high as Sour Mash managed to climb on the greasy pole of musical stardom. Our luck was better when it came to friendship. Chuck had his own circle of intimates and rarely hung out with us after work, but Greg, Ken, and I soon became all but inseparable. After every gig, we headed straight for the nearest truck stop, where we ate biscuits and gravy and talked about everything under the sun: the meaning of life, the place of Merle Haggard in the history of American music, the best spot to order chicken-fried steak. Then we climbed into my station wagon and cruised up and down the back roads of the Bootheel, drinking beer and looking for good stations on the radio. Greg usually drove, and whenever we saw another car coming toward us, he would throw both of his hands in the air, his face a study in abject terror, while Ken, crouched down below the dashboard, reached over and grabbed the steering wheel with his left hand. We scared a lot of drivers that way.

The three of us did more than just play music and go cruising. We ate meals together. We went camping together. We spent time with each other's families. We drove out to a deserted bean field one hot summer afternoon and shot bottle rockets at each other. Losing an eye or a finger would have been a stiff price to pay for a good time, but I probably would have paid it without complaining, for I knew the value of my friendship with Greg and Ken. They did their best to teach me how to be a regular guy, taking me by the hand and leading me through the nighttime world of truck stops and chicken-fried steak. I could do little for them in return except play bass and serve as a full-time butt for their practical jokes, but that seemed to be enough. I spent hours watching them shoot pool and drink beer in a seedy dump a few miles north of the Charcoal House on Highway 61. One night I overheard Greg talking about me to a fellow at the bar who was wondering why I tagged along. "Hell, yes, he's strange," Greg said, "but who gives a shit? He can play the goddamn bass, can't he? What do you want? A quarterback?"

That was Greg's idea of a once-in-a-lifetime compliment, and he didn't mean for me to hear it, either. There was no room in our friendship for sentiment. The nicest thing we ever called each other to our faces was *shithead*. We punched each other in the crotch and played tricks on each other whenever we could get away with it, which was fairly often. Shortly after sunrise one Saturday morning, Greg and Ken showed up at the back door of 713 Hickory Drive and sweet-talked my mother into letting them into my bedroom, to which I had retired two hours earlier. They slipped in on tiptoe, pulled out a pair of police whistles, counted to three and blew them as hard as they could. According to Greg, I flew four feet into the air, covers and all, and was swearing like a sailor before I came back down again. My mother laughed louder than anybody.

I don't remember where we had been the night before, but I suspect it was the Matthews truck stop, a place where we went once or twice a week to play pinball. Greg and Ken taught me to enjoy sitting in truck stops late at night. The food isn't great, but it's never awful, either. Good or bad, you eat it anyway, talking unhurriedly as you eat, knowing that nobody is waiting for your table at two in the morning. You mop up your gravy with a piece of biscuit and eavesdrop on the people in the next booth. The accents change from hour to hour, but the accompaniment stays the same: a tinny-sounding jukebox that plays cheating songs and truck-driving songs. When you're finished eating, you get a handful of quarters from the man at the cash register and wander over to the other side of the building, strolling down aisles full of junky souvenirs that nobody ever buys, looking for the pinball machine at the back of the room. You pop a quarter in and try out the flippers. Then you shoot a silver ball up the chute and get down to business, nudging the sides of the machine in order to coax the ball into a high-scoring pocket without tripping the *tilt* light first.

Ken and Greg usually teamed up when we played pinball, each taking charge of a single flipper. Since I was no better at pinball than at drinking beer, I stood by and watched them play. One night, Greg told us that he felt lucky and wanted to play alone. He was lucky, all right, for he racked up point after point, chortling to himself as the machine clicked and jingled in response to his infallible touch. After ten minutes, he got the score up to 100,000, and the scoreboard lit up and stayed lit, a sign that Greg had earned himself a bonus game.

"We've got it now!" he said, his voice filled with self-satisfaction.

"Have we really got it?" I asked.

"You bet your *ass* we've got it!" he said.

"Have we *really* got it?" I asked again, with a gleam in my eye.

"*YOU'RE GODDAMN RIGHT WE'VE GOT IT!*" Greg shouted at the top of his voice. Then I socked him right in the crotch. He fell to the floor, retching and laughing at the same time. I looked over at Ken. He was doubled up with laughter. After rolling around in pain for a minute or two, Greg got up, coughed twice, and dusted himself off. "Nice work, you little shithead," he said. Then he played his bonus game.

I went to a lot of parties with Greg and Ken. We brought along our instruments, providing free entertainment in return for all the beer we could drink. I never drank any, mostly because I didn't like beer but partly because somebody had to drive home afterward. Ken got so drunk at one party that he couldn't walk. After dragging him to the car, Greg and I decided that it would be unwise to let Ken's father see him in such a state, so I took him home with me and put him to bed in the basement. We took such favors for granted. Once I asked Greg to go out to Diehlstadt with me to visit my great-aunt, a plucky woman who had been crippled for decades with arthritis and had finally been forced to take to her bed. He grumbled, but he did it, and he brought his violin, too. We spent the whole afternoon playing hymns and hoedowns for Aunt Fronie, and she talked about it until the day she died.

The four of us knew (though we never said it out loud) that graduation would bring the good times to an end, so we decided to go out with a bang: we spent a week in Nashville the summer after Greg and Chuck graduated from high school. We called it a vacation, but we talked half-kiddingly about becoming famous, and I think all four of us must have nurtured the secret hope that we would stumble across a talent scout and end up playing at the Grand Ole Opry. For all I know, Nashville may be crawling with talent scouts, but the only musician we met during our stay there was a pianist whom we ran across in the bar of our hotel one night. He gave us his card, which read as follows:

DEAN DAVIS

(real name, David Seligman)

"Piano with Guitar Effect"

Sour Mash did make it to the Grand Ole Opry, though not to the stage. We bought four tickets, sat in the uppermost balcony, and watched the show. The only thing I remember about it was that Ryman Auditorium, the converted tabernacle that served as the Opry's home until 1974, was incredibly big and incredibly hot. After the show, we stopped by Tootsie's Orchid Lounge, a seedy celebrity hangout across the alley from the Ryman stage door, but we didn't meet any famous musicians there. Then we drove back to Sikeston, laughing and talking and punching each other, doing our best to pretend that nothing had changed, knowing in our hearts that it wasn't so.

Greg and Chuck went off to Southeast Missouri State University in Cape Girardeau in the fall of 1972. I visited them in their dorm one weekend. After chugging a few beers, they tore off my clothes, tied me to a chair, put me in the elevator, pushed all the buttons, and waved goodbye. Greg dropped out of school a few months later and became a salesman, something he did superbly well, even better than he sang cheating songs; Chuck stayed in school and started a Blood, Sweat & Tears–type rock group made up of his fellow music majors. His heart belonged to rock and roll, and he played with us less and less often as his new group began to get work. Greg, Ken, and I played a few gigs on our own, but it wasn't the same without Chuck, and so we called it quits.

Ken graduated from high school in 1973, eventually settling down to a career as a registered nurse. I left Sikeston a year later, and Greg and I fell out of touch not long after that. Ken and I visited each other fairly regularly throughout the eight years I spent in Kansas City, and he served as best man at my wedding. Then I moved to Illinois and, later, to New York, after which we saw each other at increasingly rare intervals. I called him up from time to time, but telephone calls cannot sustain a once-intimate friendship, and the time came when we, too, fell out of touch. I think I was afraid to call him, afraid that I had lost something precious and unwilling to confirm my fears.

A half-dozen visits to Sikeston went by. Then I came home for Christmas, and the phone rang as I was sitting at the kitchen table eating dinner with my parents. "Is that you? Well, get your ass over to my house *right now*," Greg said, and hung up. I walked through his front door ten minutes later and saw Ken sitting on the couch, a guitar in his lap, looking irritated and happy at the same time. We hugged each other. The front door opened again, and there stood Chuck Hanna. It was the first time in twelve years that the four of us had been in the same room. We looked at each other in silence. Then we all started talking at once. Chuck said he had a couple of surprises waiting for us at his house, so we piled into our cars and screeched off into the night. When we got to Chuck's, we found a banjo and a bass guitar propped up against a big black amplifier. We stumbled through a few of our old numbers, groaning loudly every time one of us got lost. Then Chuck produced his second surprise: an off-the-air tape of the concert we gave in Bertrand with Earl and Roy. We swapped stories as we listened, and we parted in a warm glow of nostalgia.

The next time I came home, I borrowed my mother's car and spent an afternoon cruising around town. As I drove past the American Legion post, a pickup truck swerved in front of me, came to an abrupt halt and started backing up. Just as I was about to turn the car around and get the hell out of there, I saw that the driver of the pickup was wearing a green baseball cap. Ken parked the truck, walked over to my car, and started banging on the window. "Hey, shithead," he yelled, "why didn't you tell me you were in town?"

I drove out to Ken's place that night. We spent a few minutes admiring his newborn son. Then Ken went into the kitchen, returning with a pipe in his mouth and a can of soda in each hand. We went outside, set up a pair of camp chairs in the front yard and sat and talked until three in the morning. It was as if we had never been apart. We reminisced about the old days, sharing memories of Earl and Roy, our ill-fated trip to Nashville, the nights we spent playing pinball at the Matthews truck stop. Then I put a hand on his arm. "Wait a minute, Ken," I said. "Let me talk. There's something I've been wanting to tell you."

Haltingly, I told him for the first time how much he and Greg had meant to me. I spoke of how horribly shy and inhibited I had been as a teenager and how playing with Sour Mash had helped me overcome that shyness. I told him that he and Greg were the best friends I ever had. I went on for several minutes before I finally stopped talking. *If I'd ever started blathering like that back when we were in high school,* I thought to myself as I drained my can of soda, *Ken would have laughed in my face.*

Ken Harbin, married man, registered nurse, and father of two, puffed on his pipe and looked out into the darkness. Then he said: "I felt the same way, you know. It wasn't the music that mattered. It was fun, but it wasn't the point. It was the other thing that mattered. Being friends. That was the way it was for me, too. But I guess I figured you knew that." We sat quietly for a while, listening to the distant thunder of the eighteen-wheelers roaring down the highway. Then we started talking about babies and married life and our plans for the future, secure at last in the knowledge that the youthful idyll we had shared would always be there for us, untouched and untouchable by the passage of time.

7 | *Goodbye, Annapolis*

If I had to pick a season of my life to live over again, I'd probably choose the first semester of my senior year in high school. I spent most of my Friday nights that fall playing in the marching band and watching the Sikeston High School Bulldogs get beaten. I had no business marching in the band, for I played double bass, a monstrously large wooden box that is only slightly easier to carry around than a grand piano. Pat Curry, the high school band director, wanted to add a bass to the band for the concert season; I was eager to help him out, but he insisted that I march with the band, too, and so I ended up substituting for kids who got sick at the last minute and had to stay home. I lugged a lot of instruments up and down the football field that year: clarinets, flutes, trumpets, even a big white fiberglass sousaphone. It was quite a change from playing violin in the school orchestra. I usually marched without rehearsal, and that was the only part I didn't like, for I had never marched before, and I was certain that I would look up from my lyre one night and find myself tramping away at a 180-degree angle from the rest of the band. It never happened, but only because I was lucky, not because I knew what I was doing.

Despite my perfectly understandable fear of marching off in the wrong direction, I can't think of another bad thing about the fall of 1973. I loved eating hot dogs and watching the twirlers and rooting for the home team. I had spent most of my high school days sneering at the home team, and nobody bothered to tell me what I was missing. I might never have found out had it not been for Pat Curry's stubbornness. It's been a long time since I went to a football game, but I still feel a rush of anticipation when the air turns crisp and bright red leaves start to drop from the trees. In my memory, fall in Sikeston begins with a visit to the Southeast Missouri District Fair in Cape Girardeau, an evening filled to overflowing with small-town delights: dinner at the Lutheran Men's Auxiliary hamburger stand, a ride on the double Ferris wheel, stuffed animals and blue-ribbon pumpkins and a big box of sticky saltwater taffy to take home. It ends with Thanksgiving dinner in Diehlstadt, gateway to the greater glories of Christmas. But my sweetest memories of fall in my home town will always be of the halftime shows in which I marched, clad in a gaudy red-and-black uniform, happy to be, for once, just like everybody else.

I suppose you can't really like fall unless you like school, but there, too, I have been lucky. Some people are made for summer vacation; I was made to write essays about what I did for my summer vacation. For me, fall was the most exciting of seasons, full of the promise of new teachers and new friends. Going back to school has only let me down once. It happened in the fall of 1974, the year I went off to St. John's College in Annapolis, Maryland. I didn't like St. John's, and I only stayed there for a semester. When I packed my bags and came back to the Midwest, I swore that I would never again set foot in Annapolis, a vow I have kept. It was a childish promise, but everyone deserves to indulge himself in at least one irrational whim, and that is mine.

You could argue, I suppose, that I used up my lifetime quota of whims when I decided to go to St. John's in the first place, since I knew next to nothing about it until the day I got there. I certainly don't blame my parents for letting me go to St. John's. They knew little about modern-day college life and were glad to let me choose my own school when the time came. It didn't help that I had no idea of what I wanted to do for a living. I had just been named editor of the *Bulldog Barker*, the high school newspaper, but even though I was having an enormous amount of fun chasing down stories and writing headlines, it never occurred to me that I might do that sort of thing for a living, undoubtedly because it was so much fun. The same prim logic kept me from considering music as a career. I *enjoyed* it too much. How could I earn a living doing something I loved?

Choosing a college posed a similar problem. An Ivy League school probably would have been my best bet, but I had never known anyone who had gone to Yale or Harvard or Columbia, and I knew nothing of the dozens of prestigious schools outside the Ivy League that might have suited me just as well, if not better. Most of the kids I knew went to Southeast Missouri State College in Cape Girardeau, and I took it for granted that I would go there, too, though I briefly considered going to William Jewell College, a liberal-arts school in Liberty, Missouri, a small town just outside Kansas City. William Jewell sent a recruiter named Clyde Gibbs to Sikeston one day, and I spent half an hour talking to him. He painted a handsome picture of life at Jewell, and the brochures he left with me made it sound even better. It would have simplified my life had I taken Mr. Gibbs up on his offer then and there, since Jewell was where I finally ended up. Instead, I kept on tossing and turning, trying to make up my mind.

Things became more complicated after I broke up with my girlfriend, a brown-haired piano player named Theresa Schuchart. This catastrophe had an immediate bearing on my choice of school, for Theresa and I had been talking about going to college together, possibly in Cape Girardeau. Now that we were no longer speaking to each other, I would have to find a more appropriate reason to choose a college. In addition, breaking up with Theresa had a less immediate but considerably more far-reaching effect: it made me feel for the first time that Sikeston might be too small a stage on which to play out the drama of my unlived life. I suspect I wanted to prove something to Theresa; I know I wanted to prove something to my classmates. Either way, it was clear to me that I would have to leave the Bootheel if I wanted to do something big.

All of this made me a sitting duck for the tastefully designed brochure from St. John's College that turned up in the mailbox of 713 Hickory Drive one fateful day. I had never heard of St. John's, but the more I read, the more exciting it sounded. St. John's, I learned, was founded in 1696, making it the third-oldest school in America. (Chalk one up for snob appeal.) Only five hundred students went there, and the academic program was ideally suited to self-styled young intellectuals like me, for St. John's was and is a liberal-arts school of the very first chop: no majors, no electives, no academic options of any kind. Every student at St. John's learned Greek and French and read a list of Great Books as long as my arm. Going there would prevent me from immersing myself in music to the exclusion of more important things. (Chalk one up for priggishness.) And St. John's was in Maryland, far away from Sikeston and Theresa Schuchart and all of the small-town ways at which I was beginning to look askance.

I told my parents that I had found the school of my dreams and that no other place in the world would do. Instead of pouring a pitcher of cold water on my head, my father agreed to fly to Annapolis with me and look the place over. It was my first plane ride, and some of the excitement I felt must have carried over to my first look at St. John's, though the campus was impressive enough in its own right. I had never seen so many ivy-covered buildings in one place. The professors were impressive and agreeable, and the town seemed pleasant enough. What more could an ambitious boy like me have possibly wanted? I signed on the dotted line and flew back to Missouri, ready to get my senior year over with as quickly as possible and start rolling down the road to glory.

It was, to my surprise, a good year, perhaps the best one I have ever had. I marched in the band and cheered lustily for the Bulldogs; I got back together with Theresa for four golden months; I inched past Melodie Powell, my archrival, to graduate at the head of the class of 1974. When it was all over, I collected my diploma from Buddy Clayton and tossed my mortarboard hat in the air. I spent the summer working as a bank teller, buying Great Books and new clothes with the money I made. Before I knew it, September had arrived. My parents filled up the back of the station wagon and drove me to Annapolis. Then they unloaded my things and drove off. It was the first time in my life that I had ever spent a night on my own outside the borders of the Bootheel, and it was a long night. I had chosen St. John's on a whim. Now I would have to make the best of it.

The day after my arrival in Annapolis, I made a momentous discovery: I spoke with an accent. My fellow students, most of whom came from the East Coast, were sure that it was a southern accent, an understandable error which nonetheless reminded me that I was a long way from Missouri. Nobody I met at St. John's was from the Midwest; nobody I met came from a town that sounded anything like Sikeston. Most of the kids in my class had been born in big cities and educated in private schools, where they had acquired a surface polish that I found frighteningly impressive. Worst of all, they were smart, fully as smart as I was. I was just another bright kid thrown among five hundred equally bright kids, on my own and far from home.

I was not the only freshman at St. John's College to feel the jolt of anonymity. Most of us felt it at one time or another, and we reacted in various ways. Some kids found it liberating, for St. John's offered plenty of opportunities to kick up your heels in whatever way suited you; others tried to make a name for themselves by browbeating less aggressive students, both in the class-room and in casual conversation. I was one of the less aggressive students. My friendship with Greg and Ken had eased me part way out of my shell, but I lost a lot of hard-won ground during my brief stay at St. John's.

A week after I came to Annapolis, I stopped eating at the school cafeteria. Though there was nothing particularly oppressive about the cafeteria, which was housed in an old colonial-style building at the center of campus, I found it terrifying, mostly because I didn't know anybody and found it difficult to sit down with total strangers. I ate there a couple of times, sitting by myself in a distant corner. Then I quit going altogether. I started eating lunch off campus, dining on cheese and crackers in my dorm room at night. It was one of the most foolish things I have ever done. Had I forced myself to go to the cafeteria three times a day, I'm sure I would have started to make friends; had somebody noticed that I wasn't eating and asked me about it, I might have gotten up the nerve to admit that I was desperately homesick. Like most teenagers, I had no idea that adolescent angst looks far worse from the inside than it does from the outside, and it would have done me a world of good had a sympathetic tutor taken me aside and told me that. But nobody did, and I kept my troubles to myself. The fear of experience I had tried so hard to overcome had returned, and I had no guitar-playing friends to help me deal with it this time around. Unwilling to confide in any of the indifferent strangers with whom I now lived, I was doomed to face my fear alone.

The only place where I saw my fellow students at all regularly was in class. Freshmen at St. John's were split up into groups of a dozen students or so. Except for the twice-weekly evening seminars, you saw the same students in all your classes, and you saw no other students unless you made a point of seeking them out. I made no friends among the students in my group; I don't remember any of their names, and I can't imagine that they would remember mine. The classes themselves were something of a mixed bag. Mathematics, in which we rehearsed the theo-

rems of Euclid, and Laboratory, in which we studied the theory
of measurement, seemed to me an absolute waste of time, for I
had done all that in high school. Greek was different. I had never
studied a foreign language before, and I found the St. John's
method of teaching Greek, which emphasized discussion over
drill, to be little short of disastrous. I soon began to fall behind,
though nobody found me out, since tutors at St. John's had no
use for such bourgeois pedagogical refinements as pop quizzes
and letter grades.

Seminar was more interesting. Two nights a week, St. Johnnies (as we were encouraged to call ourselves) assembled in groups
of forty to discuss the works of Homer, Plato, Herodotus, and
Aristophanes. The tutors who led the seminars claimed to employ
the Socratic method, meaning in practice that they sat in their
seats and said as little as possible, asking only an occasional
question to keep the ball rolling. Students were tacitly encouraged
to dive in and make fools of themselves, all in the sacred name
of self-discovery. I may have been lousy at Greek, but I knew
how to talk, and I did so every night, holding forth at great length
on whichever Platonic dialogue we were discussing that week.
The only thing to be said for my prattling was that it was no less
half-baked than that of any of the other kids whose parents were
paying five-figure sums so that their children could sit around a
large table twice a week, doing their best to intimidate their peers.

I held my own in seminar, but I didn't look for friends there.
I thought I might have better luck striking out on my own. I had
originally hoped to make friends at St. John's in the same way I
had gotten to know Greg and Ken: through music. It seemed as
if my wish had come true when I met a freshman named Randy
Rothenberg. Randy had a stubbly black beard and wore a black
beret and black horn-rimmed glasses, making him look rather
like a character out of a Jack Kerouac novel. He saw my Bassman
Ten, introduced himself as a jazz guitarist, and asked if I wanted
to jam. We plugged our instruments into my amplifier and played
haphazardly for a few minutes, after which we spent a couple of
hours talking about musicians we liked and people we knew. *At*

last, I thought, *a friend.* But my acquaintance with Randy failed to ripen into intimacy, or anything like it. I was too shy for that to happen, and I spent most of my spare time reading, an occupation that left little time for companionship.

The campus library was small and inadequate, and St. Johnnies were encouraged to make use of the U.S. Naval Academy library across the street. Unlike our neighbors, we had a lot of free time on our hands, since we attended only three regular classes during the day, and I spent hours on end in the Naval Academy library. I read hundreds of books that semester, some of them Great Books and some not so great, and I spent almost as much time listening to music. I had brought a couple of hundred albums of my own, and there was a well-stocked record library on campus from which I checked out several albums each week. I systematically worked my way through the music of the masters at night, reading about their lives during the day. I made many musical discoveries that fall. It was at St. John's, for instance, that I first heard the Brahms Clarinet Quintet. I checked out a battered old recording of that melancholy piece once or twice a week, and the reticent keening of the clarinet could often be heard in my room late at night.

Midway through the semester, I received an unexpected invitation. I had been friends two years before with a handsome girl named Anne Matthews, a Navy brat who spent a few months living in Sikeston while her father was between postings. At the end of our junior year, Anne and her family moved to a farm outside Mechanicsville, Maryland, within commuting distance of the Pentagon. One day my mother casually mentioned to Jo Sikes, Anne's aunt and an old friend of the Teachout family, that I was going to be stuck in Annapolis for Thanksgiving. (Air fares were too high for me to fly home twice in one semester.) Aunt Jo snapped at the bait and called up her brother, and I soon found myself invited to spend Thanksgiving in Mechanicsville. Anne lived in a poorly heated old farmhouse, and I nearly froze to death in my upstairs bedroom at night, reading a copy of Boswell's *Life of Johnson* so ancient that the pages crumbled as

I turned them. But her father treated me regally, even going so far as to insist that I hop on his tractor one morning and plow a few rows. He showed me how to work the clutch and turned me loose, and I whooped with joy as I ripped up his cornfield. I wish I had a picture of that.

Anne was unchanged: tall and willowy, earthy and completely unintellectual. I adored her, and she found me amusing. As usual, she was surrounded by her fair share of male admirers, some of whom I met during my visit. Obliging as always, she tried to set me up with a blind date, but I managed to talk her out of it, explaining that I was devoted to Theresa Schuchart. This, I am sorry to say, was a total fabrication. My real reason for turning Anne down was that I was afraid to sit in the back seat of a car with a stranger chosen for me by a carefree young woman. But Anne and I did get together with a couple of her father's farmhands and some other friends in a shack at the edge of the cornfield late one night. One of the friends passed around a joint, which I declined with thanks. I had brought a guitar with me, and I played a song called "Louise" that I first heard on an old Leo Kottke album. Whenever I hear that song now, I think of a little shack at the edge of a Maryland cornfield, and I smile at the thought.

St. John's College seemed like a blissfully safe haven after a few days in the company of Anne and her friends. When I came back to Annapolis that Sunday night, I felt for the first time that my situation might not be altogether hopeless. Had I promptly set about trying to make some friends, I might well have spent the next three and a half years at St. John's. Instead, something completely different happened: I met a girl who urged me to go back to Missouri, and I took her advice.

Studying the campus bulletin board one morning in November, I found a handwritten message from a flutist who wanted someone with whom to play duets. I liked her handwriting, so I carried my violin to the women's dormitory (it was my first visit there) and knocked on the door of a girl named Allie. She was short, soft-spoken, and curvy, and her long brown hair framed a plain but oddly appealing face. She was in my seminar, but she never said a word there, and so I had never noticed her. I only had time for big-mouthed students who whacked each other over the head with polysyllables. But Allie was a good flutist, and by the time we had worked our way through a book of Mozart duets, we had become friends.

Befriending Allie was a tricky proposition. She was slightly humorless and painfully sincere, qualities I shared with her but had never sought out in other people. She was also accustomed to saying whatever happened to be on her mind, and one day she told me, apropos of nothing, that I wasn't nearly as bad as she had expected me to be. I innocently asked her what she meant. She said that I was one of the most outrageously pretentious students in seminar, exactly the sort of person that had put her off St. John's, which she was planning to leave once she decided where to go next. "I can't understand," she added crisply, "how somebody who acts like such a pompous ass in seminar can be such a nice guy."

This statement was open to several different interpretations. I might well have decided on the basis of Allie's indictment that I was exactly the sort of person who belonged at St. John's, which is probably what I would have done had Allie been a boy. But she was a girl, and a sexy one at that, and so instead of slamming my violin case shut and stalking out of the women's dormitory, I blurted out to Allie that I, too, was thinking about leaving St. John's. It was the first time I had ever said anything of the kind to another St. Johnnie, and Allie lost no time in egging me on. She told me that dropping out of St. John's was the best thing that could possibly happen to me and assured me that she would admire me all the more if I went through with it.

Excited by Allie's fiery certainty, I decided to leave St. John's as soon as I could figure out how to do so without precipitating a full-scale family crisis. I resolved in the meantime to become a nicer, more sincere person, one whom a girl like Allie might someday find wholly satisfactory. I started by working on my behavior in seminar. Not being one to do things by halves, I stopped talking altogether. As my fellow students jabbered on about the good, the true, and the beautiful, I sat in stony, self-righteous silence, basking in Allie's occasional glances of approval and plotting my escape from St. John's.

My plot revolved around Theresa Schuchart, who was going to school at the University of Kansas and to whom I was writing once or twice a week. Susceptible though I was to Allie's austere charms, I still considered Theresa to be my steady girlfriend, and I felt it necessary to do something dramatic in order to make up for the time we had spent apart. After much thought, I decided to give her a Christmas present to beat all Christmas presents: an autographed letter by Claude Debussy, her favorite composer. I was sure that it would sweep her off her feet, though a few minor details remained to be worked out first, starting with the fact that I was broke. I had already spent most of my first semester's allowance on meals, and I was too proud to ask my father for more money. How would I have explained what I had spent it on? Clearly, I needed a job, and I started looking for one at once.

A few days later, I became part-time legal secretary to an Annapolis lawyer who was resuming his practice after a long illness. His office looked like something Raymond Chandler might have dreamed up after a week-long bender, and our professional relationship was no less peculiar. I did not tell him that I knew no shorthand; he did not tell me that his illness, a stroke, had left him incapable of dictating at anything faster than a snail's pace. We got along beautifully. When I got my first paycheck, I sent away to New York for an autograph catalogue which offered a single-page Debussy letter for $125.00. (A letter of comparable quality would cost at least five times as much today.) I went straight to my bank, bought a money order for $125.00, and sent it off to New York. Within a week, I held in my hands a letter by Claude Debussy. I remember it perfectly: it was written in dark purple ink on lavender stationery. It was exquisite. It was also the most expensive thing I had ever bought with my own money. How could it possibly fail to turn the trick?

The day the letter arrived, I called my parents and told them that I was unhappy and that I wanted to come home. I expected trouble, but I didn't get it. My father, bless him, didn't yell or scream or say *I told you so*; he simply told me to come on home. I hung up the phone, marched across the campus to Allie's room, and told her that I was dropping out of school. Naturally, she was delighted. What eighteen-year-old girl would not have been? She had persuaded me to change the course of my life, and she didn't even have to sleep with me in order to get me to do it.

I called Theresa and told her I was coming home for good. My plan was for us to meet in St. Louis and fly down to Cape Girardeau together; I was also thinking about transferring to the University of Kansas, though I said nothing about it to Theresa. She went along with everything I suggested, but she did so with a distinct coolness. Had I pressed her for an explanation, I would have found out that she, too, was keeping a secret: her plans for the future no longer included me. Theresa was having a marvelous time at the University of Kansas. She had made lots of friends and met lots of interesting boys and was even thinking of joining a sorority, and the last thing she needed was for her hometown boyfriend to come roaring back to the Midwest to complicate her life. Her cover didn't slip until I sprang my Christmas plans on her, and even then I was too pleased with myself to suspect that I might be in for a surprise.

The time had come for me to plan my actual departure from St. John's, a fairly simple undertaking. Just before Christmas break, every St. Johnnie met with his tutors in a face-to-face conference held in lieu of a report card and known as the "don rag." After Christmas, students returned to campus for a week of miscellaneous activity, followed by a long weekend holiday. The second semester began on Tuesday. My parents decided to drive me back to Annapolis at the end of Christmas break and collect my belongings, leaving me with just enough clothing to make it through the last week of the semester. After that, I would be free. With the end in sight at last, I stopped studying Greek altogether; unable to control my elation, I even started talking again in seminar.

After the don rag was over, I flew to St. Louis and met Theresa, and we boarded a commuter plane bound for Cape Girardeau. I gave her a neatly wrapped package containing the Debussy letter and told her to open it. She turned pale when she saw what it was. We went for a long drive in the country a few days later, and Theresa told me as gently as she could that things had changed. She offered to return the Debussy letter; I asked her to keep it. We parted without rancor. My heart was broken, but my thoughts were already turning to the future, for something important had happened shortly after I came back to Sikeston: I had found my new college.

When I told my parents that I wanted to drop out of St. John's, I suggested that the best thing for me to do might be to spend a semester working at a local bank, collecting my thoughts and contemplating my next move. Though my father made non-committal noises, he actually thought my idea was absolute non-sense, and he quietly arranged for the two of us to pay a visit to William Jewell College, the school I had turned down a year before. He kept his plans to himself until I got home. All he had in mind, he said, was a quick look around the place. Of course I could take the semester off if I wanted, but surely it wouldn't hurt to take a look before I made up my mind?

We drove up to Liberty a few days later, where I met Phillip Posey, a soft-spoken conductor with a slight southern accent who served as William Jewell's director of instrumental music. Dr. Posey gave me a tour of the brand-new music building and told me all about the various programs. Then he told me that William Jewell would be delighted to have me as a music major. Was I interested? Years later, my father confessed to me that he had already told Dr. Posey that I was miserable at St. John's and that he wanted me to transfer to Jewell at once, adding that it might take a certain amount of finesse to bring me around. He overestimated my resistance. I was relieved to learn that I was not damaged goods, that William Jewell actually wanted me. Besides, I liked the sound of the place. It was small, but not so claustrophobically small as St. John's; it was located in a small town, but was only twenty minutes away from Kansas City; it was affiliated with the Southern Baptist Convention, but prided itself on its high academic standards. And it was only one long day's drive from Sikeston.

This time, I got it right. Abandoning all thoughts of working at the Bank of Sikeston, I accepted Dr. Posey's invitation on the spot. I rode home with my father in a haze of pleasure and spent most of the following day thumbing through the Jewell catalogue, making long lists of exciting-sounding classes (a luxury St. John's had denied me), and deciding exactly how I would spend the next three and a half years of my life. My previous unwillingness to immerse myself in music was long forgotten. My false start was over, and I was more than ready to begin making up for lost time.

A few days later, I returned to Annapolis with my parents, who loaded up my belongings and drove back to Sikeston that Sunday. I officially withdrew from St. John's on Monday morning; I received a written summary of my don rag in Wednesday's mail. Though it no longer mattered what my tutors thought of me, I was still curious, and I was pleased with what I read. My Greek tutor reported on me as follows: "Decent, regular, capable, sound." (Boy, did I have him snowed.) My math tutor found me no less satisfactory: "Eager to demonstrate, does it well." Brother Robert, the Jesuit priest who taught my lab class, praised me as "pleasant, helpful, imaginative, and lively." And Elliott Zuckerman, the fabulously urbane pianist who led my seminar, the man on whom I would have modeled myself had I decided to give St. John's another try, wrote this: "Very promising at beginning, then withdrew. Interest elsewhere? Came back." Very smart, Mr. Zuckerman.

I said goodbye to Allie and Randy on Friday night. I got up before sunrise the next morning, threw my clothes on, and walked

down to the corner, a denim laundry bag in one hand and my
guitar case in the other. I had arranged for a cab to pick me up
at five-thirty and take me to the Baltimore airport. The cab pulled
up and I tossed my things in the trunk. Then I took one last look
at the snow-covered buildings of St. John's College. I wanted to
fix them in my memory, for I hoped never to see them again.
As I glared at the bell tower of the main building, the driver
honked his horn. I got in and didn't look back.

Thirteen years went by. I graduated in due course from William
Jewell College, and after many adventures and much confusion,
I got a job as an editorial writer at the New York *Daily News*.
Reading the papers one morning, I noticed the byline "Randall
Rothenberg" in *The New York Times*, and I wondered if that was
the same Randy Rothenberg I had known at St. John's. In any
other city, you'd probably dismiss the similarity of names as
coincidence, but not in New York. Every typewriter jockey in
the world comes to Manhattan eventually, and it seemed entirely
plausible that Randy Rothenberg should have been writing about
advertising for *The New York Times*. But I did nothing to satisfy
my curiosity until I received a black-jacketed St. John's alumni
directory in the mail one day, looked up the class of 1978, and
saw that Randall Rothenberg was living in New York City.

I was hesitant to get in touch with Randy. Even though St.
John's had been sending me literature for the past decade, I had
never had any contact with the college or the people I had known
there since the day I left. I felt like someone who, as they say in
novels about Oxford, had been sent down under a cloud, and
yet nothing of the sort had happened. I had attended St. John's
for a semester; I transferred to another school in the Midwest.
That was it. I had not been expelled, had not flunked out, had
undergone no dreadful humiliations. In fact, nothing much had
happened to me at all, and that was the whole problem: I was
not altogether sure that I wanted to get in touch with a person
who might not remember me, and I was reluctant to remind

myself so bluntly of the semester I had spent hiding from the world.

After thinking it over for a week or so, I typed out a short note on my *Daily News* letterhead: "If you are the Randy Rothenberg with whom I shared an amplifier during jam sessions at St. John's College during the fall of 1974, we're both in the newspaper business. Why not give me a call?" The note sat on my desk for a couple of days before I sent it off. I got a call three days later. It was my Randy, all right, and we made a date for lunch. I recognized him immediately, beardless and beretless but unmistakable all the same. He had a surprise for me: it turned out that he, too, had dropped out of St. John's, the semester after I left. St. John's, he said, had simply not been right for him. I wanted to laugh out loud. I thought to myself: *I may have been crazy, but at least I wasn't alone.*

As I sat down at my desk after lunch, I thought of the name I had been trying to recall ever since the alumni directory had arrived: *Allie.* A crowded decade had erased her from my memory, but now I remembered her clearly. Where had she gone? What had she done? I looked her up in the directory. Her name was there, but her address and telephone number were missing. She had not seen fit to inform the St. John's alumni office of her current whereabouts.

I wasn't surprised. It was hard for me to imagine Allie in the role of a loyal St. Johnnie. But I was disappointed all the same, for I wanted to talk to her. I wanted to tell her that I had been far too immature to handle the stresses of life at St. John's College; I wanted to thank her for giving me the courage to say goodbye to Annapolis and return to Missouri, there to do the rest of my growing up under the watchful gaze of comforting, certain, all-knowing midwestern eyes. Most of all, I wanted to tell her that I no longer viewed my stay at St. John's as a mistake. I had learned that even the bad parts of a life, the mishaps and misfortunes, are an indispensable part of the chain of coincidence that leads you to the place where you belong.

It's easy enough to cultivate a philosophical attitude a decade after the fact. Any fan of the novels of P. G. Wodehouse can tell you that. On one of the many occasions when Bertie Wooster unexpectedly found himself engaged to Madeline Bassett and sought the counsel of Jeeves, his valet and mentor, Jeeves attempted to soothe Bertie with the noble words of Marcus Aurelius, the great philosopher-emperor of ancient Rome: "Does aught befall you? It is good. It is part of the destiny of the Universe ordained for you from the beginning. All that befalls you is part of the great web." To which Bertie replied: "He said that, did he? Well, you can tell him from me he's an ass." I admire Jeeves, but I sympathize with Bertie. Had one of my tutors told me midway through my semester at St. John's College that I was caught in the great web of destiny, I probably would have called him an ass, along with a few other names of even higher voltage. But he would have been right. I wouldn't willingly live very many moments of that semester over again; I wouldn't dream of wiping any of them off the slate of my life. The fall of 1974 is as much a part of me as the fall of 1973.

I would have liked to say all these things to my friend Allie, the only person I met during my short and uneventful stay at St. John's to whom they might possibly have meant something. I'm sorry that I wasn't able to do so. Every web contains a few loose strands, and Allie is one of mine. I like to think that she has a fond memory or two of the poor scared boy whom she charmed so long ago with her flute and her small, curvy body and her doggedly sincere talk, but I doubt it. She was an agent of destiny, and one can hardly hope to make an impression on such people. They have, after all, so very much to do.

8 | *On College Hill*

I flew into Kansas City on a business trip one sunny Sunday morning not long ago. I got off the plane, fetched my suitcase, and rented a car. Once I had watched my father do these things, marveling at his poise and authority and wondering if I would ever be old enough to do them myself. Now, as I handed my driver's license and credit card to the clerk behind the rent-a-car counter and scribbled my name at the bottom of a sheaf of papers entitling me to drive a compact car wherever I pleased for the next three days, I remembered the child who wondered if he would ever become a man. *Here I am*, I thought, *all grown up. It must have happened.*

I strode briskly out of the airport, bag in hand, looking exactly like a fully grown adult on a business trip. But I was only pretending, and I stopped pretending as soon as I started the car and pulled out of the rental lot. I didn't head straight for the hotel, as my father would have done. Instead, I nosed the car out onto the highway, turned on the radio, and started driving toward nowhere, just as I had so many times during the eight years I lived in Kansas City. Kansas City is well-suited to such drives. It is big and flat, bisected by the Missouri River and crisscrossed by a dozen highways. You can circle the city in air-conditioned comfort at fifty-five miles an hour; you can pull off the interstate, open your windows, and cruise down one of the long, shady parkways lined with fountains and expensive houses.

I fingered the buttons of the radio until I found a good rock station. A good rock station is a station that plays the songs you liked when you were a teenager, and this one fit the bill to perfection. As the front seat vibrated to the sounds of Steely Dan and Linda Ronstadt and the Beatles, I thought not of the scenery, or even the music, but of my college days. I had nothing to do until dinnertime, and so I turned east on I-70 and headed straight for Highway 291, the road that leads to Liberty, Missouri.

To get to Liberty, you turn south on Highway 291 at Independence Center, a huge shopping center that sits serenely in the middle of a sea of concrete and asphalt. Judging by the boutiques and fast-food joints that line the road, you could be anywhere in America. But four lanes soon squeeze down to two, and the boutiques give way to rock quarries and drive-in theaters and tiny churches with wry proverbs posted on the signs out front. ("The emptier the pot, the quicker it boils. WATCH YOUR TEMPER.") Then you cross a bridge and turn a corner, and you are in Liberty. Many people consider Liberty a suburb of Kansas City, but that's not quite right. I should know, for I spent eight years here, during which I shared three dormitory rooms and two apartments with four roommates and a wife. Liberty is no suburb: it's a small town. Just look around. Wal-Mart is having a special on house paint today. The parking lot of Hardee's is full of pickup trucks with gun racks mounted in the rear windows. If I didn't know better, I'd swear I was in Sikeston, Missouri, three hours south of St. Louis, not Liberty, Missouri, twenty minutes north of Kansas City.

But Liberty is no ordinary small town. It is also a college town, and on a high hill just beyond the center of town you will find William Jewell College, my old school. I came here for the first time sixteen years ago. My father brought me here to take a look around; then, a week later, he brought me back to stay. I came to William Jewell a scared, unformed eighteen-year-old, bruised by my semester at St. John's College, looking for friends and solace and a design for living; I left four and a half years later, possessed of a diploma and a fiancée, ready to plunge into the white waters of adult life. I loved nearly every minute of the time I spent on College Hill. That is why I have come back for a visit. It has been a long time since I was here. I have the morning to myself, and I want to look around.

William Jewell College is surrounded by two-story houses and a thousand trees that cover the ground with a crumbly blanket of dark red, fiery orange, and dirty brown when autumn comes. Snow falls every winter, and if you have the nerve to pinch a serving tray from the cafeteria, you can slide down the hill, dodging trees, stumps, and other people on trays. William Jewell was built on this site in 1849, and it wouldn't surprise me at all to learn that its students have been sliding down College Hill since the first time snow fell on it. The hill is high enough to cut the college off from the old houses and older churches spread out at its foot, and it is possible to spend four years at Jewell without getting any sense whatsoever of the special qualities of Liberty, Missouri. It wasn't until I graduated and moved off the hill and beyond the gates of the college that I learned what Liberty was like.

To get to William Jewell, you drive through a pair of old stone gates and make a sharp left at the top of the hill. I rode up that road in a chartered bus at the end of a half-dozen choir and band tours, and no matter how late it was or how tired we were, we sang the alma mater as the bus passed through the gates. Since we were music majors, we sang in four-part harmony, and it is a tribute to the closeness of a small college that every one of us knew the man who, three decades before, had harmonized the song we sang: Ed Lakin, Jewell's much-loved music theory teacher. Now I am driving up the hill in a rented car. I pass through the gates and turn left, and I suddenly find myself in the midst of grass, trees, flowers, and old brick buildings. The uncomplicated beauty of William Jewell College took my breath away the first time I saw it, for it embodied all of my long-frustrated fantasies about college life. *This time,* I thought, *I've found the place where I belong.* The longer I stayed there, the more I took it for granted. Today, though, I have recaptured something of the surprise I felt when I first turned left at the gates of the college and saw, stretched out before me, my new home.

Sunday morning is a good time to wander around the campus. William Jewell is peopled by two kinds of kids. Some sleep in on Sunday morning; others get dressed, straggle to the cafeteria for breakfast, and go to church. If you come to Jewell at ten-thirty on a Sunday morning, the churchgoers will be long gone and everyone else will be in bed. I park my car, trudge up a steep set of steps, and find myself on the edge of the quadrangle, near the summit of College Hill. The grass on the quad is an implausibly rich shade of green; it looks as if each blade had been individually stained and trimmed by a platoon of gardeners. A tall flagpole stands at the center of the quad, surrounded by five buildings, one very old, one fairly old, three fairly new. I spent much of my time at Jewell shuttling among these five buildings, and four of them are old friends.

The building that mattered most to me was John Gano Memorial Chapel, built in 1926. A shabby, comfortable monument to high culture and higher thinking, Gano is equipped with stained-glass windows, old theater seats, an ancient stage, a four-manual electronic organ, and a Steinway concert grand that is kept in superb condition. A brass plaque in the lobby describes John Gano as "preacher—patriot—pioneer—Christian citizen," adding that he lived from 1727 to 1804, during which time he founded the First Baptist Church of New York City and served as a chaplain in the Continental Army and a "missionary in Kentucky." The plaque supplies another important piece of information: John Gano's great-granddaughter paid for the building that was erected in his name. I sometimes offer a short prayer on behalf of John Gano's great-granddaughter, for I spent many hours making music in the building she paid for, most of them deeply satisfying.

Only two things have been added since my last visit to Gano Hall. At stage left is a plaque announcing the fact that Harry S. Truman, Lyndon B. Johnson, and Jimmy Carter each spoke from this stage. At stage right is an identical plaque with the following inscription: *On February 1, 1973, LUCIANO PAVAROTTI presented the first recital of his distinguished career on this stage.* William Jewell College sponsors a lavish concert series, one of the few outright extravagances of this quintessentially Baptist school, and it was in Gano that I first heard Pavarotti and Sherrill Milnes and Victoria de los Angeles and Elly Ameling and Frederica von Stade lift their silver voices in song. I hid in the balcony one afternoon and heard the Russian pianist Lazar Berman rehearsing for a recital that evening, surrounded by gun-toting KGB agents. When I got a little older, I came to Gano to review concerts for the Kansas City *Star*, the same concerts I had once attended so greedily, snapping up the free tickets available to every Jewell student who takes the trouble to queue up and ask for them.

Across the quad from Gano is Jewell Hall, erected in 1851. The oldest surviving building on campus, it has the hefty, squared-off look familiar from Civil War daguerrotypes, and one crumbling brick wall is almost completely covered with thick ropes of ivy. If you look to the south, you can see the neat skyline of Kansas City in the hazy distance; on this quiet Sunday morning, you can hear the lazy chirping of birds and the faint rumble of trucks rolling down the highway. Off to the right is the college library, out of whose second-floor windows I used to drop books into the bushes on warm spring afternoons. I retrieved them later, saving myself the expense of paying overdue fines. I took a lot of books out of this library, one way or another, when I was a student at Jewell.

Yates College Union lies in the corner between the library and Gano Hall. It houses the cafeteria, where I ate most of my meals, none of them as bad as I liked to claim; it also houses the Cage, the campus snack bar, where I appeared twice in dinner-theater productions. Upstairs is KWPB, the campus radio station, where I worked as classical music director and, on Wednesday nights, late-night jazz disc jockey, in which capacity I obligingly played makeout music for my jazz-loving friends. It seemed unfair that I had to sit by myself in the studio while my friends reaped the benefits of my good taste. I was particularly jealous of my roommate. Week after week, I trudged off to the studio, carrying an armful of carefully chosen albums; week after week, he spirited his girlfriend up to our room, turned on the radio, and allowed nature, assisted by the saxophone stylings of Paul Desmond, Gerry Mulligan, and Stan Getz, to take its course, knowing that I wouldn't come back to bother him until he heard me play "The Star-Spangled Banner" and sign off for the night.

Across the alley from Gano Hall is the rambling house in which the president of William Jewell College lives. The annual all-campus picnic is held on the rolling lawn of the president's house. Had you strolled across that lawn in 1861, you might have been mowed down by fire from a line of Union rifle pits. The Civil War also left its mark on Jewell Hall, which was pressed into service as a Union hospital and barracks. The summit of College Hill is occupied by a shady graveyard whose oldest plots were dug long before the Confederates started firing on Fort Sumter. Time and weather have worn many of the stones too smooth to be read. You could stage the last scene of *Our Town* in the Jewell graveyard with little difficulty. I played a different kind of scene here as a junior: I entered the graveyard late one night, flashlight in hand, looking for a particular headstone. Earlier that day, an anonymous voice on the telephone told me to come to the graveyard at midnight, where I would be met by a representative of the senior honor society and escorted to an induction ceremony. The graveyard was full of winking flashlights that night.

Just past the graveyard are the dormitories. I lived in two of them, Browning Hall and Eaton Hall. College Hill drops off steeply behind the dorms, and narrow concrete steps take you down to the student parking lot, where I used to neck with my wife-to-be in the front seat of my station wagon. If you look through the trees at the foot of the hill, you will see a complex of brick buildings, isolated and almost invisible. This is where those married students live who are lucky enough to get an apartment. I never set foot in any of these modest apartments until a year after I graduated, at which time I moved into one with my new wife, who had a year to go before she earned her diploma. Off to the north are thousands of acres of farmland, stretching across the prairie into infinity, merging at the horizon with the pale purple sky. I saw this view whenever I looked out the window of my dormitory room in Eaton Hall; it reminded me that I was in Missouri, back home again. Whenever I want to summon up the beauties of the Midwest in my memory, I think of the view from Eaton Hall.

The music building, located due east of the quadrangle, was only a semester old when I came to Jewell, and the newness never quite wore off in all the time I spent roaming its corridors. On the top floor is the recital hall, unchanged since I was a student except for a plaque on the door that now identifies it as the Wesley L. Forbis Recital Hall. Dr. Forbis, known to everyone at Jewell as "Doc," was head of the Jewell music department. Doc was a born conductor who could coax thrilling sounds out of the Concert Choir simply by peering over his half-glasses and making a few inexplicable gestures in the air. He suffered from chronic back trouble, and every aspiring young choral conductor in the music department used to walk around slightly hunched over, emulating the posture Doc adopted out of sheer pain. He left Jewell shortly after I graduated, moving to Nashville to become an executive in the music division of the Southern Baptist Convention. You don't see anybody imitating his walk in the halls of the music building anymore. There is precious little immortality to be had at a college, save as a name on an unnoticed plaque.

I trot down the front stairs of the music building to the practice room floor, open a door, and find myself in the commons, the meeting place where music majors went in search of relief from the labors of practice. On the wall of the commons is a plaque inscribed with the names of every music major and faculty member resident at William Jewell on the day the music building was dedicated. Had I not spent the first semester of my freshman year at St. John's, my name would be on it, too. I knew most of the people whose names are on display here. I played music with them, toured with them, befriended them. It's been years since I last saw any of them. Are they happy? Are they still making music? Do they ever come back to Jewell and gaze at this plaque and think the same thoughts I am thinking? I spent hours sitting in the shadow of this plaque, flirting and gossiping, solving the problems of the world, even getting my hair cut by a pretty bassoon player who made a little extra pocket money by setting up shop in the commons and trimming the heads of music majors. Now I am alone, for nobody in his right mind practices on Sunday morning. All I have for company are an empty wastebasket, a candy machine, two wooden benches, and a hundred names.

This building was the center of my life throughout the four and a half years I spent at William Jewell. I made very little music at St. John's College. When I got to Jewell, music was all I wanted to make, all I wanted to study, all I cared about. At one time or another, I played or sang with every performing ensemble in the music department except the Concert Choir, which was open only to kids with good voices. In time, I figured out that I was performing so much solely because I wanted to prove to myself (and everybody else) that I was indispensable, and I scaled back my activities drastically. But no hour spent making music is wasted, and I remember most of the hours I spent making music at Jewell with undimmed affection, especially the night that Cat Anderson, Duke Ellington's famous high-note trumpeter, came to Liberty to play with the college jazz band and went out with us afterward to eat pizza and talk about life on the road.

I envied Cat Anderson, for I enjoyed touring with the concert band and Chapel Choir more than anything else I did at Jewell. I loved giving concerts in unfamiliar halls and spending the night in the homes of unfamiliar people; I loved riding on the bus, making new friends and becoming even closer to old ones. My last tour at Jewell was with the concert band. We wandered up and down Texas and Oklahoma, playing in churches and high schools and spending a couple of days at a resort hotel on Padre Island in the dead of a Texas winter. Phillip Posey, the band director, and Phil Schaefer, his assistant, went down to the hotel restaurant to eat dinner early one evening, and as they looked out at the beach through the glass windows of the restaurant, they saw me walking along the Gulf of Mexico in the freezing rain, holding hands with a freshman from Trenton, Missouri, named Liz Cullers. They were amused but not surprised, for I had been keeping steady company during the previous two months with Liz, a pretty piano major with a dizzy sense of humor who played clarinet in the band for fun. I suppose you could say we owe our marriage to the William Jewell music department. I owe many good things to my alma mater, but that is the best one of all.

As I come out of the music building, sleepy sorority girls are rising from their beds and walking to Yates College Union to line up for lunch. The churchgoers are on their way back to campus. The sidewalks are already crowded with students, and it seems impossible that I cannot recognize any of the faces I see. I return to my car and drive slowly back down the hill, passing the young men and women of William Jewell College as I go.

I do not know Liberty the way I know Sikeston, for I did not live there long enough. While I know every square foot of Sikeston, Liberty is for me a patchwork quilt, a vaguely familiar pattern with a few squares that I know intimately. William Jewell, small as it is, is something of a patchwork, too, for there were many parts of the campus where I seldom set foot. And the same is true of Kansas City: I loved it, but I only knew part of it. I knew the bank where I worked after graduating from college; the Kansas City Public Library, where I went every day at lunchtime; the Kansas City *Star* building, where I came late at night to file reviews; and several dozen concert halls and theaters and restaurants and stores and nightclubs. That was my Kansas City. Had I stayed longer, the whole town might have been mine, but I left Kansas City at the end of five good years and three bad ones. It was a long time, a third of my lifetime up to that point, but not quite long enough.

Still, there are many places in Kansas City that I know and love, and since it is noon, I decide to visit one of them: Winstead's Drive-In, just across the street from the Country Club Plaza, the oldest shopping mall in America. Kansas City is home to half a dozen Winsteads, but this is the one where I used to go after concerts to eat hamburgers fried on a greaseless grill and served with icy limeade. I find an empty stool at the counter and order a single with cheese. Seated next to me are two burly men who look as if they might raise cattle for a living. I eavesdrop and discover, to my surprise, that they are talking about local jazz musicians with whom I used to play. One of them mentions Paul Smith, the best jazz pianist in Kansas City, a tall, handsome man who taught band at a small high school up the road from Liberty and played bebop with Stan Kessler and His Flat Five at night; the other speaks well of Gary Sivils, the trumpeter who gave me my second gig. I could be eating biscuits and gravy at Bo's Pit Bar-BQ in Sikeston, Missouri, listening to a couple of farmers talk about people and places I know as well as the back of my right hand.

I finish my single with cheese and jump in my rented car and start driving off toward nowhere once again, up and down the tree-lined boulevards of Kansas City with their gaily splashing fountains. As the car radio blasts away in the background, familiar places stream past me in an unbroken procession: the church where I got married, the shopping center where I bought Liz a simple band of gold, the Italian sandwich shop where we went on our first date. This is not home, not quite; Sikeston is my home, now and forever. But Kansas City will always have a special place in my heart. The land is flat and the accents are right, and I never have to drive very far to find a memory. If I can't be at home, Kansas City will do just fine.

9 | *A Trophy for Molly*

In the course of the last eighteen years, I've worked for one high school newspaper, three college newspapers, and two real newspapers, every one of which caused me no end of irritation. I keep coming back for more, mainly because working for a newspaper makes it possible for me to write a piece on Tuesday and see it in print on Wednesday, a form of stimulation to which I am highly susceptible. Still, my experience has taught me to read the morning papers with a suspicious eye. Newspapers are produced by men and women whose chief stock in trade is knowing just enough about a lot of things, and most of them are more than willing to fill in the gaps in their knowledge with guesswork, a weakness that leads inexorably to what H. L. Mencken, himself an old newspaper hand, dryly described in his memoirs as "the synthesis of news." This is a process that only two kinds of people can truly appreciate: those who write for newspapers and those who are written about in them.

What goes for real newspapers goes double for college newspapers, many of which are kept firmly under the thumb of a faculty adviser who views them as fitting repositories for official press releases and glowing accounts of the joys of campus life. I can think of worse things. A tightly supervised campus paper may not be as much fun to write for as, say, the Berkeley *Barb*, but you probably learn more by filing routine stories under the supervision of an iron-willed disciplinarian. Back when I was on the staff, the William Jewell *Student* was run by a tough customer named Georgia Bowman who saw no reason whatsoever to send her student reporters out to cover the seamy side (such as it was) of life on College Hill. Dr. Bowman was a birdlike woman on the eve of retirement, and I could have picked her up with one hand and tossed her out the nearest window without difficulty; instead, I followed her orders to the letter, for she had perfect taste and was sparing in her praise, a combination of qualities that invariably inspires loyalty in young writers.

Despite my admiration for Dr. Bowman, I'm well aware that the back files of the *Student* should be approached with caution by anyone wanting to know what life at William Jewell was like. I know this not only because I wrote for the *Student* but because I was one of the people who helped to make an important piece of campus news to which the *Student* devoted a great deal of ink during the spring of 1978. Although my name never appeared in print in connection with the story in question, I was in it up to my ears. The last time I visited Jewell, I stopped by the library and spent an hour flipping through back issues of the *Student*, reading about the events of that spring. I wasn't surprised to see how much had been left out of the stories; I was far more surprised at how many details I had forgotten. But I had no trouble remembering what a good time I had that spring, or that I had some of it at the expense of my best friend.

It's funny what you remember from your school days. I couldn't tell you the names of more than a half dozen of my college teachers, but I still recall the names of every fraternity and sorority at William Jewell, even though I never joined a fraternity and paid little attention to Greek life on campus. Having spent a semester at St. John's College, I missed rush, and I didn't bother with it in later years. I was too busy making music to have time for toga parties, and I made more than enough good friends in the music department to keep me from feeling any need for the special brand of companionship that a fraternity provides.

Since I never went through rush, I never ran the risk of being passed over, but I knew quite a few people who failed to receive bids, and I still feel sorry for them. Life, of course, is unfair, a lesson that I suppose ought to be learned as early and as efficiently as possible, but I find it hard to forget the brutality with which that lesson was taught to those friends of mine who offered themselves up to the Greek system at William Jewell and were spurned by it. Some of them took it in their stride, but many more were scarred by the experience of seemingly arbitrary rejection and made no secret of it. Rejection is bad enough in and of itself, but failing to get into a fraternity or sorority also had important social implications. Because Jewell was so small, the Greek system played a pivotal role in many aspects of campus life. If you weren't a Greek, a regular churchgoer, or a major in one of the clubbier departments, you were pretty much out of luck. You had no opportunity to belong and, even worse, no opportunity for revenge on those who did belong.

There was only one exception to the iron law of social exclusion: Tatler Revue, William Jewell's oldest continuous all-campus ritual. Every year, Jewell's eight fraternities and sororities paired off to produce musical-comedy skits, and the non-affiliated students put together a skit of their own. The skits were performed at a show that ran for three nights in early February, and the profits were used to underwrite the publication of *The Tatler*, the Jewell yearbook, which was distributed free to all students. Tatler Revue was the principal instrument of pan-Hellenic rivalry. Every fraternity and sorority on campus spent a lot of money on its Tatler skit and devoted a lot of time to rehearsing it. Tatler was also, at least in theory, the only chance non-affiliated students had to strike back at the fraternities and sororities that had, in some cases, rejected them.

Unfortunately for the theory, the non-affiliated students were incapable of producing a winning skit. When I came to Jewell, the non-affil skits were being produced by Phi Mu Alpha and Sigma Alpha Iota, the honorary societies for campus musicians. Neither group was ever in a position to raise enough money to cover the costs of a decent production; more to the point, the members of Phi Mu Alpha and Sigma Alpha Iota simply weren't very good at putting together the kind of skit that Tatler Revue audiences liked. The Greek Tatler skits were structured along rigidly conservative lines: male chorus lines, mildly bawdy puns, pretty blond ingenues singing innocuous show tunes like "Ten Minutes Ago." The non-affil skits, by contrast, tended to be rather on the recherché side. I remember the non-affil skit at the first Tatler Revue I ever saw. It was accompanied by a string quartet. It didn't win any prizes.

After a long string of defeats, the presidents of Sigma Alpha Iota and Phi Mu Alpha threw in the towel, announcing in the April 1, 1976, issue of the *Student* that "we will not financially support the non-affiliated skit in the 1977 Tatler Revue." Eight months later, the inevitable happened, and it, too, was duly reported by the *Student*. The headline was "Revue Loses Non-Affil Skit," and the story makes for pathetic reading: "A Monday meeting of non-affil students concerned with the breakdown of the now-defunct non-affil skit made comments and plans on how this can be avoided in the future. . . . Only $57.52 had been raised. At least twice that much would have been necessary to cover the most basic expenses. . . . Group opinion was that a committee of an informal, non-binding nature be formed to organize and promote participation in school activities."

Two weeks later, a non-affiliated student named Steve Krause wrote a letter to the editor of the *Student* in which he complained that Tatler Revue had degenerated into "a production of professional proportions in which the only apparent goal is to win a trophy. . . . This trivial goal, and the distorted dollar demands which are a direct result, have finally forced the exclusion of a large segment of the student body." Steve's letter summed up the disappointment that every non-affil at William Jewell College felt that year. Such was his purpose, and his letter might well have closed the books on the whole affair had it not been for a Greek coed who sent a letter of her own to the *Student* the following week: "If those students who have 'chosen to remain independent of sororities and fraternities' wished to be 'allowed' to participate in Tatler as Steve indicates, they had only to make the same financial sacrifices that the participants made." This letter, accurate enough as far as it went, nevertheless suggested more than a touch of hubris on the part of the author and her fellow Greeks, and that was a fatal mistake, since Hubris, as the real Greeks knew and as I learned during my brief stay at St. John's College, is always closely followed by Nemesis.

Nemesis made its first appearance in the pages of the *Student* two weeks later in the form of a short news item: "About 20 students met together Monday night to form the Non-Affiliated Student Association (NASA). Its purpose: to organize non-affil participation in school events. The need for a loosely structured group became apparent after this year's Tatler Revue, according to Jan Evans, spokesman for the non-affils." That was the whole story. My churchgoing friends might well have described it as a cloud no bigger than a man's hand. But it was important all the same, for the sole purpose of NASA, as everybody knew, was to put together a winning Tatler Revue skit or die trying. As far as NASA was concerned, the non-affiliated students of William Jewell College had been humiliated by the Greeks, and not for the first time, either. Several of the prime movers of NASA had failed to receive bids at the end of freshman rush, and they wanted revenge.

This is where I came in. In the fall of 1977, I was invited to serve as music director of the first NASA Tatler skit. Many of the students behind NASA were drama majors whom I had met while working on plays, and some of them were among my best friends. While it would never have occurred to me to *join* NASA, helping my friends put on a show was different. I had happy memories of the nights I spent in the Middle School gym; I knew that a good music director would make all the difference between a professional-sounding production and yet another pretentious flop. The thought of revenge never entered my head. Nobody had ever done anything to me. All I cared about was having a good time, and working on a Tatler skit sounded like a perfect way to have one.

I signed on and was instantly plunged into four solid months of frenzy. The NASA Tatler team held regular meetings in Cardinal House, one of the off-campus residence houses for female honor students and the home of the chief instigator and co-director of the NASA skit, a talented young actress named Karen Kerr. Within a few weeks, we had roughed out a script based on *Alice in Wonderland*. Our version was set in a supermarket, with all of the characters dressed as packaged foods. Since we didn't have enough money to build an expensive set, we decided to spend what we had on colorful homemade costumes that would divert the attention of the audience from our cheap backdrop. As music director, my job was to make our skit sound like a professional musical-comedy production, something that no Greek Tatler team had ever managed to do and that could also be done on the cheap as long as enough music majors joined forces with us.

The book and lyrics of "Alice in Wonderway," as we called our skit, were quickly approved by the faculty censors, who must have been relieved to find that NASA had put together such a sweet-sounding skit. (The censors spent most of their time scissoring double entendres out of the Greek skits.) It was time for a cattle call, and we posted notices all over campus announcing auditions. Unwilling to leave matters to chance, I quietly approached two friends of mine and invited them to try out for the female leads. One was JoAnna Evans, a fine singer whose husky voice and dark beauty had made her a mainstay of the Jewell theater department. The other was a winsome-looking freshman named Donna Bohannon, whom I had auditioned for Chapel Choir, of which I was the student conductor that year. I suspected that Donna might make a perfect Alice, for she had long hair, silver braces on her teeth, and a Barbra Streisand–like voice. Donna and JoAnna quickly grasped the significance of my invitation and showed up at the audition, along with a hundred other kids, most of them music and theater majors. Only a handful were NASA members.

To no one's surprise, Donna was cast as Alice, with JoAnna playing the wicked Queen of Pop-Tarts. Phil Briggs and Byron Motley, our male leads, were both voice majors; Phil was tall and handsome, and Byron was a pretty good tap dancer. Everybody in the chorus knew how to read music. It was a far cry from the chaotic approach of the Greek skit teams, who treated Tatler Revue as something of a lark. Not us. We were out to have fun, but we meant business, too, and we knew what we were doing. All told, the members of the NASA skit team had acted in some sixty-odd high school and college plays. Now we were putting our experience to work.

In order to make the NASA skit sound as professional as possible, I decided to write all-new musical arrangements. Tatler skits were customarily accompanied by whatever sorority sister played piano best, but that wasn't good enough for me, either, so I put together a trio of piano, bass, and drums. Determined to do the job right, I approached Lynda Walker, the best accompanist in the music department. Lynda was a frail-looking girl with a pale, sober face and a wickedly dry sense of humor. Married and several years older than her fellow music majors, Lynda had never had much of a chance to get involved in campus life, and I knew she would jump at the chance to play piano for "Alice in Wonderway." Kenn Blurton, drummer for the Jewell jazz band, rounded out the NASA "orchestra," by far the slickest-sounding instrumental ensemble that had ever accompanied a Tatler skit.

As a pianist, Lynda's only drawback was that she couldn't improvise, which meant that I would have to write her piano parts out note for note, along with the vocal arrangements and choral parts. I had previously informed Karen Kerr that I was an old hand at writing arrangements, the most shameless lie I have ever told in my life. I had never written an arrangement of a hymn tune, much less a Broadway-style production number, and "Alice in Wonderway" contained four production numbers, a short overture, and various snippets of music to be played under dialogue and during scene changes. I was in over my head, and I knew it, but that didn't stop me. One Friday night, I locked myself in a studio on the first floor of the music building and worked for two days straight, coming out only for sketchy meals and an hour or two of sleep. I emerged on Sunday afternoon clutching a ring-bound notebook containing the entire musical score to "Alice in Wonderway." I thrust it into Lynda's capable hands, staggered back to Eaton Hall, and fell into bed, where I remained, snoring loudly, for the next eighteen hours.

As soon as the musical score was finished, we started rehearsing, for it was essential that we set the running time of the show at once. Tatler skits could run no longer than twenty minutes; skits that ran long lost points. Karen and I figured that if we could hold the music and dialogue down to seventeen minutes, it would give us enough time to change sets and allow for stage business without going over the time limit. After a week of sectional rehearsals, the entire NASA ensemble assembled in the choral suite of the music building for the first run-through of the complete score. Karen gave a short pep talk. Lynda clicked a stopwatch. Then we went straight through "Alice in Wonderway." The skit ended with a sugary ballad called "Home" which I had lifted from the score of *The Wiz*, confident that Donna could put it across like a Broadway star. Donna and the chorus sang their hearts out. I gave the cutoff and the room fell silent. Lynda looked at the stopwatch. "Seventeen minutes on the nose," she said matter-of-factly. Then the entire cast of "Alice in Wonderway" started dancing around the room.

After Christmas, we went to work in earnest, rehearsing every night in a union hall in Claycomo, a small town ten minutes south of Liberty. The only people who knew the full extent of our preparations were the cast and crew of "Alice in Wonderway." Fifty people can't keep a secret, and word quickly got around campus that NASA had a surprise up its sleeve, but nobody believed it. The horrible skits that the non-affils had been putting on for the last several years, coupled with the fact that there had been no non-affil skit at all in 1977, provided adequate camouflage for our activities. But the gossip was hot enough to cause a great many students to wonder exactly what we were up to, and one of them was my best friend, a loyal sister of Delta Zeta.

Molly was a girl born to wear tweeds and plaids and saddle oxfords. She was tall and slender, with long blond hair, a pretty, slightly boyish face, and a flat midwestern accent. Molly tended to keep to herself, so much so that casual acquaintances often thought her haughty, but her prim reserve concealed a sharp tongue and a well-developed sense of the ridiculous. Cindy, Molly's sister, was a coloratura soprano with a dishy figure, silky waist-length hair, and a coy, aren't-I-adorable speaking voice. She was one of the best-known voice majors at William Jewell and a prominent member of Delta Zeta. Molly probably would have done better to choose a different college, but she insisted on going to Jewell, where she majored in piano, played clarinet in the band, and sang in Chapel Choir, which is how I came to know her.

One Sunday evening, Molly and I found ourselves sitting together in the basement of an Independence church, forced to wait for half an hour before the choir could sing its three numbers, board the bus, and return to Liberty. I introduced myself and struck up a conversation, and I found it surprisingly easy to make her laugh. We sat together on the bus after the concert and talked our heads off. Within a week, we were fast friends. Molly's boyfriend was a percussion major at the University of Missouri at Kansas City, and I was unattached, so there was nothing to keep us from sitting together at recitals, taking our meals together, doing our homework together. Molly later introduced me to a friend of hers named Pam Jackson, a piano major from Villa Ridge, Illinois, a town even smaller than Sikeston. The three of us drove all over Kansas City in Pam's pickup truck that winter, shopping for clothes and eating pizza and going to movies, slipping and sliding through wet snow and screaming in mock terror every time the truck started to spin out.

My friendship with Molly was sealed when we shared a seat on the bus during the winter band tour. Choosing a seatmate for a band tour is a delicate business fraught with uncertainty. You can ask someone to sit with you, running the risk of getting turned down, or you can wait for someone to ask you, running the risk of getting stuck with an unsatisfactory seatmate. (The possibility of not being asked to sit with anyone is too awful to contemplate.) I invited Molly to sit with me, and she accepted with pleasure. We talked for hours on end during the long hauls from town to town, and we quickly settled into the comfortable intimacy that often springs up between new friends who have much in common. Molly and I had both been bright children and shy teenagers, and music had freed us from some of our many inhibitions. By the time we got back to Liberty, I felt certain that we would be friends for life; I told her so one day at lunch, and she nodded in firm agreement. A month later, she pledged Delta Zeta.

I was stunned by Molly's decision, not merely because she didn't seem the type but because her sister Cindy was a DZ. It would be hard for Molly to follow in her footsteps. But she wanted to do it, and I was so taken aback when she told me what she had in mind that I had little to say about it. I suppose I had not fully understood how difficult a time Molly had had as a teenager or how badly she wanted normal people to like her in a normal way. I liked her in an utterly normal way, but I was, after all, not altogether normal myself. Molly desperately wanted to make the acquaintance of the larger world of nice girls and regular guys, and I could hardly blame her for that.

Molly's decision to go Greek had no immediate effect on our friendship. She performed her mysterious rituals at night and told me about them every morning at breakfast, giggling at the absurdities of sorority life; we continued to eat together and pass notes to each other at recitals. Jarring phrases like "my sisters" occasionally crept into her speech, but I teased her about them and we laughed them off. Molly was amused when I told her that I had gotten roped into serving as music director for the NASA Tatler skit, and I was pleased when she told me that she had been cast in the DZ Tatler skit. When Molly first pledged Delta Zeta, I had feared that she would be pigeonholed as Cindy's younger sister, the one who studied hard and played piano, but she had turned into something of a beauty in her own right by that time, and I hoped that the experience of playing a part on stage would give her the poise and self-confidence she lacked.

I saw no reason why my work on the NASA skit should intrude on my friendship with Molly. But collective passions can sweep away innocent bystanders who stand too close. I was spending virtually every night in the company of good friends who would have walked over their grandmothers in order to scoop up the Best Skit of 1978 trophy, and their zeal was contagious. I was working hard on "Alice in Wonderway"; I felt personally responsible for the success of Donna and JoAnna. The temporary intimacy of the rehearsal hall gradually cast its familiar spell on me, and what started out as a lark became far more serious. It was, I suppose, inevitable that I should have gotten caught up in the anti-Greek feelings of my friends, but it was by no means inevitable that I should have allowed those feelings to eat away at the best and most important friendship I had, and that, sad to say, is what happened.

One day late in January, Molly and I bumped into each other on the quad. We hadn't seen much of each other lately, immersed as we were in our Tatler skits. I was cutting classes right and left, and Molly, prim and proper as she was, was doing exactly the same thing. We were both tired and overworked. The situation was ripe for quarreling, and a quarrel quickly blew up. I don't remember who started it, and I don't remember everything that was said, although I know I described some of Molly's sorority sisters as "scummy." It was a preposterous charge, for I knew none of them at all well. It wasn't me talking, of course: it was my NASA friends. But Molly could hardly be expected to have understood that. She said a few cutting words of her own, and we parted angrily.

Our encounter was far from unusual. Similar exchanges were taking place all over campus, for Tatler rivalries were at an all-time high. It was generally known by this time that NASA had put together a crack team of theater and music majors and was conducting all-night rehearsals in order to perfect its skit. (A slight exaggeration, but not by much.) Not surprisingly, many Greeks were as mad at us as we were at them. One day, I passed a well-known fraternity bigwig who shouted four-, six-, and twelve-letter words at me as I ducked into Gano Hall for a rehearsal. These tensions came to a head when the four fraternity-sorority teams and the NASA team met for dress rehearsal on Wednesday night of Tatler Week. It was the first time that any of the participants had seen each other's skits, and it was definitely a night to re-member, or to forget as quickly as possible. We ran through all five skits. Then, after a long and noisy intermission, we ran through all five skits again in order to iron out technical problems. The seats of Gano Hall were jammed with cast and crew members, all looking hungrily at each other's skits, hoping that theirs was the best, sure that it wasn't.

Molly sang well and made a charming impression. I should have sought her out at intermission to tell her so, but I didn't. I told myself that I had too many problems to fix to waste time on Molly. That was absolute nonsense, not least because the NASA team really didn't have any major problems to fix before the second run-through. We had gotten it right the first time. For us, dress rehearsal was the real opening night, the moment when our enemies would be forced to witness the fruits of our labor. *Our* enemies, mind you. I had completely succumbed to the fever that had seized my colleagues. As I sat on my stool, waiting for the stage manager to give me the signal to start the overture, I would have been glad to machine-gun every Greek in the hall, Molly included, as long as I could wait until they had seen our skit first.

The stage manager cued me, I gave Lynda the downbeat,

and the NASA team sailed through "Alice in Wonderway" like the practiced professionals we were. Twenty minutes later, we came to the end of "Home." Donna and the chorus filled the hall with sound. Lynda and Kenn pounded away at their instruments. The song soared to a climax, and I gave the cutoff. The last chord of "Home" rolled through Gano Hall, followed by an unearthly silence. Nobody ever applauded at Tatler dress rehearsals, and for anyone to have broken the custom on our behalf would have been highly unlikely, since NASA had just delivered a loud and public slap in the face to every fraternity and sorority at William Jewell College. But we knew what we had done, and we were proud to have done it.

Tatler Revue opened the following night. All three performances of "Alice in Wonderway" went smoothly, and the enthusiastic applause from the packed houses told us that we had done well. The Greek skits were perfectly respectable, but ours was in another league altogether, and everybody knew it. On Friday afternoon, I ran into Molly on the quad and she told me that our skit was wonderful. Everything else about those three days is a blur. My memories resume with the cutoff that I gave at the end of "Home" on Saturday night. As the curtain went down for the last time on "Alice in Wonderway" and the crowd clapped and whistled and cheered, I hugged Lynda Walker. She handed me the score. I handed it back and told her to keep it.

I remember the endless wait for the judges to make their decision. I remember the bad jokes the master of ceremonies told in order to kill time. Most of all, though, I remember the awards. The DZs claimed the best-actress trophy, and I was furious that my Donna had been beaten. But that was the only award that slipped past us. Under normal circumstances, Molly would have had a better-than-fair shot at winning the award for best supporting actress, but these were not normal circumstances. I had spent hours tailoring a sensational arrangement of "Ease on Down the Road" for JoAnna Evans, who sang it like the trouper she was and stopped the show every night, just as I had planned.

JoAnna won best supporting actress, Byron best supporting actor, Phil best actor. A one-hitter seemed within our grasp.

When the MC tore open the last envelope and announced that "Alice in Wonderway" was the best skit of 1978, the crowd went wild. Karen, Donna, JoAnna, Phil, and Byron charged up on stage to collect the trophy. I hung back. No award had been given for best music director, and I wasn't even a member of NASA, just an outside consultant, a hired gun. I felt strangely out of place. Then Karen waved at me and I clambered onto the stage. We passed the trophy around and hugged each other and basked in the waves of applause, sweating under the hot stage lights. A thought popped into my mind: *God, I haven't done any homework for a month.* It didn't matter. We had won.

The rest of the story can be found in the pages of the *Student*. The customary two-page spread of Tatler photos was accompanied by a signed editorial whose implications were impossible to overlook: "And now that Tatler is finished until next year, I sincerely hope that there are no bad feelings (as has unfortunately been the case in the past) concerning the judging—or anything else." Everybody at Jewell knew what that meant. NASA was the *anything else* of the 1978 Tatler Revue, and it was widely felt that we had played dirty. Anyone who thought otherwise need only have read the letter to the editor that appeared a little farther down the page, signed "A Concerned Greek":

> It amazes me to see these people who are affiliated non-affils doing Greek things. If they are so against Greeks and Greek activities, why do they insist upon participating in everything that the Greeks do? . . . Maybe the Greeks should just drop Tatler completely and let the non-affils do it themselves.

"A Concerned Greek" went on to accuse NASA of having engaged in flagrantly unethical conduct by bringing in nonmembers (like me) and of having overprofessionalized Tatler Revue. The whispers that had been heard all over campus for the past week were now set up in cold type for everyone to see. It was quite a jolt. I was surprised that the *Student* had printed the letter, and not merely because it was unsigned. It was a dramatic departure from the code of restraint that Dr. Bowman normally imposed on her student reporters. I knew, too, that "A Concerned Greek" would have had to sit down immediately after Tatler, write her letter, and hand-deliver it to the offices of the *Student* in order to get it into the following Wednesday's issue. I wonder to this day if the editor of the *Student*, who was a non-affil, made a special point of slipping that letter into the paper.

Whatever the motives of the parties involved, the result was an immediate, campus-wide uproar. The *Student* was distributed on Thursday afternoon, and nobody could talk about anything else in the cafeteria that evening. The general consensus seemed to be that though NASA had gone too far, "A Concerned Greek" had committed an even greater breach of civility. A week later, the *Student* ran another long editorial and printed three representative letters, one from a NASA official, one from a non-affiliated student not connected with NASA, and one from a Greek who had taken part in one of the Tatler skits. The first letter told off "A Concerned Greek" in polite language. The second letter told off "A Concerned Greek" in considerably blunter language, inadvertently revealing in the process the actual motivations of several of the people behind "Alice in Wonderway": "Almost all the non-affils involved with the skit went through rush, some even twice, and of that number well over half would have gone Greek, if they had received bids." It wasn't quite true, but it was close enough to the knuckle to draw blood.

The third letter was by far the most sensible. Unlike "A Concerned Greek," this sorority sister took a remarkably even-handed approach to the events of Tatler Week. On the one hand: "How can anyone dismiss well over half the student body from any sort of campus activity, simply because they are not a member of a Greek organization?" On the other hand: "I, too, think it unfair that NASA is able to pool their resources from such a large number of people, while we Greeks are strictly limited." She closed by sounding a note of compromise: "This problem and many others will never be solved if NASA and Greeks alike spend all their time back-stabbing each other. . . . I hope that in next year's activities, both Greeks and non-affils will strive for friendly competition to promote a common cause, instead of heated rivalry to win a coveted trophy."

The letter was signed by Molly.

Molly and I had a talk shortly after the letter from "A Concerned Greek" appeared in the *Student*. She had found the letter appalling, and I listened soberly as she told me how she felt about the whole affair. The only thing she neglected to tell me was that she planned to share her thoughts with the entire student body. Now, as I read them in the *Student*, I realized that "A Concerned Greek," for all her ugly spite, had a point. The cold-eyed professionals of NASA had come roaring in and broken up a well-loved campus ritual, all for the sake of settling a score. My own motives may have been pure, but I, too, had ultimately been swept up in the understandable desire for revenge that had driven my colleagues. The fact that we had put on a terrific show was beside the point, for I knew that "Alice in Wonderway" hadn't been just another show. It was the climax of a blood feud, the kind that nobody really wins, no matter who walks away with the trophies on closing night.

Molly, as it turned out, had the last word. NASA's Tatler Revue victory was listed as one of the top ten campus news stories of the year in the April 27 *Student*, along with such items as "Poisoning of campus birds" and "Reshuffling of the administrative staff." With that, the story of the 1978 Tatler Revue disappears from the pages of the *Student*. As for the winning team, none of us had anything to do with the following year's non-affil skit. Further involvement in Tatler Revue would have been graceless. We had done exactly what we set out to do, and that was the end of it.

It was also the end of my friendship with Molly. Not that

there was anything melodramatic about it. We continued to see each other and to talk whenever we did, but we no longer sought each other out, and our former intimacy quickly dwindled away. It would be too easy (and too melodramatic) to say that Tatler Revue was solely responsible for the breach in our friendship. Molly and I had come to the end of our junior year in college, and our lives were picking up speed as we began the long downhill run to graduation day. We had plenty of other things on our minds. Molly broke up with her drummer and began to date around; I met my wife-to-be and began spending every spare minute with her. Molly and I had simply grown apart, a perfectly natural process. That, at any rate, was what I told myself.

Molly and I had one last just-like-old-times chat toward the end of our senior year. We ran across each other in the library late in the spring. I told her that I had met the girl I hoped to marry. Molly didn't know Liz very well, and so I had the rare pleasure of talking to one girl about the good points of another one. I went on at length about Liz's beauty, her musical talent, her quick wit. Molly was pleased that I had finally managed to snag myself a first-class girlfriend, and said so. Little was said about the days when she and I had sat together in the cafeteria and shared our hopes and fears. Nothing at all was said about Tatler Revue.

I saw Molly in a Kansas City shopping mall a year or so after we graduated from Jewell. She had married and was working for the phone company, and she was visibly pregnant. We were glad to see each other and promised to get together soon. It never happened. We talked to each other on the phone a few months later, and it was the last time we ever spoke. I lost track of Molly after that, just as I lost track of all my classmates except Pam Jackson, the girl with the pickup truck, with whom I have remained in unbroken contact to this very day. Pam and I see each other every year or so, and when we get together, we sometimes talk about Molly, recalling with affection the movies we went to see and the meals we ate together.

My only souvenir of Molly is a color snapshot taken midway

through her senior year in high school, at the exact moment when she began to emerge from the chrysalis of adolescence, shortly before we met and became friends. Though it is only a head-and-shoulders pose, I know she must have been wearing knee socks and a plaid skirt and black-and-white saddle shoes. Sometimes I look at that picture and think about the lovely days of our friendship. More often, though, I remember the day I said cruel things to Molly for no good reason; I remember, too, how I did my best to deprive her of the trophy she might well have won had I not allowed myself to become caught up in a passion I did not share. My wish came true: Molly never got her trophy. But, then, I don't have a trophy, either. I don't even have a program from the 1978 Tatler Revue. All I have is a snapshot of Molly. It's funny how little it takes to remind you of the things you wish you hadn't done.

10 | *My Friend Harry*

In a small town, news is something you hear from a neighbor over a cup of coffee and read about in the local paper a few days later. I don't mean to knock the *Daily Sikeston Standard*, my old hometown paper, which I always used to read loyally and regularly. It's just that word of mouth is a more efficient way to find out about the things that really matter in a small town: love and marriage, hirings and firings, births and deaths. As a rule, small-town newspapers exist not to dig up embarrassing secrets but to sanctify matters of established fact, in much the same way that the president of the school board gives you a diploma on graduation day to prove that you went to school for twelve years. You're glad to have it, but it isn't exactly news.

The *Standard* wasn't much quicker on the uptake when it came to events that took place beyond the city limits of Sikeston. If you wanted to know what had happened in the world during the day, you turned on the television after you got home from work and watched the evening news. At our house, that meant

The CBS Evening News with Walter Cronkite. Walter Cronkite seemed to me a man of absolute probity, probably because his accent contained audible hints of a childhood spent in St. Joseph, Missouri, and I took the soundness of the rest of his team for granted. As far as I was concerned, it hadn't happened until Walter Cronkite announced it and Eric Sevareid analyzed it.

For me, though, the best thing about *The CBS Evening News with Walter Cronkite* was Charles Kuralt, a balding, paunchy fellow from North Carolina who spent his days driving around America in a white motor home, stopping along the way to file feature stories about plainspoken, good-hearted men and women who made bricks out of mud, carved merry-go-round horses by hand, and led tranquil, undisturbed lives in towns even smaller than mine. I thought Walter Cronkite honest and Eric Sevareid wise, but I was sure that Charles Kuralt had the finest job in the world, and I still think so. Years ago, I promised my brother that I would buy him a houseboat if I ever became rich, and he promised in return that he would buy me a white motor home. Neither one of us has collected, but we continue to remind each other of our solemn pact.

I used to hope that Charles Kuralt would someday get around to doing a story about Sikeston. In fact, I once thought about sending him a postcard and inviting him to drop by for a visit. I felt certain that he would appreciate the unspectacular virtues of my home town, and I would have been more than happy to show him around and introduce him to all the local characters. But it wasn't until after I left Sikeston that I met the man I would most have liked to introduce to Charles Kuralt, a man who embodied the things I love about my part of the country more completely than anyone I have ever known. His name was Harry Jenks, and he used to play piano every Saturday night in a pizza parlor in Independence, Missouri, the quiet suburb of Kansas City that was home to another Harry, Harry S. Truman. He died eleven years ago, and not a week has gone by since then that I haven't thought about him.

I owe my acquaintance with Harry Jenks to the stubbornness

of my friend Pam Jackson. Pam was introduced to Harry by her best friend, a fellow piano major named Dee Dee Hunter who had studied with Harry as a child. According to Pam, Harry had been a fixture on the Kansas City jazz scene until his eyesight started to fail, after which he lapsed by degrees into semiretirement. He now made his living by teaching piano to the children of Independence and giving concerts at retirement homes with a banjo player named Epp Roller; Harry and Epp also had a weekly gig at a Shakey's Pizza Parlor in Independence, where they played on Saturday nights for anybody who felt like listening. Since both men were as bald as cueballs, they called themselves "The Skinheads." Epp was good, Pam said, but Harry was the one I had to hear, because he sounded just like Art Tatum.

That got my attention. Art Tatum, a blind piano player from Toledo, Ohio, was considered by most of his colleagues to be the greatest pianist in the history of jazz. Oscar Peterson, himself no slouch in the technique department, called Tatum "a genius who had no respect for the impossible." George Gershwin and Vladimir Horowitz used to go to nightclubs to hear him play. Fats Waller is supposed to have introduced him as follows: "Ladies and gentlemen, I play piano, but God is in the house tonight." I never heard Art Tatum play, for he died ten months after I was born, but I owned enough of his records to know how special he was, and I found it unlikely that an old man who had been Dee Dee Hunter's first piano teacher and who was currently taking requests from drunks at a suburban pizza parlor could play half as well as Art Tatum had played on the worst day of his short life.

I brushed Pam off the first time she tried to talk me into going to Shakey's to hear Harry. But she kept after me, insisting that he was really that good, and it was sheer exasperation that finally made me give in. I was fond of Pam, but I had to show her that I knew better. "All right, Pam," I said one day. "You win. Let's go hear your friend Harry."

"How about Saturday night?" she replied.

Pam, Dee Dee, and I drove out to Shakey's that Saturday. We ordered a pizza and sat down on a bench next to a tiny bandstand where two men seated on barrels and dressed in white shirts with garters and string ties were playing "Nola," a hoary old popular song from the twenties. Epp Roller, the banjo player, was a short, bullet-headed man with a big nose. His banjo, which he strummed skillfully and with obvious pleasure, was fitted out with flashing lights. All I could tell about the man at the piano was that he had a broad back and that his playing was clean, straightforward, and ragtimey. The piano was an ancient upright that looked as if it had been bought at a garage sale for a sum in the low two figures. The room was dark and half empty. A sign on the piano informed listeners that copies of "The Skinheads," a homemade cassette containing such tunes as "Bye Bye Blues" and "Twelfth Street Rag," were available for five dollars apiece.

Harry turned around on his barrel and said hello to Pam and Dee Dee in a cheerful midwestern twang. He had a massive head and wore a pair of horn-rimmed glasses with one opaque lens. "What do you kids want to hear?" he asked.

"How about 'Sweet Lorraine'?" I said, with studied casualness. I had chosen my request carefully. "Sweet Lorraine" was an Art Tatum standby, and I hoped that it would prove my point to Pam without bringing needless embarrassment to the kindly old man at the piano.

Was it something in the tone of my voice? Had Pam and Dee Dee tipped Harry off? Or was it just that the place was nearly empty and he felt like playing to suit himself? I don't know, because I never asked him, but I remember the smile he flashed at me, an irresistible mixture of good humor and a mouth full of gold teeth that gave off more light than Epp's banjo. "Sure," he said, "glad to oblige." Harry spun around on his barrel and settled his heavy hands on the yellowed keys of the old upright. I leaned back and crossed my arms. He began to play, note for note, the introduction to Art Tatum's 1940 recording of "Sweet Lorraine." Then, with Epp strumming softly in the background, he moved gracefully from the impressive to the impossible: he launched into an original improvisation on "Sweet Lorraine" in the style of Art Tatum. It didn't come from any of Tatum's recordings of "Sweet Lorraine." I knew all of them cold from beginning to end, and this was different, unmistakably so. This was the way Tatum *might* have played the song: the same rich, full tone, the same fluttering downward runs, the same iridescent harmonies. Only Harry was making it all up on the spot. My head began to spin. I felt myself in the presence of something inexplicable, perhaps even supernatural. It was as though the spirit of Art Tatum had taken up residence in the body of an aging, half-blind white man from Independence, Missouri.

Harry brought the song to an end and turned around again to take a bow. Pam and Dee Dee were clapping; I was sitting there with my mouth hanging open. I pulled myself together and asked Harry to play "Tea for Two," another Tatum specialty. He laughed and said he'd be delighted. Harry and Epp spent the next hour taking our requests. After the last set, I asked Harry if I could bring my bass along and sit in some time. "Oh, sure," he said. "We'd be *glad* to have you. Just don't try to do it before the last set. We don't want anybody from the musicians' union coming by and finding you up on the bandstand." My plan, of course, was to come back the very next Saturday and play with Harry and Epp for as long as they were willing to put up with me, and that was what I did.

The first time I sat in at Shakey's, a friendly drunk sitting near the bandstand asked Harry if he knew "the Marine song." Harry looked at Epp. Epp slipped Harry a big wink. Without further ado, they launched into a very fast version of "The Caisson Song." At the end of the first chorus, they changed keys and started playing "Anchors Aweigh." I had to scramble to keep up, but I managed to follow them faithfully through all four service songs. Our improvised medley sounded as if we had spent a good half hour rehearsing it that morning, and as we charged through the coda of "Off We Go into the Wild Blue Yonder," I was grinning like a fool.

.   .   .

I spent the next few months hanging out at Shakey's whenever I had a free Saturday night. Harry liked to reminisce, and he gradually worked his way through the story of his career between sets. He had first heard Art Tatum on record in the late thirties and was so impressed that he resolved to learn how to play like Tatum. That, he told me, was the only way to play the piano. (He said this in a perfectly matter-of-fact tone, as if anyone in the world could learn how to play piano like Art Tatum if they tried hard enough.) When World War II started, he joined the merchant marine and served as entertainment director of a troop-transport ship. After the war, he came back to Kansas City and got a job as staff pianist for KMBC, Kansas City's biggest radio station, back in the old days when radio stations still employed staff musicians. When KMBC let its musicians go, Harry became the organist at Royals Stadium, a job he held until he could no longer see well enough to read the scoreboard, at which time he retired and started working with Epp Roller. He lived alone in a neat frame house in Independence and devoted himself to his students, all of whom idolized him.

As I got to know Harry better, I realized that there was much more to him than the fact that he could play piano exactly like Art Tatum, impressive as that fact was. He was a man of singular sweetness of character. He was also wholly lacking in personal ambition. Harry had once been something of a local celebrity, but his fame had faded long before I met him, and though he was vaguely remembered by many of the older jazzmen in town, I never met a Kansas City musician under the age of forty who knew his name. I was appalled, but Harry couldn't have cared less. He had never cut a record and wasn't interested in doing so; the homemade cassette he and Epp hawked at Shakey's every Saturday night was good enough for him. His idea of a really good time was to stay home and listen to records by his three favorite piano players: Erroll Garner, Nat Cole, and Art Tatum.

I found it hard to understand Harry's lack of ambition, partly because I couldn't imagine not being ambitious and partly because the hours I had spent on the bandstand with him had made me fully aware of how extraordinary a pianist he was. If I had taped him on one of his better nights and sent it to a few well-chosen people in New York and Los Angeles, the record companies would have been pounding on his door. But Harry simply didn't care enough about fame to pursue it, and I wouldn't have dreamed of trying to tell him what to do with his life, at least not at first. In fact, it wasn't long before I started thinking of him not as a reclusive genius but as a member of the family, a kind of honorary uncle. Harry wanted to see me get ahead in the world of jazz, and I think he came to look upon me as something of a protégé. I found myself turning to him for advice, which he was glad to give. Most of the time, though, I learned by following his example, and he taught me a lot that way.

I was twenty-two years old when I first met Harry. I was the bass player and musical linchpin of the William Jewell College Jazz Band, a well-meaning but chronically shaky institution that never seemed to be able to hold on to a good drummer for more than one semester; I was also the jazz critic of the Kansas City *Star*, in which capacity I was pleased to pan such distinguished artists as Sarah Vaughan and Dizzy Gillespie. I went to great pains to conceal from my readers the fact that virtually everything I knew about jazz came from reading books and listening to records. To be sure, I had read dozens of books and listened to hundreds of records, but I had never played a professional gig in my life, and I had never worked regularly with anybody who was better than I was, the most important experience a young jazz musician can have.

Cocky though I was, I knew a good thing when I heard it. I had developed a genuine passion for the jazz of the thirties and forties, and I knew how very lucky I was to have stumbled across a pair of old masters who were happy to teach an admiring young boy everything they knew. Harry and Epp treated me with unfailing kindness; I repaid them with open admiration. They never tried to embarrass me by playing obscure tunes in difficult keys at impossibly fast tempos, the usual way in which experienced jazz musicians administer lessons in humility to cocky kids. I knew I had no right to be cocky about anything in the presence of these two men, and I noticed with surprise that they, who had earned the right to be as arrogant as they liked, chose instead to be modest and unassuming.

Harry and Epp would never have described themselves as jazzmen. They spoke of themselves as "commercial" musicians, meaning that they were prepared to play whatever people asked for, as long as they knew, more or less, how it went. This attitude was new to me. I had been brought up on beboppers like Miles Davis, a man who refused to announce the tunes he played, turned his back on the audience between solos, and spat obscenities at anyone foolish enough to request a song. No musician of Harry's generation would ever have behaved like that. That simply wasn't the way things were done. Harry took pride in pleasing his audiences. He was an artist, just like Miles Davis, but his relationship with the people who paid to hear him play was a different matter altogether, and I soon found that I preferred it to the studied disdain of so many of the younger musicians I knew.

As I got to know Harry better, I began to change my mind about Epp. At first I had found his banjo playing corny, and I winced every time he took a solo. But Harry, the most gifted musician I had ever known, admired Epp, so much so that he was happy to let Epp take the lead whenever they played together. I came in time to understand that Epp was a master in his own right, a brilliant exponent of the ragtime banjo style developed at the turn of the century by virtuosos like Vess Ossman and Harry Reser. He was also a superb showman, something at which neither Harry nor I were any good at all. Without uttering a single word of reproach, Harry taught me to listen to Epp, and one day my ears opened up and I heard for the first time the old-fashioned beauties to which I had previously been deaf.

Harry never let me down. There was, for instance, the rainy night that my mother and father drove from Sikeston to Kansas

City to pay me a visit. After eight hours on the road, they were worn out and ready for bed. Instead, I bullied them into driving out to Independence to hear Harry and Epp, who played like angels and charmed the socks off them between sets. But the kindest thing Harry Jenks ever did for me was to come to the William Jewell College Dinner Theater production of A *Thurber Carnival.* I was playing piano in the pit band because there wasn't anyone else in the music department who could play jazz well enough to get through the part. Next to Harry, my playing was hopelessly amateurish, and I would never have dreamed of inviting him to come. Pam and Dee Dee didn't bother to ask me: they just brought him along one night. He cleaned his plate, laughing heartily at the actors he could not see; he praised me to the skies afterward, giving me a bear hug that made me want to cry.

The only things I wanted from Harry that I was unable to get were things that his retiring temperament made it difficult for him to give. I wanted to play real jazz with him, and I wanted to make him a celebrity again.

Harry and Epp played very little jazz at Shakey's. They ground out three choruses of "Somewhere, My Love" for every chorus of "Sweet Lorraine." That was what the people wanted to hear and that was what they got. It was as simple as that, and as frustrating. Then Pam and Dee Dee had the brilliant idea of throwing a party at Harry's house. One Sunday night, a dozen music majors drove out to Independence and took over Harry's music studio, a converted garage that contained a baby grand, a Hammond organ, an overstuffed couch, plenty of chairs, and a thick rug. We supplied the food and drink. I brought along my bass, figuring that Harry would welcome the opportunity to stretch out and play some real jazz. It didn't work out that way. Harry's desire to entertain was so deeply ingrained that he spent most of the evening accompanying the voice students in show tunes. We all had a marvelous time, Harry included, but hardly any jazz was played that evening.

I was no better at pushing Harry into the spotlight, mainly because I never understood how little he wanted to be there. Had some terrible catastrophe left invisible scars on his psyche? Or was it simply that Harry, sure of his own worth, knew that the praise of strangers means nothing next to giving pleasure to a roomful of intimate friends? Whatever the reason, Harry had no desire whatsoever to get ahead, and the conflict between his modesty and my inability to accept it led to an uncomfortable episode in which Harry, for the first and only time in the course of our acquaintance, embarrassed me. By that time, my Sunday jazz column for the Kansas City *Star* had become a fixture on the local music scene, and I used my influence to persuade the Friends of Jazz, a concert series sponsored by the Jewish Community Center, to book Harry for their spring jazz piano festival. Harry went along with the idea; he generally went along with anything anybody suggested. Then, to my astonishment, he pulled out three weeks before the concert, explaining that some old friends of his were coming to town that weekend and that he would be just too busy to make the gig.

I never tried anything like that again. Unable to fathom Harry's modesty, I learned at last to respect it. In time, I would learn that Harry's situation was far from unique. The medium-sized cities of America are full of great jazz musicians who are all but unknown. Some are frustrated, others deeply content. Harry Jenks was content. He made me think of a line from Thomas Gray's "Elegy Written in a Country Churchyard": "Full many a flower is born to blush unseen/And waste its sweetness on the desert air." But Harry knew better than that. He knew that the sweetness of his art was not wasted merely because he lavished it on audiences of ten, or of one.

That was why I was so surprised when Harry called me up one evening in the spring of 1980. "Terry," he said, "Epp and I have decided to make another record. That old Skinheads cassette is getting a little tired, and there are some new tunes we want to do."

"That's just wonderful, Harry," I said, meaning every word.

"Well, I'm glad you think so." He paused. "Oh, there's one other thing. Would you like to play bass for us? Not your electric bass. I hate that damn thing. Get an old stand-up bass and bring it down to the house next Saturday afternoon and we'll rehearse." He paused again. "You know, maybe we'll even find a studio and make a real record one of these days."

I hung up the phone and started jumping up and down. I was going to get to play real jazz with Harry and Epp, as much as I wanted. We might even make a record. I was thrilled, and honored, too, for I sensed that the barriers of age were coming down at long last, that I could now claim Harry not merely as an admired mentor but as a beloved friend.

I showed up at Harry's house on Saturday. Epp was already there, tuning up a hollow-bodied electric guitar. There was no banjo in sight. I was amazed. I had no idea that Epp played jazz guitar. I unpacked my bass and slipped a cassette into the tape deck, and Harry stomped off "Sweet Georgia Brown." As we began to play, Harry and Epp threw off the shackles of commercial music and started to jump. Harry sounded like a cross between Art Tatum and Nat Cole; Epp's slightly choppy playing became smooth and bluesy, just like Oscar Moore, the great guitarist of the King Cole Trio. I stayed in the background, content to accompany two masters at work. Ever since I had first heard the King Cole Trio, I had dreamed of playing in a light-footed combo consisting solely of piano, guitar, and bass. Now it was happening, and I was dancing on air.

I could tell that Harry and Epp were a little rusty. Neither one of them had played straight jazz for years, and they occasionally fumbled for riffs and changes. I was fumbling, too, trying to settle into the easy, loping groove that had come so naturally to Johnny Miller, Nat Cole's bassist. But our playing got tighter as the afternoon wore on. We did "Some of These Days," an old Skinheads standard, and it sounded exactly like the Art Tatum

Trio. I suggested "Whispering," a tune as ancient as "Nola," and it came out sounding fresh as a daisy. Epp and I took a break and Harry rippled through "Time on My Hands," milking every last drop of sentiment out of that lovely ballad. "Terry," he said as the last chord died away, "you won't remember this, but you had fifteen-minute programs and thirty-minute programs back in the old radio days. I had a fifteen-minute program every afternoon. It ran from three o'clock to three-fifteen. That was my theme song."

As afternoon gave way to early evening, Epp and I packed up our instruments and prepared to head for home. For once, I didn't think about how I was going to make Harry Jenks famous again. All I cared about was the sheer pleasure of playing, and the prospect of doing it again. I plucked my cassette out of Harry's tape deck and slipped it into the pocket of my windbreaker. We didn't bother to make a date for our next rehearsal. There was no hurry.

I rang Harry up a couple of weeks later. When did he want to rehearse again? And would he be interested in playing host to another party? We'd bring the food and drink, just as before, but this time we'd ask Epp to come over and make it a proper jam session. Harry sounded enthusiastic, but he also sounded uncomfortable, as if he were in pain. He asked me to hold on for a moment. The phone was silent for two full minutes. Then he came back on the line. "Terry, I'm not feeling well," he said. "The old stomach is acting up. Something I ate at lunch, I guess. But call me in a couple of days, would you? It's about time for another rehearsal. And we'll have that party. Soon."

Pam called the next day to tell me that Harry had died in the night of a bleeding ulcer. I hung up the phone and stared out the window. Then I sat down and wrote a new draft of my jazz column for that coming Sunday. It was an obituary, the first one I had ever written about a man I had known. It was short and to the point, and it ended with a reference to the record that would now never be made: "His friends all thought fame finally had Harry pinned down. Instead, he'll have to settle for the memories of his friends. There were hundreds of them, so perhaps that's not such a bad monument after all."

A few days later, I took the afternoon off and drove out to Independence for Harry's funeral. The church was large, and the parking lot was jammed. Most of the people inside were middle-aged and older, although dozens of Harry's students showed up. Epp and a four-piece band were seated in the balcony, playing a slow blues. I took no part in the ceremony. I was a recent addition to Harry's life, and I knew that this funeral belonged to those who had known him for longer than that. I was satisfied with my memories.

The pastor spoke warmly of Harry's kindness and generosity. Then he told a story. During World War II, he said, Harry had visited New York City on an overnight pass. As soon as he got off the boat, he headed straight for Fifty-second Street and sat in at the Three Deuces, one of the hottest jazz clubs in town. Art Tatum was sitting at the bar. After Harry finished playing, Tatum strolled up to him and said, "Boy, you play just like me, only you're white!" A leathery-faced old man sitting next to me shook his head and smiled. He had heard the story before. I smiled, too, but for a different reason: Harry, modest to a fault, had never bothered to tell me about the night he played for his idol. I heard the story for the first time that afternoon. I suppose he saw no reason to tell me about it, and he was, as usual, right. It would have impressed me, but to no real effect, since I couldn't have admired Harry, or loved him, any more than I already did.

Space for mementos is usually at a premium in a small apartment, and I keep mine in a large cardboard box in the corner of my bedroom. I was sifting through the box not long ago, throwing out things I no longer wished to save, when I ran across a few relics of my friendship with Harry Jenks. I found the column about Harry that I had written for the Kansas City *Star*, in all likelihood the first time his name had appeared in print in decades, except for the formal obituary that the *Star* had run a couple of days before. The clipping was tucked inside a *Thurber Carnival* program.

I also found two cassettes. The first one bore a clumsily printed label that said "K.C. Skinheads." Harry had given it to me after a night at Shakey's. It contained crudely recorded versions of all of Epp's specialties: "Dill Pickle Rag," "Maple Leaf Rag," "St. Louis Blues," "Waiting for the Robert E. Lee," "Havah Nagilah," "Dueling Banjos," even "Nola." Harry soloed only once or twice, preferring to lay back and accompany Epp with his customary elegance. I remembered how I used to wish that Epp would lay back and let Harry shine. I knew now that Harry had wanted it that way, that this discretion was more characteristic of the Harry Jenks I had loved than a hundred flashy solos.

The second cassette was blank except for a single word scrawled in pencil on the label: "Harry." I recognized it at once. It was the tape of our last rehearsal. I played it on the night of Harry's funeral, after which I tossed it into the cardboard box and forgot about it. Now I placed it on my desk, but I didn't listen to it. Pam came to visit me a few weeks later, and I made a copy of the "K.C. Skinheads" tape for her, but even then I couldn't bring myself to listen to the other cassette.

A few months later, I flew out to Kansas City on a business trip and dropped in on Pam. She showed me three photographs taken during our college days. One was of me sitting in a dunking booth at the William Jewell College Band Carnival, soaked to the skin. Another was of me on graduation day, standing next to Liz. The third was of Harry and Epp, standing on either side of Dee Dee.

"I only have one copy of that one," Pam said, "but I'll make a print of it and send it to you if you'd like."

"I wish you'd do that," I said. "I'd like that a lot."

I flew home to New York the next day. The cassette was still gathering dust on my desk. I dropped it into the tape deck and turned up the volume, and all at once my living room was full of the joyous sounds of a bright spring day ten years before. There was Harry, batting out "Sweet Georgia Brown" in crisp, twinkling octaves; there was Epp, strumming four steady beats to the bar; there was I, ten years younger, laying down a simple bass line in the background. I listened to two bald-headed old men and an eager young boy exchanging cries of delight, talking happily between songs about the record they were planning to make, sure that they had all the time in the world in which to make it. Nothing, I thought as I listened, tears at our hearts so much as remembered pleasure. Every bright spring day ends with a grown man standing in his living room years later, shaking his head sadly, knowing at last that there is never, never enough time in the world to do the things that make us happy and to be with the people we love.

11 | *Elegy for the Woodchopper*

LeMars, Iowa, a small farm town about thirty miles north of Sioux City, is swinging tonight. It is Founder's Day at Westmar College, a United Methodist school with an enrollment of 430, and the college is throwing a Saturday-night dinner dance in honor of the occasion. The picked-over remnants of a hundred platefuls of prime rib have been cleared away. Fifteen men are settling themselves on a folding bandstand, tuning up their instruments, and idly leafing through thick folders of music. Most of them are in their twenties and early thirties. Their leader, who is waiting for his cue in the hall outside the dining room, is seventy-four.

The drummer strikes a crisp roll on his tom-tom, the trombonists wave white plastic mutes in front of their golden bells, and Woody Herman's Thundering Herd swells confidently into the slow, mournful strains of "Blue Flame," the band's theme song. The odds are that I am the only person in the room under the age of fifty who recognizes it. I own two recordings of "Blue

Flame." I have heard the Thundering Herd play it in an Independence, Missouri, shopping center, in the auditorium of a suburban high school, and on a warm summer night at an outdoor concert in Kansas City. I have traveled a thousand miles to hear it tonight.

Without further ado, a short, stooped man steps quietly from the wings and begins to make his careful way to the bandstand. He does not smile. He is too tired to smile. I saw him backstage before the dance, bent almost double under the weight of a half century of one-night stands, and I felt my throat catch at the sight. Every wrinkle on his deeply lined face seemed to stand for another year of bumpy bus rides and cheap motels. Forty years ago, he was a matinee idol who packed movie theaters and ballrooms from coast to coast. The crowds are smaller now, the ballrooms less glamorous, the jumps from job to job longer. LeMars is the Thundering Herd's fourth gig this week, and it seems impossible that this old man will be able to shake off his weariness and face the three hours of hard work that lie before him.

But the throaty, growling sounds of "Blue Flame" are working their nightly miracle, and Woody Herman seems to grow more confident with every cautious step. As the room swells with the applause of expectant dancers, the last of the big-band leaders reaches center stage, picks up his clarinet, and begins to play the blues. This is the moment I have waited for. This is the beginning of my dream come true.

The word *no*, spoken at the right time and in the right place, can change the destined course of a lifetime. I like to think that my father had this in mind when he told me not to touch the old phonograph records in the basement closet. Whatever his intentions, the fact remains that as soon as the back door slammed behind him that Sunday afternoon, I was halfway downstairs, and by the time he was out of the garage, I had pulled the rollaway bed out of the closet and dragged six crumbling cardboard boxes out from behind it.

Had those boxes been full of records by, say, Shep Fields and his Rippling Rhythm, I would have shoved them back behind the bed without a second thought. But my father had been young once, and the music that he favored in his youth was, by and large, the swinging kind. It's true that he loved the music of Glenn Miller, which is perfect for dancing but not very likely to speed up the pulse of a young boy raised on the Rolling Stones. But he had a roving ear, and along with his battered copies of "Moonlight Serenade" and "Perfidia" and "American Patrol," he had preserved dozens of records by Artie Shaw and Stan Kenton and Tommy Dorsey and Claude Thornhill—and Woody Herman.

After he came home from the Philippines at the end of World War II, my father bought many of the records that Woody Herman made in 1945 and 1946 with the band that would later become known as the First Herd: "Laura," "Apple Honey," "The Good Earth," "Your Father's Mustache," "Caldonia," "Woodchopper's Ball." Once he had danced to them with my mother. Now I held them in my hands, those red-label Columbias, thickly covered with cardboard shavings, unplayed for twenty years and more. I took them over to the basement phonograph, a cast-off Philco portable. I had just read *The Good Earth*, so I put on "The Good Earth" first, wondering what this dusty antique could possibly have to do with Pearl Buck's slow-moving tale of life in China. Curious and mildly expectant, I changed the speed of the turntable from 33 to 78, flipped the needle over, and eased the heavy tone arm onto the record.

Children born in the age of the laser-scanned compact disc will never know the crackle of a steel needle briskly scratching its way through the grooves of a shellac 78, a sound as evocative for the jazz buff as the tuning up of a symphony orchestra is for the lover of classical music. I heard it for the first time that afternoon. Then strange music came crashing out of the speakers, the loud, piercing, joyous strains of a big band in full cry. I heard it plain, unfiltered by nostalgia, unobscured by memories of make-believe ballrooms and the girl you left behind. I turned up the volume as far as it would go, feeling the lift of the rhythms in my bones. I was hooked. The big-band era, decades after its demise, had reached down the corridors of lost time and grabbed a piece of me.

I borrowed a bass from the music room of my junior high school on the first day of summer, carried it home, and played along with my father's records until school started again in the fall. I played every record in the basement a hundred times and memorized all five of the books in the Sikeston Public Library about the big-band era. One of the musicians I read about that summer was Woody Herman. I learned that Herman played clarinet and alto saxophone; that he had survived every change in musical fashion, even the ruthless choke hold of rock and roll; that he was still spending ten months out of the year on the road with his current group, which he now called the Thundering Herd. Hundreds of celebrated musicians had passed through Woody Herman's bands, which thereby acquired a reputation as the great finishing schools of jazz. I learned that he was universally regarded as one of the kindest and most decent men in the business. None of his alumni, I read, ever had a bad word to say about him. The younger ones even had a nickname for him: "Road Father."

I wanted it to be 1945 again, so that I could play bass with Woody Herman. But it was 1975, and so I went off to William Jewell College, played with the college jazz band and wangled a part-time job writing about jazz for the Kansas City *Star*. At the urging of Harry Jenks, I went down to the union hall one afternoon and joined Local 34-627 of the American Federation of Musicians. My first gig was at a bar called the Lucky Penny. The Lucky Penny had recently been bought by a bartender who liked jazz and who decided to book us without bothering to check with his regular customers, most of whom would have rather gone on listening to country music on the jukebox. The band consisted of a shaky clarinetist whose red face bore the unmistakable signs of hard drinking, an accordion player who spent most nights working in polka bands, a cocktail drummer, and a scared young Southern Baptist on bass. All four of us were jammed onto a bandstand the size of my mother's kitchen table. The clarinetist, who knew that this was my first gig, never bothered to call any tunes. He just glared at me through bloodshot eyes, stamped his foot and started playing.

I must have done all right, for I began to get calls from bandleaders around town. After Harry died, I started working two or three times a week with a plump, red-faced piano player named Bob Simes. A veteran of the bebop era, Bob knew exactly how to handle kid bass players who thought they knew a thing or two. He liked to sip Scotch and soda between sets, and as we sat together in a quiet bar one night taking five and swapping stories, he started reminiscing. Swirling the Scotch around in his glass, he cocked his head and said, "The first time I played with Charlie Parker . . ." No particular stress was placed on the word *first*, but I got the point anyway. Bob had played with the king of bebop *more than once*. Any questions, kid? I shut up and spent the next two years doing exactly as I was told, and I had the time of my life doing it.

Most of the musicians I met during my two years with the Bob Simes Orchestra had day jobs and played jazz strictly on weekends, though a few of them did nothing but grind out dance dates and wedding receptions night after night. One or two were nasty drunks, but most were intelligent, well-spoken, and honest to a fault. Theirs was a nighttime world of friendship and mutual admiration, of unexpected kindnesses and extraordinary generosity, of hard times and empty pockets and four-in-the-morning courage. I learned a lot from them, about jazz and about other things. I learned to take people as they were, bark and all. I learned what it was like to get home in the middle of the night on a regular basis. I learned how it feels to get blown off the bandstand at a crowded jam session. (In case you're wondering, it feels like hell.) I learned everything except how to drink on the job, something that comes only with age and practice.

It wasn't long before I started to think about trying to play bass for a living. It wouldn't have been very hard to do. I was good enough at what I did and getting better every night. I was being offered twice as many gigs as I had time to play. My colleagues treated me with warmth and tact. But even though I loved playing bass as much as anything I had ever done in my life, I knew in my heart that I didn't quite belong in the world of jazz, that a small-town boy like me could never be truly comfortable living on the after-hours margins of respectability.

Not long after I got married, my wife told me in a wistful voice that it would be nice if we could occasionally see each other on weekends. I promised to quit playing so many gigs. I did not yet know that you can't play only when it suits you, that if you're not there when the contractor calls, the contractor starts calling somebody else. What turned out to be my last gig was a quartet date with Bob, a hard-driving drummer named Abel Ramirez, and the best tenor saxophonist in Kansas City, a baby-faced lawyer named Mike White, who liked his jazz fast and hot. We were playing for an Oldsmobile dealers' convention, and none of the dealers were sober enough to know what we were doing up on the bandstand, so we played for our own pleasure and ignored the crowd. Had I known I was quitting music for good that night, I would have called for Horace Silver's "Sister Sadie," Mike's favorite song, at the end of the last set. But I didn't know, so we played "The Party's Over," the tune Bob always played at the end of the last set, and I loaded my bass in the back of my station wagon and drove off to join the middle class.

By the time I came to New York some ten years later, I had learned a lot more about jazz, and about myself. I had played enough lousy gigs to know that I didn't have the true fire in my belly, that I didn't want to play jazz passionately enough to do nothing else. But jazz was in my blood and bones all the same, and I missed it badly. Most of all, I missed the one thing I had not done in my two years as a professional jazzman: I had never gone on the road. The tours I went on in college had given me a taste of what it feels like to live out of a suitcase and play for a different crowd every night. A dozen autobiographies had taught me the miseries of life on the road: broken-down buses charging across rickety bridges, greasy food and crummy pianos and hostile crowds. I could not forget Charlie Barnet's pithy summing-up: *You stay tired, dirty, and drunk.* I had no wish to do any of those things. But I never stopped wondering what else I had missed out on because I had not gone on the road.

One morning, I put my feet up on a desk in an assistant editor's cubicle in lower Manhattan, started sifting through the daily pile of unread magazines, and ran across a short article in *The Atlantic* about Woody Herman. It mentioned in passing that Woody was preparing to celebrate his fiftieth anniversary as a bandleader with a concert at the Hollywood Bowl. I didn't even stop to think twice. I called up a friendly editor at another magazine and started talking very fast. *How about a profile of Woody Herman? Good guy, everybody loves him, fiftieth anniversary, last of the great big-band leaders. I could even spend, oh, a couple of days traveling with the band. . . .*

It is four minutes after noon. I am standing in the parking lot of a run-down motel on the outskirts of LeMars. Those who eat breakfast have long since boarded the band bus. A handful of stragglers, some of whom have all too clearly just stumbled out of bed, are scrambling on board for the long haul to Kansas City, where the Thundering Herd has a night off. Woody Herman has already left for the Sioux City airport. Too fragile to endure the day-to-day stresses of life on the bus, he will fly to the next gig. No one grumbles about it. Woody paid his dues long before most of the musicians in the band were born.

"This is home, man," one musician says to me as we climb on board. If so, then the Thundering Herd is in desperate need of a housekeeper. The back of the bus, where the rowdier Herds-men sit, is littered with books, pillows, and old newspapers from various cities. A huge double bass, snugly wrapped in its black canvas case, is balanced gingerly in the seat ahead of me. The overhead luggage racks are crammed with suitcases and overnight bags of every imaginable size and color. Someone has hung a hand-lettered sign on the toilet door: CONTAMINATION! HAZARDOUS WASTE MAY BE HARMFUL TO YOUR HEALTH.

The door hisses shut and the driver pulls out of the parking lot. As the cornfields of southwestern Iowa slip by, the players swap battered paperbacks, play Trivial Pursuit, and trade notes on the restaurants of LeMars. One man is banging away at a pocket calculator, working feverishly on his tax return. A cassette of the rough mix of the band's next record album, taped three weeks ago at a concert in San Francisco, makes its snail-like way from seat to seat; I have brought along my own homemade cassette of Woody Herman's forties recordings. To my surprise, I discover that most of the people sitting around me have never heard any of Woody's old records. Indeed, my interest in them strikes the tenor saxophonist in the seat across the aisle as somewhat pe-culiar, perhaps even a mark of squareness. Why should he care about Woody Herman's old stuff? *He* plays with Woody every night. But the other musicians are curious, and my cassette is soon being passed through the bus along with the rough mix of the next Woody Herman album. "Goddamn, man, that stuff holds up *really well*," the tenor saxophonist says to me a few minutes later, shaking his head as Woody's 1945 trumpet section wails its way through the last chorus of "Northwest Passage."

Sitting behind me is Mark Lewis, a youthful-looking trum-peter who has played with the Thundering Herd since 1980. He is thirty-one years old, my age. Cappy Lewis, his father, played with the Herman band more than forty years ago. (He plays the muted trumpet solo on Woody's 1946 recording of "Woodchop-per's Ball," one of the tunes on my homemade cassette.) "Dad took me to hear the band one night," Mark tells me. "We went up to meet Woody afterward, and when my father told him that I played trumpet, Woody said, 'So when are you going to play in my band?' "

I ask Mark about the daily grind. "The road," he says, "is the same thing every day. You don't have much time to yourself. You eat bad food a lot of the time. You're stuck on a bus eight hours a day. You wash your underwear in the sink. When you get sick, there's nothing you can do but ride the bus and play the gigs and feel rotten all the time. But I like it. I really do. I know it sounds crazy, but there's a freshness to our work that makes it worthwhile, especially when we get a young crowd. That's what we look forward to. They *make* us want to play. And there's Woody, you know. He lets you be yourself. He keeps things relaxed. You're never afraid to go up on the bandstand with Woody. And he really loves to hear us play. That's why he's there."

Six hours later, the skyline of Kansas City begins to fill the windows of the bus and the members of the band begin to discuss their plans for the evening. A rumor that a convention of beauticians is being held in our hotel ripples through the back of the bus. One group of Herdsmen wants some real Kansas City barbecue. All the musicians with wives or girlfriends at home decide to get together and watch a little television. "Eight o'clock call, guys," says the road manager as the bus pulls into the Downtown Howard Johnson parking lot. A chorus of groans greets his announcement as the Thundering Herd streams off the bus and heads for the front desk in search of room keys.

I leave the bus by myself. I chose this particular weekend to travel with the band because I knew it would be passing through Kansas City, and I have been looking forward to spending a quiet night in my old college town. Italian Gardens, a familiar downtown haunt where I had intended to give myself a good dinner, turns out to be closed on Sundays, so I trudge back to the restaurant of the Downtown Howard Johnson for lack of a better idea. As I chew on a stubborn piece of hotel steak, the words of

"Sweet Kentucky Ham," a song by a jazz pianist named Dave Frishberg, flash into my mind, and I realize for the first time that Frishberg wasn't trying to be funny:

> *It's six P.M.*
> *Supper time in South Bend, Indiana*
> *And you figure, what the hell*
> *You can eat in your hotel*
> *So you order up room service on the phone*
> *And you watch the local news and dine alone*
> *You got to take what little pleasures you can find*
> *When you've got sweet Kentucky ham on your mind.*

At 8 A.M., the same people who barely made it onto the bus in LeMars are barely making it onto the bus in Kansas City. The rumor about the beauticians' convention was true. The married men quiz their bachelor colleagues closely as we pull onto the highway and start our long drive across the prairies of Kansas to El Dorado, an oil town where Butler County Community College is hosting an afternoon clinic and an evening concert. The clinic is for the members of the college jazz band and other student musicians from the area, while the concert is open to the general public.

The afternoon clinic begins with a short performance by the Thundering Herd. About forty students, trumpets and trombones and saxophones in their laps, are scattered around the bleachers of the college gym. Many of them look skeptical. I eavesdrop and learn that a few of them have never even heard of Woody Herman. Dressed in a windbreaker and sneakers, Woody makes his slow way to center stage and offers a few terse words of greeting. The first tune, he says, will be a new arrangement of Duke Ellington's "It Don't Mean a Thing." (How many of these kids, I wonder, know who Duke Ellington was?) The rhythm section pumps out a fast four-bar introduction. The saxophones enter with the theme and the brass fire back a crisp riff. A massive wave of sound rolls off the bandstand and washes over the bleachers. I can see that the students are surprised at how *loud* the Thundering Herd is. It is a special kind of loudness, a kind they have never encountered before. It comes not from tall banks of shrieking amplifiers but from sixteen jazz musicians playing in bold, fat-toned unison, and it quickly sets their feet to tapping.

After the concert, Woody heads for the men's locker room, where a table loaded with cold cuts and soft drinks awaits the band. I have arranged to spend the next hour with him. As he pours himself a glass of orange juice, I ask him about some of his less well-known alumni from the forties and fifties. This is a gesture of homage, a sign that I have taken the trouble to learn about him, that I am a member of the fraternity of jazzmen, a respectful insider. Woody notices at once. The friendly mask and the polite, unreflective answers of a thousand hurried interviews with general-assignment reporters are promptly laid aside. His worn face shines with enthusiasm. In his soft, buzzy voice, he begins to tell me elaborate tales of epileptic drummers and heroin-soaked baritone sax players and tough times on the road. "The highways are better now," he says with a crooked smile, "so you get to drive even further every day."

Why, I ask, is he still on the road after fifty years? "There's a reason for the road," Woody tells me. "As long as you're doing one-nighters and moving every day, you have the most freedom for your music. You don't have to answer to the people you worked for yesterday. You're not going to be there tomorrow night. You can play the music *you* want to play. That's why I keep going. Because it's still fun. That's the reason I'm here, and that's why all the guys are here. Sure, they gripe like hell. They go through all the motions of being unhappy people. But then they start playing, and they realize that this is the only thing they want to do. I know I can't think of anything else *I* want to do."

Woody pauses. He is clearly ready to get back to his motel room and rest. I start to trip over my words. Up to this moment, I have been prompting him with ease, but the thing I want to tell him most now will not come out. *My God, Mr. Herman, I* want to say, *I admire you so much. You can't imagine how hard*

*I schemed to get to where I could sit in this grubby locker room
and watch you drink lukewarm orange juice. I called my father
last night to tell him about this trip. He used to drive for eight
straight hours to come hear me play jazz in Kansas City. He was
so proud of me, Mr. Herman, and you did that, you and Stan
Kenton and Artie Shaw and Claude Thornhill.*

"Mr. Herman," I say nervously, "do you ever play 'The Good
Earth' anymore?"

He shakes his head. "Nope." He rises slowly to his feet. "But
I'll see if I can work it in tonight."

That evening the band returns to the gym for a full-length
concert. The crowd is a mixture of middle-aged couples and
younger fans, including most of the students who came to the
clinic that afternoon. Woody offers them his usual concert program, one I have heard a half-dozen times over the years. There
are five numbers from the books of the First and Second Herds:
"Blue Flame," "Woodchopper's Ball," "Four Brothers," "I've
Got the World on a String" and "Early Autumn." There is a
rock version of Aaron Copland's "Fanfare for the Common Man"
and a jazz version of Gabriel Fauré's "Pavane." There are a half-
dozen numbers from the Thundering Herd's forthcoming record
album. The band plays them so beautifully and passionately that
even the older members of the audience, the ones who came to
touch up their memories, give in happily to the new and unfamiliar sounds.

Woody announces that he will play an old First Herd tune
by special request. The players fumble through their music folders. Then he kicks off "The Good Earth." The tempo he sets is
a shade too fast for comfort, and the performance is ragged. I
know sight-reading when I hear it, and I also know it is unlikely
that many of these young players have even heard the tune before,
unless they happened to listen to my cassette as we drove to
Kansas City. But it is with my forgiving inner ear that I hear
Neal Hefti's chart the way it sounded in a New York recording
studio on August 10, 1945, at the beginning of the atomic age
and the end of the big-band era. I hear Dave Tough's flashing

cymbals, Flip Phillips' surging tenor saxophone, Pete Candoli's brazen, slightly acid lead trumpet, Chubby Jackson's springy five-string bass lines. I wonder if Woody can hear them, too.

Nine Herdsmen hang around the gym after the concert to play basketball. The others, too beat to join in, board the bus and return to the motel. I am among them. "Back in the old days," one trumpeter says to me in the lobby, "musicians used to shoot heroin. Now we shoot baskets. Wild life, isn't it?"

As I flew back to New York the next day, I thought about the many aging performers I have known who refused to retire. Some of them could not get up in the morning without the certain knowledge that they would hear applause before they went to bed that night. I don't doubt that Woody Herman liked applause, but that wasn't why he stayed on the road. I knew, although I didn't ask him about it, that he toured because he owed the government money. Back in the sixties, Woody's manager, a fat man named Abe Turchen, spent three straight years gambling away the money for Woody's income tax and the band's withholding. By the time anyone else knew what was going on, Woody owed the IRS $1.6 million in back taxes, penalties, and interest. For the rest of his life, all of his profits and all of his record royalties went straight to the IRS. That was why he kept touring. His choices were limited: he could trade one prison for another.

As the seventies gave way to the eighties, Woody's life started to fall apart. Charlotte, his wife, died of breast cancer. Illness caused his clarinet playing to grow shrill and uncertain. He scaled back his solos to the barest possible minimum. Sometimes a critic would knock him in print, leaving a foaming wake of hatred among musicians who read the cold, tactless words and cursed critics, cursed the IRS, cursed the idiot fate that saddled Woody with a merciless financial burden and simultaneously took away his health.

"It's strange," Mark Lewis told me as we drove from LeMars to Kansas City. "I started listening to big bands when I was thirteen. All the old guys were still going strong then, guys like Ellington, Basie, Stan Kenton. Now it's down to Woody. Believe me, there'll be an empty feeling when he quits." But he didn't quit. In fact, he stayed on the road for several months after I returned to New York. As he continued to fly from gig to gig, I tried to write my magazine piece. My first draft was bounced back. *Not enough details,* the editor said. I knew what kind of details he wanted, and I didn't want to put them in. I knew that this story would not have a happy ending.

The fiftieth-anniversary concert at the Hollywood Bowl came and went. Then Woody got really sick, too sick to stay on the road, and he flew back to Hollywood. When the money stopped coming in, the IRS seized his house and put it on the auction block. A real estate speculator bought it for a song and offered to rent it back to Woody. When Woody couldn't make the payments, the speculator hit him with an eviction notice. For the first time in his long life, Woody Herman found himself on the evening news. A band of alumni held a benefit concert in Los Angeles to pay their old leader's rent. He was too far gone to know or care. My editor called me up. "I think that circumstances may have caught up with your piece," he said gently.

Woody Herman died on November 29, 1987. I was sitting in my office when the news came over the wires. As I read the bulletin, I remembered a scene from my first night on the road with the Thundering Herd. It was twelve-forty in the morning. The dancers were gone, the autographs signed. The pianist and bassist were jamming together on "Willow Weep for Me" as the other musicians, tired and bedraggled from another long night's work, knocked down the music stands and took apart their instruments. Woody was standing alone near the bandstand, listening to the music, idly snapping his fingers to the beat. He picked up his clarinet and tossed off a low, breathy chorus of "Willow Weep for Me." Then he put it down, did a stiff little dance step, and slipped out of the room. Homeless, wifeless, and futureless, Woody Herman was still taking what little pleasures he could find. His music had sustained him for five decades, and it would comfort him until the very end.

I thought about my own youthful dreams of playing bass with the Thundering Herd. Could I possibly have cut it? Now I would never know. My bass had been gathering dust in the bedroom closet for years. I knew I would never play seriously again, that my casual decision to give up jazz had been carved in stone by the passage of time. Most of the time I didn't think about it very much. Sometimes, sitting in a nightclub in Manhattan, I would feel a desperate longing for the life I had so briefly led. That longing gripped me again as I thought about Woody and Harry Jenks and Bob Simes and the Lucky Penny and a hundred dismal country-club dances. I thought about what I had missed by having been born a couple of decades too late, by having opted for a loving wife and a middle-class job over the constant scuffle of a jazzman's life.

I struck a balance in my mind for the ten-thousandth time and noted, as usual, that the life I had chosen came out squarely in the black. Then I said a silent farewell to Woody Herman and remembered, not without a touch of rue, the last verse of "Sweet Kentucky Ham":

It's one A.M.
They're serving up last call in Cincinnati
But it's still a nighttime town
If you know your way around
And despite yourself, you find you're wide awake
And you're staring at your scrambled eggs and steak
And you must admit your heart's about to break
When you think of what you left behind
And you've got sweet Kentucky ham on your mind,
*   on your mind*
Nothing but sweet Kentucky ham on your mind.

12 | *One Killed,*
One Wounded

One of the best things about growing up in a small town is that you're never very far from a clump of trees. As a child, you can climb far above the surface of the earth and dream of snow-capped mountains; as a teenager, you can wander into the woods and take potshots at wild rabbits. I climbed my fair share of trees as a young boy, though I never shot any rabbits, something for which I probably have my father to thank. He grew up in Omaha, Nebraska, which is by no means a small town, and while he readily encouraged me to mow the lawn and join Little League and climb all the safe-looking trees on our block, it never occurred to him that I might want a gun of my own, though he would certainly have gotten me one had I asked for it. Since I was musical, he bought me a piano instead.

Despite my failure to travel the well-worn path that leads most small-town boys from BB gun to .22 rifle to double-barreled shotgun, I gloried in imagined violence. I checked the complete works of Raymond Chandler and Dashiell Hammett out of the

Sikeston Public Library. I owned a closetful of toy guns, my favorite being a sleek black Luger that fired red plastic caps. I ate my mother's beef stew happily, unembarrassed by the knowledge of how the main ingredient got from the pasture to my plate. Late one Saturday afternoon when I was eleven years old, my friend Mark Deane and his older brother Bill returned from a hunting trip with the bloody carcass of a deer strapped across the back of their father's pickup truck. I examined it with admiration, though it never occurred to me that I might want to shoot a deer myself, any more than it occurred to my father to buy me a gun in the first place, or to Mark to ask me along when he later went hunting on his own.

My only hunting trip, such as it was, took place during the summer of my fifteenth year. I was camping with Greg and Ken, and they insisted that I at least try to shoot something for our evening meal. We had spent the better part of a hot day wandering around pretending not to be lost, and I was as hungry as they were, so I found a squirrel, pointed a borrowed shotgun in its general direction and pulled the trigger. Rubbing my bruised shoulder and watching the squirrel scoot up the nearest tree, I decided then and there that hunting was not for me.

I was even less enthusiastic about the idea of shooting at people. The Vietnam War was still winding down during my high school days, and I decided to become a conscientious objector at one point during my freshman year. I even talked it over with Wade Paris, my preacher. But this was nothing more than a typical piece of adolescent posturing. The simple fact was that never having spent much time around guns, I failed to acquire any particular interest in them one way or the other. I knew quite well that my squeamishness at the prospect of shooting people, while reasonable enough on the face of it, derived entirely from my fear of being shot at first. The hard reality of guns, their sound and smell and power, remained alien to me, and the shotgun I fired so ineptly at the age of fifteen was the last gun I heard go off until I grew up and moved to Kansas City, where one was fired at me.

This shot was one of the few noteworthy events that took place during a gap in my résumé which began with my graduation from William Jewell College and ended when I left Kansas City four years later. Unexplained gaps in a résumé sometimes conceal major disasters, more often aimless stretches of drift and dullness. On the surface, mine was of the latter sort. Having left college with a bachelor's degree in music and no very firm convictions about what I wanted to do for a living, I found myself working during the week as a teller in a bank on the edge of downtown Kansas City and playing jazz on weekends in bars and country clubs. At night I worked as a part-time music critic for the arts section of the Kansas City *Star*; I ground out magazine articles, some of which were published, in the brief intervals between work and sleep. It was a peculiar existence, one into which I fell with little planning and less forethought. I had already been writing about music for the *Star* for two years and expected to be hired as a full-time writer as soon as I graduated from college. To my surprise, there were no openings, so I took the first job I could find and settled down to wait for a place to open up at the *Star*. It never did.

In the beginning, I saw my work at the bank as strictly temporary, a stopgap until the *Star* came through. I have only myself to blame for the fact that it went on for so long and that I was so bad at it. "Proud and lazy men," George Orwell once said, "do not make good waiters." They don't make good tellers, either, and I should know, for I was proud, lazy, and the worst teller imaginable. My lunch break was a case in point. I was supposed to eat between ten forty-five and eleven-thirty, coming back in time to work straight through the noon rush hour. In practice, I usually managed to get away no later than ten-thirty, wolfing down a BLT with cheese at the greasy spoon around the corner and spending the rest of the hour wandering through the stacks of the Kansas City Public Library, picking out the books that I read in my cage when not waiting on customers. I read constantly. I was reading when a robber came into the bank one spring morning and started shooting at everybody in sight.

I was lucky, though I didn't know it at the time. The average bank robbery, according to industry statistics, takes place between half-past ten and eleven in the morning. If ours hadn't been on the early side, I might have met the robber on my way out the back door. Lacking a getaway car of his own, he hailed a taxi and was taken to the rear entrance of the bank, where he asked the driver to wait. He marched through the door at ten twenty-six, pulled a pistol out of his pocket, and fired a shot at the forehead of one of our guards. The noise made me jump, but never having heard a real pistol, I was curious rather than fearful. A pistol fired indoors sounds nothing like the outsized handguns that actors shoot off in movies; it sounds more like a large paper bag being popped. As more shots rang out from the east alcove, the hidden camera in the bank lobby began to take a series of still photographs. In the first picture, three startled-looking tellers were visible. In the second one, all the tellers were safely out of sight except for me. I was leaning out of my cage, trying to get a good look at whatever was going on.

"Get down, for God's sake!" someone screamed. A strange half silence, broken only by the hum of the automatic teller machine and the bland prattle of canned music, settled over the lobby. I ducked down inside my cage, jabbed at my alarm button, and reached for the telephone. I dialed 911 and told the dispatcher to send the police right away.

"We just got your alarm," the dispatcher replied. "They're on the way." A high-pitched *beep* in the background signaled the watchful presence of a tape recorder. "Could you please try to look around and see what's going on?"

"Look around? Are you crazy? Jesus Christ, lady," I snapped, "just what in hell do you think is going on here?"

"Please don't get hysterical, sir."

"I'm *not* hysterical," I shouted. By this time I could hear sirens outside. No more than a minute or two had passed since the first shot was fired. Uniformed policemen, detectives in trench coats, and a couple of FBI agents in nylon windbreakers came running into the lobby. I hung up on the dispatcher and called my wife. "Honey," I said, "listen carefully to me. There's been a shooting at the bank. I'm not hurt. Did you get that? Ignore anything you hear on the radio." As I spoke, one of the guards came through the door to the teller line, sat down heavily at a cluttered desk behind me, and picked up another telephone. "Listen, honey," he said, "don't worry about what you hear on the radio. We had a little trouble over here, and I had to kill a man." He paused. "No, honey. We had some trouble, and I had to kill a man."

"I need three ashtrays to cover the slugs," a man outside the door called out, and I pulled it open gingerly to see if I could help. The other guard lay just beyond the doorway, blood pouring from a gash across his bald spot. I could hear one of the tellers sobbing loudly in the distance. ("I kept wanting to yell at her," the guard told me later. "I wanted to tell her to shut up, that I was all right, but it hurt too much for me to say anything.") Lying next to the guard was a young black man, surrounded by paramedics, with a tourniquet wrapped around his right arm and a neat little hole in the shoulder above it. His shirt had been cut off, his eyes were closed, and someone in a white jacket was squeezing a plastic bag that covered his nose and mouth.

I saw the gun then, a bright chunk of metal lying uselessly against the wall. A policeman knelt to pick it up. The floor was littered with plastic syringe covers that seemed to be floating in heavy pools of blood. *I must notice all of this*, I thought. *I've never seen a real shooting before.* I was transfixed by the slender figure on the floor before me. His chest rose and fell in halting rhythms. I wanted to kick him in the head as hard as I could. I wanted him to die.

"Don't you ever get tempted," I was asked at least once a week during the four years I worked at the bank, "being around all that money?" I always scoffed at the idea. The idea of emptying my cash drawer and running off to South America was too ridiculous to entertain, even for a moment. But I thought about money constantly, not merely because I did not have enough of it but because my daily life was constantly shaped and reshaped by its presence.

Everyone who enters a bank knows, whether or not he chooses to admit it, that the men and women with whom he is dealing know at least some of the embarrassing truth behind his financial hypocrisies. When, long after I left the bank, I read Trollope for the first time, I thought not of Dickens or Queen Victoria but of an older man who came to my window two or three times a month to make a withdrawal from a savings account. He was self-confident, even overbearing, but there was no way he could hide from me the well-thumbed paper label taped securely inside his passbook. *John Doe,* it read, *is entitled to the full use of the funds in this account during the lifetime of Mrs. John Doe.*

Rich or poor, anyone who deals regularly with servants who know his secrets eventually lapses into erratic behavior. This is why tellers live by an elaborate calculus of servility in which the principal variable is money. On one side of the equation are the large depositors, whose every whim, however bizarre, is honored faithfully; on the other are the tellers, who are expected to treat every customer with a degree of tact bordering on obsequiousness, yet never cash a bad check. Cashing a check for the distinguished-looking gentleman who closed his account yesterday in preparation for an extended trip abroad is a guaranteed ticket to the nearest unemployment line. So is brusquely requesting identification of a seedy-looking fellow with a six-figure balance in his checking account. A teller must be prepared to swallow any amount of personal abuse without flinching or backtalk, for he knows that the bank will not back him up if he provokes the wrath of a rich man.

The people with whom I worked, nearly all of whom were women, found it easy enough to deal with the tensions inherent in the job. They had no real stake in it. Most were married, and those who weren't were looking. Getting fired would cause a temporary hitch in their lives, but one with which they could deal, for they knew who they were. I did not. At night I was a writer, on weekends a jazz musician. During the day, though, I was a servant. My nameplate was displayed for the world to see, and strangers, seeing it, called me by my first name. I despised them for their casual familiarity, but I despised myself even more. Once I had been a young man of unlimited promise. My teachers had predicted great things for me. Now I spent my days making change. My promise was running dry, my great expectations turning sour. I was sure I had gone as far as I could go. I expected to spend the rest of my life punching a clock.

Looking back, I find it hard to explain the spiritual paralysis that gripped me throughout the four years I worked at the bank. It goes without saying that I could have quit at any time. Why, then, did I choose to stay? The only answer I have to offer is as straightforward as it is unflattering: I was afraid. People who grow up in small towns often have narrow senses of possibility, and I was no exception. The *Star*'s failure to hire me had been a crippling blow, for I could not imagine myself making a living as a writer outside the tightly structured framework of a full-time job. I was too fearful of the unknown horrors of joblessness to consider leaving Kansas City to look for work at another paper; I was too middle-class to give up my day job and try to play jazz for a living. Since there was nothing else I knew how to do, I continued to trudge to and from the bank every day, to review mediocre concerts for the *Star* every night, to play for drunks and bad dancers every weekend, to send my essays and articles off to New York every month, waiting vainly for a miracle that I knew would never come. It says something about my state of mind that my wife never saw the inside of the building where I worked for four years, not even once.

My misery was magnified by the fact that I had never before been confronted with the ordinary frustrations of working for a living. As a student, I had repaired clarinets, shelved library books, spun records. I even worked in a couple of friendly small-town banks during summer vacations. But I never went out and found a real job, and that was my downfall. A bank is no place for a frustrated young man who has not learned how to deal with the public, and my fellow tellers, companionable though they were, had no notion of the choking fear that kept me from striking out on my own. One day I showed up for work to be greeted with the news that the morning paper contained a column by William F. Buckley, Jr., largely devoted to a flattering summary of a magazine article I had written not long before. My colleagues were full of praise, but all I could think about was what the great Bill Buckley would say if he knew that I was a lowly teller in a Kansas City bank, a miserable, gutless creature too frightened by the world to throw open the door of his cage and walk away.

Nobody can hate himself for very long. Something has to give. Adjustments must be made, and desperation provides a long list of alternatives. I could have become a wife-beater or an alcoholic or an adulterer. Instead, I found a safer, cheaper form of release, one that cost nothing but the price of my soul.

I never used the word *nigger* as a boy. Not that I didn't hear it often enough. My barber, a good-natured man who gave me a quarter whenever I went to get a haircut, used it regularly and unhesitatingly. So did some of my schoolmates and a few of my relatives. But it was rarely used by the middle-class children with whom I went to school, except for the ones who had moved to Sikeston from the Deep South. In my circle, to speak of blacks as "niggers" was regarded as a lower-class habit, a sure sign that your own social standing was uncertain enough for you to be able to take cold comfort in the existence of people who were worse off. As for me, I was far above such vulgarities. My blacks were the legendary giants from New Orleans and Chicago who made the old shellac records from which I taught myself how to play jazz, the angry militants who wrote the angry books like *The Autobiography of Malcolm X* and *Black Boy* and *Go Tell It on the Mountain* that I read over and over again, quietly congratulating myself on my freedom from the prejudices of the white bigots who soiled their pages.

This idealism was completely rootless, since I lived in a town where blacks quite literally lived on the wrong side of the tracks and mostly kept to themselves. My black schoolmates, like the rest of the blacks who lived and worked in my home town, were shadowy figures with whom I had no meaningful contact. I usually saw them only in gym and in the halls. It wasn't until I graduated from college and began spending my mornings and afternoons in a teller's cage that black people acquired any reality for me. I use the word "reality" ironically, for the blacks I saw there were filtered through the window of my cage and the turmoil and embarrassment of my own situation. The situation was real enough, though, and so were the people on whom I waited. The branch where I worked was a hundred yards north of the concrete ramps leading to and from the highway that circled the city. It was an ideal location for customers, who came from all parts of town to do business with us. Businessmen from downtown could walk to our branch if they liked. So could residents of the Kansas City ghetto, who flocked to the bank in large numbers on those days of the month when government checks arrived in the mail.

For a year or so, I continued to believe that my stay on the teller line would be temporary, that I was there merely to view the human comedy and, incidentally, to pay the rent. During that brief time of innocence, I found everything about our black customers fascinating: their deep voices, their vivid vocabulary, their enviable lack of self-consciousness. They were romantic and unreal to me, and my youthful immersion in their music and literature further enhanced their aura of strangeness. But as my misery grew, so did my need to separate myself from my surroundings, to prove that I was better than the people on whom I waited. For the first time in my privileged life, I needed somebody to hate. To hate the wealthy is to abandon all hope of becoming like them; to hate the middle class, my own kind, made no sense to me. My destiny, then, was to hate the poor, and in the environment where chance had placed me, the poor were mostly black.

It began, modestly enough, with idle speculations about our black customers. Why did so many of them make mistakes on their deposit slips? Why were their balances always so low? Why were they always the ones with the fattest government checks? I already knew the perfectly innocent answers to these questions. The location of our branch ensured a large black clientele; it followed that the ordinary traits that tellers find irritating in the public at large should have been particularly noticeable in our black customers. But I soon managed to dismiss this obvious fact as irrelevant to my situation. The qualities I had once found mysterious and attractive in our black customers now began to seem tasteless and exaggerated. All of the foul clichés at which I had long turned up my sensitive white nose now came back to me in a sickening rush. Gradually, inexorably, the evil word *nigger* crept into my vocabulary. I never said it out loud, but I thought it with growing regularity, especially on those busy Fridays when it seemed that the entire Kansas City ghetto was lining up at my window to cash welfare checks, the proceeds of which I knew (but told no one, not even my unsuspecting wife) would be spent on cards and whiskey and whores.

I was, of course, mad, though the insanity into which I had drifted was temporary and, at least at first, voluntary. Somewhere in the back of my fevered mind, I knew that my hateful thoughts were inspired not by the customers at my window, imperfect though they were, but by my own sad cowardice. I thought of my madness as a kind of safety valve, and I knew, too, that blacks were simply the most convenient target, that under other circumstances I might have been spewing my jets of self-loathing at some other group of innocent bystanders. This secret understanding made the distinction between thought and speech all-important. To pronounce the word *nigger* in front of another human being would have been to march past the point of no return.

My mind was divided into two tightly sealed compartments, only one of which was tainted with the virus that, so far, I had kept from infecting my life outside the bank. In that larger life, I continued to function as a husband and a musician and a writer. I went on picnics and tried to write a novel and sat in at late-night jam sessions, meeting and becoming friendly with a few black jazzmen in the process. One of them, a very old guitar player named Charles Goodwin, had an account at the bank where I worked. He came into the bank once or twice a week, dressed to the nines and exuding the massive dignity of a man who has seen the worst and lived to tell his great-grandchildren about it. He came to my window to do his business, oblivious to the anxiety he touched off in the nice young white boy who took his deposits. My two worlds came together in his stately presence, leaving me filled with terror and confusion.

Juggling acts are by definition hard to keep going, and I began to drop an occasional ball when no one was looking. Driving home through heavy traffic after work, I would shout ugly words at cars that cut in front of me on the Paseo Bridge. The actual color of the driver never mattered, *nigger* by this time having become for me an all-purpose obscenity. What had begun as an attempt to find an escape from the unendurable pressure of self-hatred had turned into an obsession from which I could see no way out. I had no rich uncles, no influential friends, no kindly gods waiting to tug on the ropes and pull me into the lofty realms of fame and fortune. All I had was my talent, in which I had long ago lost faith. I was driving dangerously close to the white line, and I knew that it was only a matter of time before I ran into somebody, assuming that I didn't get run down first.

Such was my despoiled condition on the day I opened the door of the teller line and gazed upon the slender young black man who, moments before, had come through the back door of the bank firing a revolver. I stared at the ragged holes in his body. I saw the shadow of death in the sticky red pools of blood on the floor beneath my feet. The sight was so terrible that the two compartments of my mind at last split open and commingled. Part of me was sick with fear and rage; the other part was almost gleeful. *It's true*, I whispered to myself, *it's all true. I was right all along. See this vile creature? They're all like that. I hope he dies. He deserves to die. Better him than me.* I knew that I might easily have been lying on the floor next to him, and this knowledge was too much for me to bear. *If strokes are caused by mental stress,* I thought, *then I am going to have one right here. I am going to collapse and die next to a thug who would gladly have put a bullet through my head in order to get at the money in my drawer.*

Suddenly I heard a woman scream. I looked up and saw Michelle, one of the other tellers, stumbling across the lobby, supported on either side by hard-faced policemen. She was saying something over and over, but her words were distorted by huge, racking sobs and I couldn't make them out at first. Then, all at once, I understood what she was saying: the robber, the young black man whose life was draining away on the cold tile floor of the lobby, was her cousin.

I had always liked Michelle. Trim, pretty, considerate, intelligent, she existed apart from my bizarre fantasies, a concrete figure in the middle distance rather than a dim stereotype lurking just beyond the bars of my cage. I had granted her a private exemption from the rigid rules of hatred by which I had come to live. Yet there she stood, weeping hysterically, while the silent paramedic squeezed the plastic bag and the punctured chest of her cousin rose and fell haltingly in the midst of plastic syringe covers and sticky blood. It was a fantastic coincidence, the kind of thing that not even the most cynical screenwriter would dream of trying to palm off on a paying audience—but there it was. The tableau was complete, the details neat and explicit and damning. It was no longer possible for me to pretend that Michelle was anything other than a black woman whose cousin was dying a violent death before her eyes; it was no longer possible for me to pretend that I was anything other than a cowardly boy who had touched the pitch of evil and thereby been defiled. Unable to look at the bleeding body on the floor for a moment longer, I ran back inside the teller line and shut the door behind me. I sank into a chair and buried my face in my shaking hands.

A couple of hours later, I left for home. The bank had been closed for the rest of the day. Hastily hand-lettered signs had gone up in all the windows. Several employees were headed for the emergency room of the nearby hospital where the wounded guard had been taken. Only a few detectives had stayed behind to lock up, and I heard one of them talking on the phone as I waited for someone to let me out. "Do I have this straight?" he asked in a crisp, uninterested voice. "The perpetrator was D.O.A. The guard is stable. One killed, one wounded. Right. Right. Thanks."

I headed for my car, brushing off a reporter as I went, and pulled blindly onto the Paseo Bridge, driving away from the inner city toward my suburban home. I switched on the radio. The announcer was talking about the holdup. He got the names of the guards and the address of the bank wrong. As he spoke, I noticed for the first time that my shirt was soaked with sweat.

The bank was open for business the next day. The blood had been scrubbed from the floors the night before. Most of our customers did not know that an attempted robbery had taken place, but those who knew asked us about it, and we shared the details gladly, basking in the glow of our modest notoriety for as long as it lasted. The only exception was Michelle, who never said a word about the robbery and was never asked about it.

Like the bank, I looked the same on the outside, but I had acquired, among other things, a new reflex, one which betrayed me for the first time on a breezy fall afternoon some four months later. The manager had propped the doors of the bank open, and a gust of wind blew over a large metal display case in the lobby. At the sound of the crash, I instantly dropped to my knees. I had already begun to fumble for the alarm button when I heard the laughter of the teller in the next cage and struggled, red-faced, to my feet.

This reflex was the only outward sign of the healing of the fissure in my mind. Yet the healing had begun. A person in pain who uses morphine, however large the dose, does not become addicted; addiction is the result of use for pleasure alone. In much the same way, my madness quickly ebbed away after the robbery.

It had given me no pleasure, and I did not need it anymore. Purged by the awesome sight of death and the horrible spectacle of my own degraded soul, I was ready at last to crawl out of the shallow pit I had dug for myself. I didn't quit my job the next day, or even the day after that, but I gradually began to change the course of my life, and a year or so later I left Kansas City for good.

I saw no reason to share the details of my life as a teller with my new friends, though I did occasionally tell people that I had once been caught in the middle of a bank robbery and had watched the robber die. For the most part, though, I tried to forget about the whole episode. Months passed when I did not think of the four years I spent as a teller in Kansas City. But the memories were there, and I know that they will always be there. Even now, I jump whenever I hear a certain kind of loud noise, and in an instant I am standing in the lobby of the bank, unable to turn away from the sight of a slender man lying in a pool of blood. One morning not too long ago, I reached the head of a long line in a Burger King in Manhattan and found myself face to face with a young black girl who gazed coolly at me as she took my order, not bothering to conceal the contempt in her eyes. I knew what she was thinking, for I had thought it, or something very much like it, back in the days when I stared at long lines of poor black people and wished them dead.

If I learned anything during the four-year gap in my résumé, it was that I, too, shared in the common predicament, at least as fully as the young man who, had I added a couple of extra minutes to my lunch hour one fine spring day, might well have shot me dead. Though I have never killed a man, or even fired a gun in anger, I cannot forget the malign impulse that once waited patiently inside me, flowering into hatred at the touch of self-pity and then swiftly withering away. I suppose it is still there, for no man can escape the shadow of his sinful nature, the primeval calamity that touches us all. But that is something on which I prefer not to dwell, at least not for any longer than I can help.

13 | *In the Night*

My favorite time of day is the middle of the night. It's an unusual taste for a small-town boy, and I'm not quite sure where I picked it up. I know it wasn't in Sikeston, though, because my home town isn't very busy in the middle of the night. Too many people have to get up and go to work first thing in the morning. After the sun goes down, Sikeston becomes a sleepy-eyed country town, a place where the street lights barely cut through the darkness that settles in like a heavy fog well before midnight. Bedtime at our house was nine o'clock sharp when I was a child, ten-thirty when I got a little older. The first time I stayed up all night was when Apollo 11 landed on the moon. It was the last time for a long time to come.

Perhaps my taste for the small hours of the morning came from the plays I did in college, for our dress rehearsals usually ran late, leaving us too keyed up to go back to our dorms right away; most nights, we piled into a couple of cars and drove out to the truck stop on the edge of town to unwind over an after-midnight snack. Perhaps it came from reviewing concerts for the Kansas City *Star*, a morning paper with an eleven-thirty deadline. Perhaps I picked it up during the semester I spent dating a girl named Debbie Lee who lived on the south side of Kansas City. Kansas City is a big place, and I got to bed at three in the morning quite a few times that fall. I never minded, for I loved driving back to Liberty through the early-morning fog, hissing down the empty city streets with my windows open and the radio turned up, passing an occasional truck and wondering where it was headed.

Part of it, I know, must have come from working as a nighttime disc jockey at the William Jewell radio station. I found that I liked sitting by myself late at night in a tiny studio on the top floor of a deserted building, spinning records and talking softly into the microphone, my voice lowered to a near-whisper. Not that I ever had much to say. I did my best to keep the talk down, and to keep it consistent with the cool jazz and saloon songs that I played. I used to shut off every light in the studio except for a tiny reading lamp clamped to the side of the control panel. If I had a big test the next day, I would study by the light of the lamp; most of the time, though, I just sat and listened to the music I was sending out over the air.

I stopped working at the radio station after I started playing jazz. The kind of jazz I liked to play was the kind you're likely to hear in a nearly empty bar at a quarter to three, the hour Johnny Mercer and Harold Arlen had in mind when they wrote "One for My Baby." Quiet jazz goes well with quiet conversation. If you've ever been in a bar at a quarter to three, you know that people have a way of letting their guard down after a couple of early-morning drinks, especially when a piano is tinkling in the background and the brightest light in the room is the neon sign in the window:

> *You'd never know it,*
> *But buddy, I'm a kind of poet,*
> *And I've gotta lotta things to say.*

And when I'm gloomy,
You simply gotta listen to me,
Until it's talked away.

I stopped playing jazz after I left Kansas City and moved to Urbana, Illinois, where I spent two years studying psychology at the University of Illinois. Instead of exchanging confidences in half-empty bars at a quarter to three, I worked the graveyard shift at the Champaign County Mental Health Center Crisis Line, an around-the-clock service that offered a sympathetic ear to anyone who called. It wasn't ideal, but it beat working at an inner-city bank, and that was all I cared about at the time.

I didn't want to leave Kansas City. It was the right kind of place for me, a big city surrounded by cozy little bedroom towns with solid midwestern names like Independence and Lee's Summit and Overland Park. If the Kansas City *Star* had given me a job, I probably would have stayed there for the rest of my life, eating hickory-smoked barbecue twice a week and playing jazz on Saturday nights, secure in the knowledge that fate had dealt me a good hand. As it was, I had to leave. I knew it was time to throw myself into a new world full of new people, to turn away from the bad times and build a new life.

My mistake was in assuming that I would have to go back to school in order to build my new life. I probably could have found a newspaper job if I'd looked hard enough. I didn't look at all. I had not yet gotten over being rejected by the *Star*, and my confidence was still at a low ebb, so I started from scratch. Not only did I go back to school, I entered a field of study about which I knew almost nothing. I had read several popular books about psychotherapy; I had also spent a couple of months during my sophomore year paying weekly visits to the college psychologist, a bluff, outgoing man named Harles Cone, who helped to ease me through the rocky shoals of self-consciousness. Dr. Cone made a big impression on me, but that wasn't exactly reason enough for me to burn my bridges and take up the study of psychology at the age of twenty-seven. It was as if I wanted to erase not only the bad years in the teller cage but the good years that had gone before.

Looking back, I suppose my decision to become a psychotherapist was more of a convulsion than anything else, though there was a certain twisted logic to it: having been sick, I now thought myself qualified to heal others. A course in elementary logic would have shown me the kink in my reasoning, but I was too busy sailing through introductory courses in psychology to bother with logic. Going back to college, I found, was not unlike falling in love. Lost in a rosy mist of infatuation, I spent the better part of a year telling everybody I knew that I had found myself at last. All I could think about was how great it would be to hang out my shingle and spend eight hours a day giving out advice to unhappy people. I was so pleased to be an undergraduate again that I even helped to start a student newspaper, a venture into which I plunged with great enthusiasm, though I gradually withdrew from it as I became increasingly preoccupied with my studies.

Like all honeymoons, mine came to an end, though no single moment of disillusion shattered the spell of my new love. The novelty of my situation simply wore off, and I saw when I came to my senses that I was in for a long, hard slog. As a student of music, I had spent countless hours immersed in the intricate beauties of Bach and Mozart; as a student of psychology, I was spending countless hours memorizing statistical formulas and tabulating responses to long questionnaires. Most of my classes were boring, most of my teachers earnest and dull. I spent most of my evenings supervising experiments whose pointlessness was clear to everyone except the assistant professors who dreamed them up in the first place. It was a far cry from my memories of sessions with Dr. Cone and books like *Captain Newman, M.D.* and *The Making of a Psychiatrist*, and it wasn't long before I saw that I would quickly run out of patience with the plodding realities of a student's life unless I found a way to reconcile them with my brightly colored fantasies.

I was saved, as has so often been the case in my life, by a

chance encounter. Prowling the corridors of the psychology building one autumn morning, I stumbled across a sign-up sheet inviting psychology majors to volunteer for a yearlong tour of duty on the Champaign County Mental Health Center Crisis Line. I knew an omen when I saw one. My faculty adviser had made it clear to me that a résumé packed with outside activities would increase my chances of getting into a graduate program in psychology. Working on the Crisis Line would give me an immediate chance to play therapist; it would also look good on my résumé. Altruism had nothing to do with my decision, and I doubt if many of the other psychology majors who signed up did so in order to make the world a better place. We all knew that there was only a handful of first-rate graduate programs in psychology and that the sole purpose of our lives as undergraduates was to get into one of them. Besides, how could we possibly do anybody any good until we got a Ph.D., preferably from a well-known school? *First things first*, I told myself, and scrawled my name at the bottom of the sheet.

Two weeks later, I reported to the Champaign County Mental Health Center and got my first look at my fellow volunteers. Half of them were ambitious psychology majors from the university, the other half older people from the surrounding community. The training sessions went by at a dizzying pace. We learned the basic principles of crisis intervention: when to talk, what questions to ask, when to shut up and listen, when to hang up and call the cops. Then we paired off and practiced on each other. Our teacher, a bearded, soft-spoken man named Dave, passed around a bowl full of folded slips of paper on which brief descriptions of imaginary emotional disasters were neatly typed. *(You are a pregnant teenager who has just been dumped by her steady boyfriend. You want to get an abortion but can't afford it. You are thinking about killing yourself.)* We pretended to be callers, playing out the miniature dramas on our slips with all the panache we could muster; we pretended to be counselors, wondering what nightmare our partners would pull out of the bowl next.

At the end of the course, each of us received a black loose-leaf notebook containing information about the various places in Champaign County to which we could refer callers if the occasion arose. Then we signed up for our first shifts and went home. Home, to my surprise, was where we took our calls. Instead of coming to the Mental Health Center to man the switchboard and drink pots of black coffee, we stayed home and waited for callers to be routed directly to us by an answering service. We checked in by phone at the beginnings of our shifts and sat by the phone for the next four hours. After every call, we filled out an evaluation form, describing what the caller said and did and how we handled it. When our shifts were over, we mailed our forms to the Mental Health Center, where they were examined and filed. Each volunteer talked to Dave on the phone once or twice a month about how things were going. That was the extent of our personal contact with the Champaign County Mental Health Center once our training was over.

We were on our own from the moment we checked in for our first shifts. A professional counselor was on call in case we got in over our heads, but we had to hang up in order to get help, and it was tacitly understood that Crisis Line volunteers didn't hang up on a caller for any reason short of a heart attack or the sound of a gunshot. That suited me fine. I was breathless with excitement at the thought of dealing with disturbed callers. It didn't take long to wear off. My first caller was a teenager who told me that a friend of hers was feeling suicidal. After ten minutes or so, the light went on: I was talking to the "suicidal friend," and she was waiting, not very patiently, for me to grasp that obvious fact. It was the oldest trick in the book, and I had fallen for it. I promptly broke out in a cold sweat.

Such calls were rare, something that never failed to surprise friends who asked me about my work on the Crisis Line. Most people think that "crisis line" and "suicide line" are synonymous. It isn't so, at least not after midnight in Champaign County, Illinois. I heard a lot of casual talk about suicide, especially at night, but I couldn't have gotten more than a dozen serious suicide calls during my tour of duty, and I only had to talk one caller out of actually shooting himself. Still, I tightened up whenever a caller let slip even the slightest hint of what Dave had taught me to call "suicidal ideation." *Maybe I'd be better off dead,* the voice on the other end of the line would say, and all at once I would feel a cold finger running slowly down my backbone. I started to imagine what it would be like to spend the rest of my life wondering if I had been too stupid or too insensitive or too sleepy to say the right thing. My stomach shrank into a dry little ball, and it stayed that way until the caller hung up.

In time, my fear of suicidal callers leached its way into every minute I spent on duty. When the telephone rang, I recited my personal mantra: *A person who really means business doesn't waste time calling the Crisis Line. He just kills himself.* (Untrue, but comforting.) Then I picked up the receiver and started running through a long list of stock questions: *How old are you? Are you married? Are you in therapy? Are you on medication?* These questions were designed to help inexperienced counselors determine as quickly as possible whether or not a caller was at high risk for suicide. Once I ruled that possibility out, I sat back and let the caller talk. Some people sounded slow and careful, some fast and high-pitched and scared, a few hard and certain. But no matter how they sounded, I knew that I had to sound calm, and I did. I spoke in a soft, steady voice, the same voice I had used as a late-night disc jockey. The white-knuckled hand with which I gripped the receiver was like a shock absorber that swallowed up the panic oozing out of my body. I twitched and squirmed in my chair and my palms grew slick with sweat, but the caller heard only the gentle sound of my voice.

Most of the calls I got were routine. Some people were looking for a referral to a place where they could get immediate help, usually in the form of a bed for the night. Others, already in treatment at the Mental Health Center, were simply having a bad night and wanted somebody to talk to between doses of Thorazine or Valium. I used to hear regularly from a lesbian carpenter who liked to talk about her unsuccessful love affairs. I got a lot of calls from alcoholics and their wives and husbands and kids, none of whom ever seemed to have heard of AA or its offspring. I was singing the praises of Al-Anon to a woman caller one night when my wife and her best friend, just back from a party, walked through the front door, plopped themselves down on the couch, and began to titter loudly. The woman hung up in a huff.

Once or twice I got a call from a person whose name was printed in capital letters on the last page of the black notebook, which contained a "do-not-call" list of Crisis Line abusers. Some of the names on the list belonged to people in treatment at the Mental Health Center who called every night for no good reason; others were troublemakers who got their kicks by harassing the volunteers. Most of these callers were screened out by the operators at the answering service, who told them to hang up and go to the Mental Health Center in the morning, but a few of them managed to slip through. One operator told me about a longtime veteran of the do-not-call list who said he absolutely had to talk to somebody that night. She recognized his voice, told him to call back in the morning, and hung up. He called back ten minutes later and said that he'd just dumped a gallon of gasoline over his head and was holding a cigarette lighter in his hand and would she please ring one of the crisis counselors *right now?* She did.

I spent a couple of months trying out different shifts before settling on midnight to eight, the graveyard shift. The other shifts were half as long, but fewer people called after midnight. That may strike you as odd if you happen to live in a big city, but Urbana is not a big city. Besides, the Crisis Line rarely got calls from University of Illinois students, who had plenty of on-campus counseling services at their disposal. I can't remember getting a single call from a college student. My callers were townies and residents of the rural parts of Champaign County, many of them good country people who clearly found it hard to tell their troubles to a stranger, no matter how friendly he sounded. Sometimes a whole night would go by without a call. But there weren't many nights like that, and when the phone did ring, the caller usually had a lot to talk about.

During my first few weeks on the graveyard shift, I went to bed shortly after I checked in, hoping to catch a few uneasy hours of sleep before the phone rang. By the end of my tour of duty, I was staying up until two or three in the morning as a matter of course, knowing that it was pointless to go to bed any earlier. As a result, I had a lot of time on my hands. I tried studying, but I found it impossible to concentrate. Watching television was no better, for somebody always called just as things got interesting. In the end, I spent most of my time reading detective stories. I recently ran across a battered paperback copy of Ross Macdonald's *The Goodbye Look* in a box in my bedroom closet and noticed that one of the pages was dog-eared. At the bottom of the page, Lew Archer, a hard-boiled private eye with a sensitive streak, made the following remark to a psychiatric nurse: "I have a secret passion for mercy. But justice is what keeps happening to people." I have a feeling that I turned that page down in the middle of a long night on the graveyard shift.

I took calls sitting at the kitchen table of my apartment. A pull-down ceiling fixture shed a tight cone of light just wide enough to illuminate my black notebook and the yellow pad on which I scribbled notes to myself. Though my wife was usually asleep in the bedroom down the hall, I felt completely alone as I sat at the kitchen table. Sometimes it seemed as if there were only two people awake in the whole world, one talking and the other one listening. This sensation was intensified by the solitary nature of my work. I made one friend in training, a psychology major named Kathy Venn who was a dead ringer for Bonnie Harris, the frizzy-haired pianist with whom I had worked on *The Fantasticks* and *Fiddler on the Roof* back in Sikeston. Except for Kathy, I never saw any of my fellow trainees again. I had lunch with Dave twice. I helped train the next class of Crisis Line volunteers. But I rarely had the sense that I was part of a larger undertaking. The only people from whom I heard were the people who called for help. They might have been down the street; they might as well have been a million miles away.

My nocturnal solitude mirrored the loneliness I felt during the daytime. I was a stranger in town, almost as isolated from everyday life at the University of Illinois as I was from my callers. Married and living in a dowdy apartment a couple of miles off campus, I spent my days among younger men and women who lived in dormitories, went on dates, and lost their hearts every weekend. I did all I could to fit into the crowded schemes of their lives. Sometimes I felt sure that I had turned back the clock and cheated the moving finger. Sometimes I woke up long before sunrise and stared at the ceiling until the alarm went off.

One way to keep from waking up in the middle of the night and worrying about your problems is to wake up in the middle of the night and worry about somebody else's problems. In the end, that was the main reason why I continued to work for the Crisis Line: it kept my mind off myself. Before long, it was the only activity in my daily life about which I cared at all, except for the magazine articles I wrote on Sunday afternoons. My classes ceased to mean anything to me, though I continued to show up and take notes, a sleepwalker going by rote through the meaningless motions of lost ambition. The idea of becoming a psychologist seemed more unreal with every passing day.

Most psychology majors, logically enough, hung out in the psychology building. I began to stay away from the building as much as I could, preferring to spend my spare time in the undergraduate library, a spacious underground cavern full of tall bookshelves and comfortable chairs. I sat in the library for days at a time, surrounded by stacks of books on every imaginable subject except psychology, indulging in the narcotic pleasure of total immersion in the completely irrelevant. I emerged from the stacks only to cram quarters into the coin-operated vending machines that lined the tunnel between the undergraduate library and the main library building and to come home at night. I had done more or less the same thing toward the end of my stay at St. John's College, a coincidence that did not escape my notice.

Whenever my attention strayed from the book in my hand, I usually found myself thinking about the people who called me in the middle of the night, hoping to find a sympathetic ear. I had realized fairly quickly that there was little I could do for them, and it wasn't much longer before I began to suspect that there was little anyone could do for them, that their miseries lay far beyond the reach of any form of psychotherapy known to man, however ingenious or powerful. I was tempted to say outrageous things to them in order to try to jolt them out of their passivity. (*So you think you'd be better off dead? Well, why don't you try it and see?*) But I never did. I feared that it was their destiny to be unhappy, and I knew that calling the Crisis Line was in all likelihood the best thing they could do to ease their suffering, perhaps even the only thing. They were calling to complain about their destiny, not to change it, but at least they were doing something.

I didn't share my bleak thoughts with my colleagues, mainly because I saw so little of them. I preferred to spend my spare time with my wife and her friends. Liz was working on a master's degree in music, and I got to know several of her fellow music majors quite well. It occurred to me one day that of the two of us, it was my Liz who was really alive. She loved her work and her friends. My life, by contrast, was not unlike that of a vampire. I spent my days underground, waiting until sundown to come out of my cave; I lived off the tears of strangers, varying my diet with soggy sandwiches bought from a machine. The only people with whom I truly felt at home were the people I had met through Liz. Instead of a real life, I had a borrowed one, happy though it often was; instead of a real vocation, I had a false one, and I was finding it harder and harder to pretend that I believed in it.

When the devil of doubt paid me the inevitable visit, it was in the person of a professor I knew and liked, a testy, research-oriented specialist in cognitive psychology who made no secret of the utter contempt in which he held all psychotherapists. I ran into him in the hall one day. He asked me what I was up to. I said I was working on the County Crisis Line and was thinking about becoming a therapist. Without batting an eye, he casually suggested that I might want to take a look at one of his favorite books, a survey of various scientific studies of the outcome of psychotherapy. I said I would try to get around to reading it one of these days. I checked it out of the library that afternoon.

The author of the book presented his findings in a dry, tight-lipped blend of polysyllables and psychological jargon. It was as if he wished to shield the uninitiated from the implications of his discoveries. He had examined every published study of therapeutic outcomes and had concluded that virtually all forms of psychotherapy had roughly the same results. None was totally useless, none particularly effective. Psychoanalysts with medical degrees, it turned out, were no better on average at curing their patients than laymen who had been given month-long crash courses in nondirective therapy, which consists primarily of the kind of sympathetic listening that was the stock in trade of the Champaign County Mental Health Center Crisis Line.

I laid down the book with a heavy heart. I understood at last why my love affair with psychotherapy, the great secular religion of our time, had gone sour. Though I had escaped from the bank, life was still passing me by, and I feared that I would never leave my mark on the world. My classes had taught me nothing about how to deal with that fear. It was from the unhappy people who called me in the night that I learned what I needed to know: that the trials of life can only be overcome by courage. I had found the courage to leave Kansas City; I would need even more of it to leave the University of Illinois and start living my life, instead of merely waiting for it to begin. *If I really believe in what I am doing*, I thought, *then why am I not in therapy myself?* There was no need for me to answer. No false god could make me brave. I would have to do that for myself.

A few months after my brief encounter with the enemy, I pulled up my stakes, withdrew from the University of Illinois, and left Urbana. I never went back, and I never again volunteered to work on a suicide line. I had done my time, and I had lost my faith. It's been a long time since I casually suggested that a troubled acquaintance "get some therapy." Once that glib phrase was constantly on my tongue. Now it sounds hollow whenever I hear it.

My two years as a student of psychology were not a total loss. I made two good friends with whom I have stayed in touch. I learned enough about statistics to distrust people who casually throw them around. I spent many pleasant hours in the company of Liz's colleagues. The student paper I helped to start survived my departure by five years, an ample life span for ventures of that kind. All in all, though, Urbana didn't leave much of an impression on me, and I don't think I left much of an impression on Urbana, unless it was on some of the people who called the Champaign County Mental Health Center Crisis Line after midnight and found themselves, for better or worse, talking to me. I like to think I eased their pain a little, and I know that nobody committed suicide on my watch. Maybe I was doing something right. More likely I was just lucky. But at least I was there.

My year on the graveyard shift did nothing to lessen my passion for the middle of the night. One of the many things I learned in Kansas City was that it is pleasant to sit in a half-empty bar late at night and listen to music. It isn't surprising, then, that I like to put on Frank Sinatra's recording of "One for My Baby" at a quarter to three in the morning and gaze out the window of my apartment at the empty streets below. It reminds me of the lurking dangers of self-pity; it reminds me, too, that when things are really tough, it's better to drop into the nearest bar and tell your troubles to Joe than to sit outside in the night and curse the darkness, miserable and desperate and alone.

14 | *Grand Central Terminal*

Nobody comes to New York by accident, least of all the stray children of the small towns of America who flock here like stubborn pigeons. However elaborate the chain of coincidence that draws these misfits eastward, there is always a single bright thread of fascination that can usually be traced back to a youthful encounter: a scene in a movie, a tale told by an aunt or cousin, a rainy afternoon spent looking at the cartoons in a tattered copy of *The New Yorker*. The seed is planted and grows silently, and then one day you set your jaw and pack your bag and head for Grand Central Terminal, determined to prove whatever it is you have to prove.

My own bright thread can be traced back to an ancient Curtis Mathes television set that only worked if you smacked it on the right side (not too hard) with an open palm. When I was growing up, New York was still the undisputed headquarters of the kingdom of television, the home of Walter Cronkite and Ed Sullivan and Johnny Carson. Leonard Bernstein conducted the New York

Philharmonic on Sunday afternoons; Ralph Kramden lived on Delancey Street, Rob Petrie in New Rochelle, Archie Bunker in Queens. I watched them all on that old television, and in the process I wove myself a private fantasy of what New York must be like: a daily festival of operatic arias, flying bullets, and witty remarks.

Many of the wittiest remarks in my fantasy were lifted from a weekly TV game show called *What's My Line?* that I watched as often as my parents would let me. If I had been good all week, I was allowed to stay up past my bedtime on Sunday to watch *Candid Camera* and *What's My Line?* This was a powerful disciplinary tool, far more effective than a mere spanking. Watching *Candid Camera* was great fun, but watching *What's My Line?* was more than just fun. For me, it was a ceremony, a mystical rite that opened a window on the unknown world far beyond the city limits of my home town.

The ritual of *What's My Line?*, like the Christmas rituals of my mother's family, was elaborate and invariable. At nine-thirty sharp, four panelists in evening dress marched through the curtained doorway of a TV studio in New York, took their seats, and proceeded to guess the occupations of two working stiffs and a Mystery Guest, engaging in friendly chitchat between rounds for the benefit of the folks at home. Johnny Olson, the unseen announcer, always introduced Dorothy Kilgallen, Broadway columnist for the New York *Journal-American* and the first panelist; John Charles Daly, the avuncular host with the rich anchorman's voice, was always introduced by Bennett Cerf, president of Random House and the last panelist. It was years before I found out that the balding, bespectacled, good-humored man with the slight lisp who came into our living room every Sunday night was the same Bennett Cerf whose publishing house had brought out more than a few of the books I most admired.

The panelists on *What's My Line?*, I realized as I watched them week after week, *knew* each other; they were fellow members of the freemasonry of celebrity, and they convened each Sunday in a television studio in New York, capital of the world, for the sole purpose of entertaining me. As I watched them, I imagined New York to be a place that existed only for the collective pleasure of the rich and famous. To live in New York, I felt certain, was to go to opening nights on Broadway, eat at inconceivably fancy restaurants, appear on *What's My Line?*, and be friends with lots of other famous people. I could not imagine living there myself, but it was enough to watch *What's My Line?* and dream, and I did plenty of both.

In America, the impossible has a way of coming true, usually when you least expect it. Not long after I came to William Jewell College, I went on a week-long pilgrimage to the Emerald City, courtesy of Richard Harriman, the worldly professor of English who ran the college's concert series and who took a lucky handful of students to New York every December. That was the week I went to the Café Carlyle to see Bobby Short, but that wasn't all I did, not by a long shot. Rummaging through my mother's cupboard the other day, I found a manila envelope full of souvenirs of my visit to New York. There was my program from Harold Prince's Broadway production of *Candide*; there were Lincoln Center and Radio City Music Hall and Mikhail Baryshnikov, fresh out of Russia, soaring across the stage of the Uris Theater; there was a memorandum scrawled in an unformed hand on Waldorf-Astoria stationery (when you traveled with Mr. Harriman, you traveled first-class) telling where I had eaten dinner each night. The food I ate dazzled me as much as the sights I saw, for I had been raised on Kraft Dinner and Chef Boy-Ar-Dee pizza in a box, and the act of ordering vichyssoise from a haughty waiter at "21" very nearly made me swoon.

As I looked through the envelope, I remembered how giddy I felt when my plane broke through the clouds over Queens and I caught sight of the Unisphere, the glittering symbol of the World's Fair to which my father had gone a quarter of a century before. That was the moment when New York first became real to me. But the week I spent there, thrilling though it was, did not widen the compass of my ambitions, at least not by very much. Moving to Kansas City had temporarily exhausted my sense of possibility, and moving to New York seemed out of the question altogether.

I did not yet know that we are born into a vast room whose walls consist of a thousand doors of possibility. Each door is flung open to the world outside, and the room is filled with light and noise. We close some of the doors deliberately, sometimes with fear, sometimes with calm certainty. Others seem to close by themselves, some so quietly that we do not even notice. "I want to play the violin," I said to my parents one day, and nobody bothered to tell me that a half-dozen doors slammed shut at that very moment—not just the door marked BECOMES JAZZ TRUMPET PLAYER but the one that said BECOMES SMALL-TOWN LAWYER AND SPENDS LIFE IN SIKESTON, the one my father would someday encourage me to walk through, not knowing that it was already bolted shut. I went off to college, and a door marked MARRIES HIGH SCHOOL SWEETHEART AND SPENDS LIFE IN SIKESTON closed softly in the distance. I closed a few doors on my own when I met Harry Jenks, when I played my first gig at the Lucky Penny, when I met a pretty girl at the William Jewell College Band Carnival in the fall of 1978 and fell in love.

With every door I shut, the shadows in the sunny room of my youth grew longer. I was afraid to stay in the dark; I was afraid to walk toward the light. I knew that all of the doors marked SPENDS LIFE IN SIKESTON had closed long ago. I did not know that I was moving steadily toward a door of whose very existence I was unaware.

I took my second trip to New York in the spring of 1984 at the urging of my wife and her best friend, a soprano from Bronxville, New York, named Rica Julie who proposed that the three of us drive all afternoon and night on the last day before spring break, arriving in New York the next morning to spend a week doing whatever suited us. We drove through Indiana and Ohio and Pennsylvania and crossed the George Washington Bridge as the sun came up. New York stretched before us, looming over the blasted wastelands of industrial New Jersey like a vast alien presence. We spent the week shopping and listening to jazz and museum-hopping and goggling at tall buildings and eating the fanciest meals we could afford.

At night, Liz and I would lie in bed together and review the day's adventures. As we talked, an unfamiliar notion began to take hold: the thought that we might want to consider spending a couple of years in New York. Not any time soon, for I had to get into a decent graduate school and earn a degree and wrestle with a dissertation, at the end of which New York might indeed become a possibility, if nothing more than that. But the possibility had at last been acknowledged, the magic words spoken aloud for the first time.

A year later, I applied for an internship at the Champaign County Mental Health Center. I had mixed feelings about the prospect of working with disturbed adolescents, but I knew that the internship, like my work on the Crisis Line, was just the sort of thing that directors of graduate programs in psychology would be looking for when I applied for admission. I did not yet know that I had already closed the door marked BECOMES PSYCHOLOGIST when I lost my faith in the profession I sought to practice, a faith without which I would never be able to endure the wretched life of a graduate student. All I knew was that something had gone wrong with my plans, leaving me at the mercy of undefined fears and conflicting ambitions. Unsure of what to do next, I continued to go through the familiar motions of my everyday life. I wrote up elaborate experiments and memorized long lists of statistical formulas; I continued to write magazine pieces and send them off to New York. Unable to sleep at night, I signed up for extra Crisis Line shifts, spending the small hours listening to a sad parade of despairing voices.

Then, one day, I sat down at my typewriter, pecked out a résumé, and sent it to my one friend in New York, a young man named Jon Cohen, who worked for the Institute for Educational Affairs, the foundation that had underwritten the campus newspaper I had helped to found a year before (unwittingly shutting a whole row of doors in the process). I had visited Jon during my second trip to New York, at which time he had casually mentioned that the IEA was underwriting a number of yearlong internships at various newspapers and magazines around the country. I nodded, but I said nothing. No doubt I had already come to suspect that the career I had so carefully planned for myself in Kansas City three years before had by now become unworkable, but I was not yet prepared to admit it to myself. I was still not prepared to admit it when I typed out that résumé. Had I stopped to think about what I was doing, I probably would have shrugged my shoulders and thrown it away. Instead, I walked down to the corner mailbox and dropped it in.

A week or so later, my wife and I were eating lunch at home when the phone rang. It was Jon. He was surprised to have gotten a résumé from me, surprised and pleased. He thought I might want to know that the internship program had an opening: *Harper's Magazine* was looking for an assistant editor for the coming year. There was a problem, though: they needed somebody who could report right away, in six weeks if not sooner. Delay was impossible. Was I interested? "No, thank you," I said politely. "I don't think that will work for me." I hung up and told my wife what Jon had said. She stared at me blankly for a moment. Then she told me to call him back at once and tell him I had changed my mind.

Jon was waiting by the phone. He told me to catch a plane to New York at once—the very next day, if I could manage it. The foundation would pay for my ticket. I could spend the night with Jon, drop by *Harper's* the following morning to be interviewed by Lewis H. Lapham, the editor, and fly back to Illinois that same afternoon. Two days later, I walked into the Park Avenue offices of *Harper's* and met Lewis, a lean, sardonic man with a touch of Jason Robards in his face and bearing. He seemed to embody the very essence of the city I had looked on from afar as a child. We chatted for half an hour, and it was clear to me as we shook hands and said our farewells that the interview had gone well. He told me that he'd be in touch with me in a few days. I walked up Park Avenue to Grand Central Terminal, boarded a Carey bus for La Guardia Airport, and flew back to Illinois.

True to his word, Lewis called three days later. Was I still interested? Would I be able to report on June 1, or even earlier? Until that moment, I had kept an open mind about the prospect of going to work for *Harper's*. I was waiting to hear from the Mental Health Center. It was not too late for me to cross the last unburned bridge, to stick to my chosen path. Or was it? My stomach lurched. I knew that the moment to choose between the known and the unknown had arrived, that there was only one door left open, one single shaft of light illuminating a room that had become terribly dark and frightening in the course of the last few years. Fear of failure had kept me from taking myself seriously as a writer; fear of experience had kept me from seriously considering the possibility of moving to New York. Fear had brought me to Illinois, where I had spent two years charging furiously down a side road. This was my chance to get back on the main highway again.

I took a deep breath. "No earlier," I said, "but I'll be there."

I got a call from the Mental Health Center the next day. A friendly voice told me that I was accepted, that they'd be delighted to have me join the program, and would it be possible for me to start work in the summer instead of waiting until the fall? There was an uncomfortable pause. "I don't know how to tell you this," I said at last, "but something has come up."

Waiting. Walking through the neighborhood with Liz, sitting side by side on the swing set in the playground down the street and talking about the life to come. Long, silent drives through the flat farmland south of Urbana, both of us lost in our unspoken thoughts. Dozens of unwanted books to be sold to one of the campus bookstores. Hundreds of unwanted record albums to be donated to the Urbana Public Library. Businesslike conferences with the movers. Fishing through the Safeway dumpster for unbloodied cardboard boxes in which to pack our belongings. Letters to friends. Letters to magazine editors in New York. *I'm moving to New York in May. We have a mutual friend. Could I stop by for a chat?*

The hardest part was telling our parents. Liz flew back to Missouri to tell hers, sensibly leaving me behind. Mine were close enough to make a face-to-face meeting in St. Louis possible, so I called them up and told them that we'd like to get together with them some weekend—how about this Saturday? They got the idea. We went to a Steak 'n' Shake for lunch, and I blurted out my news as the waitress brought our cheeseburgers. Both of my parents were visibly shocked, but neither one dropped dead or started shouting, and that was good enough for me.

Time, which had slowed to an agonizing crawl, now picked up speed and began to roar by like an express train. Suddenly we were watching two beefy men haul the bed and the couch and the Steinway spinet out of the apartment and into a moving van, which pulled away from the curb without ceremony late in the afternoon and drove off into the sunset. We slept on the floor of the apartment that night, possessed of nothing but two sleeping bags and what little we could wedge into the trunk and back seat of our white Toyota. Blossom and Cleo, our two gray cats, wandered curiously through empty rooms that echoed with our faltering steps and fearful words.

We left town the next day, spending a night in an Ohio motel that didn't suffer animals gladly, doing our best to keep Blossom and Cleo off the windowsill and out of sight. We crossed the George Washington Bridge and made our way to Bronxville, parking the car in front of a building in which we had rented an apartment sight unseen, relying solely on the recommendation of a friend of Rica's. The building was old, the apartment bright and airy. We put together the stereo and blew up a pair of air mattresses and spent an uncertain night waiting for the movers to catch up with us. The next day, we took a trip into Manhattan to see how the train worked and try to get our bearings. We went to the Museum of Modern Art and strolled down Broadway and wandered around Lincoln Center and visited Bloomingdale's and took the subway down to Greenwich Village and ate at a Cuban-Chinese restaurant with a menu the size of a magazine, boggling at the prices. We began at last to grasp the fact that we were really going to live in New York, perhaps for a very long time.

We got up early Sunday morning and bought a *New York Times* and a bag of fresh bagels. The floor of the apartment was covered with cardboard boxes, but the bookshelves were up and the stereo was running and Blossom and Cleo had looked over their new home and chosen their turf. Blossom liked the foot of the bed; Cleo preferred the top of the bookshelf. They took our change of life in stride. The apartment may have been new, but the couch and chairs were the same, even if they were in different places, and we were the same people we had been a week before, a year before, the very same people who had picked two kittens out of a glass box shortly after we got back from our honeymoon and bought them for six dollars apiece.

I spent the night staring at the ceiling. Then I got up and dressed, walked to the Fleetwood train station, bought my first monthly pass, boarded the Harlem Line local, and peered through the window at the Botanical Gardens and the South Bronx. The tunnel swallowed us up at 125th Street, and soon we were pulling into Grand Central Terminal, the last and final stop. I bought a paperback at the downstairs bookstore. *Something for the ride home,* I told myself, pretending that I was an old hand at commuting. I took the great marble stairs two at a time and gazed at the vaulting ceiling and the twinkling beads of light far above my head. Then I went out into the June sunshine, turned right on 42nd Street, and got lost. Swept along in a fast-moving stream of self-assured pedestrians with places to go, diverted by the sight of a thousand young women dressed in neatly cut suits and dirty sneakers, I forgot where I was going and wandered off in the wrong direction. Then I became afraid, not of anything reasonable but simply of looking foolish. How could I possibly duck into a phone booth and call my boss, the only person I knew at *Harper's*, to tell him that his new assistant editor was such a rube that he couldn't find Two Park Avenue?

In the midst of my panic, I heard someone calling my name. I shook my head and kept on walking. It had to be a mistake. When I heard it again, I turned around. There, waving at me from half a block away, was the unbelievable, the impossible: a familiar face. It was Jon Cohen, the young man who had pulled me out of my disorder and misery into a strange new world. Neatly dressed in a suit and tie, he was a shining vision of order, a sign from heaven that my life up to that moment had not been a mistake.

"Terry!" he yelled. "I think you're going the wrong way!"

"I know!" I yelled back. "Why don't you point me in the right direction?"

He put a hand on my shoulder and spun me around. I saw a green street sign on the corner: PARK AVE. "Just turn right, you idiot," he said with a laugh, "and keep going until you get there." I turned right and stepped through the invisible door I had shunned for so long, toward which I had been irresistibly drawn since childhood, and began to walk down Park Avenue toward the rest of my life.

15 | *A Place at the Kitchen Table*

"**L**ast winter," Samuel Johnson wrote to a friend in 1762, "I went down to my native town where I found the streets much narrower and shorter than I thought I had left them, inhabited by a new race of people, to whom I was very little known. My play-fellows were grown old, and forced me to suspect that I was no longer young. . . . I wandered about for five days, and took the first convenient opportunity of returning to a place, where, if there is not much happiness, there is, at least, such a diversity of good and evil, that slight vexations do not fix upon the heart."

Like Dr. Johnson, I went down to my native town last summer and wandered about for five days. I rarely get to spend that much time in Sikeston. The best I can usually manage is a three-day weekend, at the end of which I return to St. Louis and fly back to New York, a place where there is, to put it mildly, a diversity of good and evil. But slight vexations rarely fix upon my heart in Sikeston, perhaps because I stay so close to home. My outings are few and fixed: a quick trip to Diehlstadt, lunch with an old friend or with my mother, dinner at a favorite restaurant, an evening with my brother and sister-in-law. I spend the rest of my time in the house where I grew up. That is why I come home and that is where I want to be, and I always have to leave sooner than I like.

But I had five whole days at my disposal the last time I came home for a visit, and so I spent a few of them looking around Sikeston and revisiting half-remembered haunts. One or two of them, I noticed with pleasure, seemed not to have changed at all. The Sikeston Public Library was one place where I found it all but impossible to tell past from present. I prowled through the stacks and saw the same books I had checked out as a boy. I sat on the tired old leather-covered sofa in the magazine section, gazing at the stuffed chairs and the unlit fireplace (has it ever been lit?) and the tall-and-short water fountains in the vestibule, all of which had been there a quarter of a century ago. The librarians were different, but they looked exactly like their predecessors, and it wouldn't surprise me very much to learn that they were whispering about the same things, if not the same people, as the librarians of my youth.

Few things in Sikeston are as completely unchanged as the library, though, and some are changed grievously. Around the corner and down the street from the library, for instance, is what is left of the old Middle School. The gymnasium is intact and in use, but the main building was condemned and torn down a few years ago. Nothing is left of it but the semicircular drive that used to fill up every afternoon at three-thirty with yellow school buses and children waiting to be picked up by their parents. The buses are gone, the children grown. What once was a school, crowded and noisy, is now an empty field covered with green grass.

That change is visible. Others are harder to see. The old First Baptist Church, for example, is no longer the Sikeston Activity Center. The black letters over the main entrance that once said

SIKESTON ACTIVITY CENTER have been pried off and discarded; the words FIRST BAPTIST CHURCH, carved into the granite of the facade in 1915, are visible once again. The south wing of the church is now the Scott County Juvenile Court, and the north wing houses the Sikeston Regional Children's Service. The sanctuary is no longer used by anyone. Little Theater stopped performing there in 1981, and it is now a storage room.

I asked a friendly-looking receptionist if I could take a look at the old sanctuary. We passed through a locked door and into a long corridor, the corridor that runs along what once was the backstage wall. Next to an Alcoholics Anonymous bulletin board is a broad brown metal door, and it, too, is kept locked. I pulled the door open and walked down three brown-tiled steps to what once was the baptistry of the First Baptist Church and which later became the stage of the Sikeston Activity Center. Now the steps lead down to nothing: no pews, no chairs, no stained glass, no congregation, no audience. Pails and buckets line the walls. The plaster is peeling. An abandoned pool table stands in the center of the room. Only the rake of the floor and the faintly ecclesiastical hue of the moldings give any hint of what this room once was; only the still-hanging stage curtains suggest its later uses. I looked around for a moment. Then I excused myself and fled as quickly as I could from the musty air of the sanctuary into the heat of a summer day.

Some of the biggest changes in Sikeston are invisible to all but a handful of people. My father had told me about one such change, so I drove out to the Garden of Memories Cemetery on the southwest side of town, just past Ferris Field, the place where I played Little League baseball so haplessly. (It is now a girls' softball field.) Verona, my father's mother, is buried in the Garden of Memories Cemetery, far from her elegant Omaha apartment. Next to the tarnished bronze slab atop her grave is a shiny new marker, installed in the certain knowledge that the ground beneath it will someday be turned in order to accept a pair of coffins. This is what it says:

TEACHOUT

H. H. "Bert"   Evelyn C.
May 21, 1926   June 14, 1929

TOGETHER   MARRIED
FOREVER   11-22-47

This *memento mori* was not, I knew, the most important change that had taken place in Sikeston, Missouri, since my last visit home. It was not as drastic as the demolition of the old Middle School or the gutting of the Sikeston Activity Center. But it was change enough for me, this silent reminder that I will come back here at least twice more, unless God in His infinite wisdom takes me first.

As I wiped the summer sweat from my forehead, I thought about another graveyard I had visited a few months before. The occasion was the funeral of Grace Crosno, my mother's mother and my last living grandparent. She died early on a Thursday morning in January. There was no way I could leave New York until late Friday night, and I would have to be back in the city on Sunday for a meeting. My parents urged me to be sensible and skip the funeral. It was only because I heard a faint but unmistakable note of regret in their voices that I spent an hour on the phone with a travel agent and came up with a solution to my dilemma: I would fly out of La Guardia into Memphis, Tennessee, at six on Saturday morning and fly back to La Guardia from Memphis at nine that night. The funeral would be held at two in the afternoon. It happened that my brother was in Memphis for a car show that weekend, so I could drive up to Sikeston and back with him. It was tricky, but it was possible, and so it was that I rose before dawn in New York and, a few hours later, stood by an open grave in a country cemetery on a raw, wet January day.

I was not there for my grandmother's sake. We had never been close. Her children had given her so many grandchildren that it was hard for her to pay much attention to any one of us.

We had had little enough in common in any case. Grace was a farmer's wife who had outlived her husband by nearly thirty years, and she had drifted into senility long before her death. No, I was there for my parents' sake, and I was glad that I had come, for I learned when I arrived at the funeral home that the rest of Grace's grandchildren, all eleven of them, had turned out to help their parents consign her earthly remains to a cold hole in the ground of the Odd Fellows' Cemetery outside Charleston.

I am the Resurrection and the life, the preacher said as we huddled together beneath the undertaker's tent. As he spoke, I cast an eye over my two uncles, three aunts, and ten cousins and thought about how far they had traveled to be here on this day. Grace's children, I knew, had mostly stayed close to home. Jet went off to Florida, but Albert stayed in Diehlstadt for many years before his work took him to a series of small towns in Missouri and Illinois. My mother had moved away, but only to Sikeston (though this, too, was a great journey in its own way), and Suzy, Dot, and Peggy were all living in Diehlstadt. It was Grace's grandchildren who had chosen to wander. Not all of them, for Peggy's children still lived in Diehlstadt, my brother David and his wife and daughter lived in Sikeston, and Annie, Dot's youngest child, lived in Cape Girardeau. But Mike had gone to Chicago to become a salesman for a shoe company, and his work took him to New York City every year or so; Bob had become a TV cameraman in Paducah, Kentucky, and Gary was managing a body shop in Memphis. None of Jet's children had ever lived in southeast Missouri, and they were all in college now, two in Memphis and one in Fort Lauderdale.

I thought: *I have traveled far from home, but I am not the only one of us who has traveled.* Most of the Crosno grandchildren had grown up and left home, just as most of our fellow countrymen now grow up and leave home. Once upon a time, the children of America stayed close to the nest and ate Sunday dinner with their parents and went to work in the family business. Now they seek their destinies in faraway lands called Chicago and Paducah and Memphis and New York, though they come home as often as they can: for Christmas usually, for funerals always.

I glanced at my watch. My brother would be doing the driving, and he drove nearly as well as my father, so I had nothing to worry about. I squeezed my father's hand and listened to the preacher. A few hours later, I looked down at the lights of New York through the scratched window of a jet airliner, marveling at the thought that I could eat breakfast in New York and go to bed in New York and, in the middle of the day, help to bury an eighty-four-year-old woman in a cemetery deep in the Missouri wildwood. Perhaps I was not so far from home as I thought. Perhaps I had not traveled so far as I thought.

Sitting at my desk in Manhattan the other day, sifting through the regular crop of bills and magazines and press releases, I found a letter from my mother. It started like this: "I hope your cold has improved." And it ended like this: "Last night when Dad and I finished dinner, I told him how much I wish I could have called you and said I had a chop left and some cranberry sauce and a serving of potatoes—why don't you come over and have them?"

Now that I have gone home and come back in a single day, I know that I could do just that if I wanted to, although the chop and potatoes would be cold by the time I got there and I would have to sit in a different chair, since my father now sits in my old place at the end of the kitchen table. If it pleased me to do so, I could sleep in the room where I slept as a child. The crickets would chirp softly outside the window and the all-enveloping stillness of the night, the hush that city dwellers never know, would wash over me just as it did when I was a child and lived at home.

Home. I still call it that, and I guess I always will. When do we acquire the grace to feel at home where we are? Do we ever? Or can we do no better than to make a home for our own children, who will grow up and do the same for their children? I cannot answer that question, not yet. But the longer I live in New York, the more I cherish the ties that bind me to a place at the kitchen table of a small house in a small town in the southeastern corner of Missouri. Once my wife and I were waiting for a train in a subway station in lower Manhattan. There was a grubby pay phone across from the bench on which we sat. "Liz," I said, "has it ever occurred to you that I could go to that phone, put in a quarter, push a few buttons, and be talking to my mother in Sikeston, halfway across the country? Isn't that the greatest thing?" She smiled sweetly at me and changed the subject.

The grip that my home town has on me is rooted above all in its changelessness. The changes that saddened me on my last trip home went no deeper than the ripples on the muddy surface of the Mississippi River. The First Baptist Church of Sikeston, Missouri, was still the First Baptist Church of Sikeston, Missouri, when the sign outside read SIKESTON ACTIVITY CENTER and the Little Theater was doing *Fiddler on the Roof* inside, and even though the Sikeston Activity Center has given way to the Sikeston Regional Children's Service and the Scott County Juvenile Court, even though the holy sanctuary that became a deconsecrated theater is now a dingy storeroom, nothing has changed. The black plastic letters on the facade are gone and the chiseled granite letters that say FIRST BAPTIST CHURCH are visible once more, and they will be visible as long as the church stands, and even after the church is torn down and the rubble carted away, there will be books and pictures and memories to prove that it once stood on a lot just across the railroad tracks from downtown Sikeston.

I know this all the more surely now that I live in New York, far beyond the reach of midwestern eyes. I know, too, that I am as changeless as the town from which I came. Whenever I try to shake off the sticky mannerisms of my adopted city, I find myself swerving back toward the plain ways of my home town. Not so long ago, I went to a retirement dinner for an esteemed colleague. I gave a toast in his honor, and my voice shook with the high emotions of the moment. The next morning, a friend who had been at the dinner called me up and said: "You know, your accent really came out last night when you were giving that toast." I chuckled at the thought. I used to wonder if I would ever start sounding like a New Yorker. I don't worry about it anymore.

Of course New York has left its mark on me. So have Annapolis and Kansas City and Urbana, Illinois. But am I really a different person because I grew up and moved away from home and fell in love and got married? Am I a different person because I have read a thousand books and played jazz in big-city dives and seen a young man bleed to death before my eyes? I don't think so. More and more, I think that I am not so very far from the small-town boy I once was, not much farther than a plane ride and a three-hour drive. And since he lives on in memory, as unchanged by passing time as a painting hanging in a museum or a fleeting image preserved in a home movie, I suppose that I am still that boy, too, even though I now live in exile in New York, pleased to write books and go to the ballet but constantly aware that home is somewhere else.

In the front yard of 713 Hickory Drive is a maple tree that casts a long, cool shadow on summer days. Once it was a slender sapling, held up by wires that led to wooden stakes driven deep in the earth, and I wondered if it would ever grow tall enough for me to climb. It is tall enough now. My niece will soon climb it, and my own unborn children, God willing, will someday climb it, too. But for me it will always be the young sapling that stands in front of the house that is my home, in the town that is my home town, in the part of the country where I was born and to which I will always return, frequently and gladly, inevitably and eternally.

ABOUT THE AUTHOR

Terry Teachout has worked as an editorial writer for the New York *Daily News*, a senior editor of *Harper's Magazine*, a music critic for the Kansas City *Star*, and a jazz bassist. He is the editor of *Beyond the Boom: New Voices on American Life, Culture, and Politics*. Born in Cape Girardeau, Missouri, in 1956, he now lives in New York with his wife Elizabeth, an opera coach. He is at work on a biography of H. L. Mencken.